A Most Revolutionary Watch

A Time Travel Adventure

By Scott M. Smith

PROLOGUE

New York: July 15, 1776

The Washingtons stood stiffly under the columned portico of the Mortier House, just north of the city gate, watching their guests disembark from horsedrawn coaches. Deep inside, slaves, attired in red and white livery, bustled. The mouth-watering aroma of roasting fowl wafted from the kitchen while an unseen harp crooned. Ribbons of peach and pink, the palette of a summer sunset, backlit the Hudson River, visible in the distance through the bay windows of the parlor.

Martha, a short woman, wore a rose gown adorned by three white bows. Her brown eyes radiated a warm welcome not always associated with Southern plantation masters. George, tall for any era, had changed from his military attire into a forest green knee-length jacket, matching breeches, and white silk stockings. His copper hair was swept back, tied, and lightly powdered in the American style.

Gary Johnson, a visitor from the twenty-first century, paced nervously in the courtyard. His round-trip ticket was not yet punched – or even in his possession.

Three couples waited ahead of Gary and his partner-in-crime, the curvaceous redhead Erin Duffy. Fortunately, Erin was as alert as a firefighter approaching a blaze. She scrutinized the commander-in-chief from head to toe as they shuffled forward. Since Gary's Watch, his vehicle for time travel, was likely lodged in one of Washington's six pockets, his fate rested in her sticky fingers.

As their turn approached, Gary noticed the general nodded to each guest, but never touched anyone, male or female. No handshakes, knuckle bumps, bro hugs, or air kisses.

"Mr. and Mrs. Gary Johnson. From Connecticut," Billy Lee, Washington's longtime Black manservant, finally announced in a deep baritone.

Gary squeezed Erin's hand for luck. She curtsied. He bowed slowly, gauging the distance to the general. Erin was good, but no one was that good.

"Do gentlemen fox hunt in Connecticut?" Washington asked, sweat glistening on the broad expanse of his forehead. The commander-in-chief barely opened his mouth as he spoke, sparing his audience the sight of his decayed teeth and gums.

"No. I think not," Gary replied, the words tumbling awkwardly from his lips like a teenager on a first date.

"Most disappointing," Washington said, turning his attention to the next couple in line.

Billy Lee ushered them inside. No lingering in his Master's presence.

"Did you...?" Gary had to ask.

"Patience, dearie," Erin replied, patting his hand.

CHAPTER 1

Connecticut: June 30, 2026

(several weeks earlier – or 250 years later)

Gary Johnson didn't plan to film videos of Benjamin Franklin taming a lightning bolt, sell teepee rights on the virgin banks of the Hudson River, or mine crypto coins of George Washington. A patriotic entrepreneur, he wanted to retrieve a copy of the Declaration of Independence fresh off the press on July 4, 1776 and bring it back to the twenty-first century, putting an exclamation point on America's 250th anniversary celebration.

Having just turned seventy, Gary knew most people thought he was too old for the journey, but he had dedicated his entire life to time travel. Graduate degree in computer science, IBM, four start-ups – each step propelling him closer to his goal. TimeR, his latest company, and its Watch would be his crowning achievement.

This one trip would justify all the hours he had stared at computer screens, chalked Einstein's relativity theories on a blackboard, begged investors for money, and explained away his failures. He might even be hailed as one of the great explorers of all time, right up there with Christopher Columbus, Lewis and Clark, and Neil Armstrong.

"Grandpa, the pitch clock is counting," his flop-haired five year old grandson, Derek, shouted, twenty feet away, swoosh-sneakered feet anchored into the batter's box, yellow plastic bat twirling over his shoulder like Aaron Judge, his favorite ballplayer. "4-3-2-1..."

While he loved his family immensely, Gary wasn't exactly comfortable being a grandfather. He adjusted his black cap, sporting the Ryder Cup logo of the famed Bethpage golf course, tucked his blue-pinstriped Yankee polo into his shorts, and stared down at Derek with all the seriousness of a major leaguer.

Yes, Gary's hair had wisped and grayed, but his eyes blazed a piercing blue. Only middling height, he still stood erect, fit enough to carry his golf clubs for eighteen holes. He hadn't bought a new belt in years. Most importantly, his mind was still sharp. For a few more years at least.

Gary went into his wind up, left leg kicking as high, or low, as might be expected for his age, just before Derek reached zero. The wiffle ball darted towards home plate, chalked in the driveway of the center hall colonial Gary now empty-nested with Lucie, his wife of forty years, in the leafy hills of Connecticut.

Derek strode forward - a bit too quickly. He swung and missed, frustration apparent on his otherwise cherubic face.

"Strike one," Gary announced as his daughter, Maribel, long-legged and Yankee-capped, fielded the ball off the garage door and tossed it back. Derek ceremoniously stomped his feet.

Maribel, thirty-eight, and her younger brother, Remy, had grown up in this house, and, more notably, still visited regularly. She assumed a catcher's crouch, swiping a lock of tawny hair from her eyes.

Gary looked in for the sign, shook Maribel off once with a mischievous smile, before aiming a juicy meatball down the middle of the plate. Derek took the pitch without swinging, much to Gary's consternation. Once again, pitcher, batter and catcher settled into their stances.

Before Gary could wind up, Lucie, three years his senior, bustled out the back door. Sporting a lavender polo and snug hiking shorts that belied her grandmotherhood, she tugged along Maribel's younger munchkin, Quincy, depositing the two-year-old a few steps behind the pitcher's mound.

"Not too much longer, *mon brave vieux*," she whispered, tapping his right shoulder as she passed by.

"My arm's fine, *mama*," Gary snapped, shooing his wife away. He couldn't pinpoint the exact date, but, sometime over the past decade, Lucie had assumed the captaincy in their marriage. Quitting on her command would set a bad precedent.

He rolled a ground ball to Quincy, waiting patiently for his grandson to field it and toss it back in his general direction. He still hadn't told Lucie he had poured all their savings into TimeR – and taken out a second mortgage. If the Watch didn't work, they might have to move in with the kids. Assuming he returned at all.

"*Le petit déjeuner est sur la table,*" Lucie called, gesturing her clan towards the kitchen. Born and raised in Paris, she deployed her native tongue strategically, a technique sharpened to perfection over the years.

"Only two outs, *grand-mere*," Derek called, tapping his bat on home plate. When Lucie went inside alone, ostensibly to answer a ringing phone, Gary smiled. He savored the small victory, even if assisted by a five-year-old.

He threw four pitches before Lucie sallied outside once again, the set of her lips signaling an approaching storm. "One more - then breakfast," he offered in surrender.

She shook her head. "Rob Mangano's on the landline."

"Mangano?" Gary's stomach clenched. Rob Mangano, a chum since middle school, was his lawyer. He never called with good news.

"He said it was urgent," Lucie added, exchanging glances with Maribel. "We'll take the kids."

CHAPTER 2

Gary hurled his glove into his cubby, his mind racing through the possible reasons for Mangano's call. Two weeks ago, he had fired Saoirse, a Dublin-based coder who wasn't up to the task. She had unleashed an indecipherable array of Gaelic, which he presumed to be profane, before Zooming out. Could she be suing TimeR?

He stomped across the oak floored living room and into the book-lined library which also served as his home office. The autographed photographs of Brooklyn Dodger greats, Jackie Robinson, Pee Wee Reese, and Duke Snyder, always calmed him, stirring memories of his parents, post-World War II immigrants who had adopted baseball as a way to assimilate to their new home.

Sitting at his desk, a pool table sized slab cluttered with family photos, Gary picked up the phone and punched the flashing button on the console. "What's the problem, Rob?"

"I got a call from a friend at the FBI."

"So?"

"He just got an order from up high to crack down on

radicals."

"Radicals? Like the kids who tore up college campuses defending terrorists?"

"No. The radicals who want to incite another revolution."

"What the ..."

"Look, the White House has been pushing America250 for the past year. The big day is almost here, but someone in the West Wing is having second thoughts."

"Second thoughts?"

"The Declaration of Independence may be too revolutionary, if you get my drift."

"All men are created equal...life, liberty and the pursuit of happiness – that's about as American as it gets, right?"

"Sort of. But keep reading."

"No one ever reads past that."

"That's the point. If you bring back the Declaration, people might read the rest of it."

"Not much there, really, is there? Just a list of grievances against mad King George."

"Well, it appears that the radicals are planning a huge social media campaign to show how many of those same grievances apply today."

"I'm a Republican - not a radical. Besides, all anyone cares about today is the economy. And their share of it."

"Look, the billionaires hate the whole War of Independence concept. They prefer to think of the Revolution as an economic dispute over tea and taxes."

"But it was a Revolution. A violent one. Fought primarily by the working class."

"The Department of Education has been tasked to come up with a new name," Mangano said, "and change the historical record to reflect the real truth."

"The *real* truth?"

"DOE wants to edit out the French involvement."

"The French involvement? You've got to be kidding me.

America would never have gained its independence without France's help."

"We'd like to forget that part now."

"It's June 30th. I'm scheduled to leave for 1776 in four days," Gary said, shaking his head. Lucie would go batshit-crazy when he told her about this conversation.

"Sit tight, friend. My guys here are working on it."

Gary had no intention of sitting tight. The Chinese were working on time travel too. The grapevine swirled with rumors that they were behind on their geo-temporal location technology but he knew they would catch up if he didn't keep moving forward.

He ended the call and hustled out to the backyard. Maribel was pitching to Quincy. Derek played first base. Lucie was catching.

"I've got to go to the office," he whispered to his wife. "It's important."

"*Allez,*" she said, tucking a strand of pearly hair under her broad-brimmed, gardening hat. "Say hello to Molly for me."

Molly Brant was TimeR's head of development. With his launch imminent, she and her team would be at their screens 24/7 to make sure the Watch worked perfectly.

"It's Sunday, dad," Maribel called out as he tousled Quincy's hair. "Where are you going?"

"Your father has work to do," Lucie answered. They hadn't told the kids, or anyone else outside of TimeR's immediate circle, about Gary's imminent departure.

CHAPTER 3

Gary had been lucky to hire Molly five years ago. Forty years old, she had grinded her way up from a hardscrabble upbringing on the Iroquois Nation reservation in upstate New York, to the halls of MIT, to the rock star status of a top-notch tech guru. As important, given Gary's advancing age, she attracted a covey of computer geeks with a shared passion for time travel.

TimeR's office was located on two floors of Building 3, situated on a leafy, seven building campus, complete with gym and cafeteria. Gary's office, as well as sales, marketing and finance, was on the main level with windows overlooking a babbling brook while Molly's lair was in the basement.

He wandered downstairs to a bullpen of eight cubicles, set in two rows of four, fronting a glass-walled conference room. The desks were empty save for a hodgepodge of monitors, hoodies, thermos jars, beer mugs and a brightly feathered Native American headdress; but the conference room was packed with programmers.

Wearing cut-off jeans and a purple Iroquois Confederacy tee, Molly waved him inside. Ebony curls framed her youthful face, still a dusky tan despite all the hours spent indoors.

Jared, bald with a diamond glistening in his right ear, held a three foot long briar wood pipe, decorated with red, white and blue needlepointed pennants. He took a deep drag before offering it to Gary.

The acrid smoke started Gary coughing, inducing titters of laughter from the tech team. "What are you smoking?" he asked when he finally caught his breath.

"Something to stir our creative juices," Molly said, standing to take the pipe. She inhaled, swirling the smoke in her mouth before slowly exhaling. "Take a hit. It's an Iroquois tradition."

When Gary shook his head, she passed the pipe to a gangly woman with coal black hair ponytailing down to her narrow, blue-jeaned hips. A full sleeve tattoo, a macabre totem pole of shrunken skulls, scrolled down her right arm. Tanner Mitchell, Gary was pleased he remembered her name, sucked on the pipe even longer than Molly had.

"You sure?" Molly asked again. She took the pipe from Tanner and walked it over to Gary. "It's a bad omen to refuse a peace pipe."

"Not on Sunday," Gary replied, even though he was tempted. He couldn't remember the last time anyone had offered him dope. Maybe in grad school. Almost a half-century ago.

Escaping the fumes, he stalked to the white board in the back of the conference room to study the flow chart scrawled in red marker. While an AI bot was doing much of the grunt-level coding now at TimeR, he had written all the foundational time travel algorithms himself and was still quite fluent in geek-speak. The puppy-dog eyes of the techies followed his every move. He counted nine faces. But there were only eight last week. And he didn't recognize two. The math didn't add up.

The room started to spin. He put his hand on the conference room table to steady himself.

Where was Jennifer Tryon, their geo-temporal location guru? Gary was initially hesitant to hire a Harvard grad, they generally shied from the dirty work of coding, but, fortunately, he had been wrong. He and Jenn had spent hours together mapping his journey along ley lines, the longitude and latitude of time travel.

Ley lines crisscrossed the globe, conveying massive amounts of energy from one site to another. They powered the construction of architectural wonders such as Stonehenge, Chichen Itza, Machu Picchu and the Great Pyramids, all built far too early to be accomplished with the technology of their eras.

"Tryon's gone," Molly said, reading his mind.

"Gone?"

"Quit on Friday."

"Friday?" Something was wrong. Gary sobered quickly, righting himself. "Where'd she go?"

"Just emailed in her resignation. No explanation – no call," Molly replied, her eyes spitting fire. "Probably got an offer to become a CEO in Silicon Valley."

Although the explanation jived with Gary's predilection about Harvard, he wasn't a happy camper. "What's TimeR going to do without her?"

"The Watch is finished. We just need to wrap up testing your route home."

"Without Jenn?" he asked again, sitting down.

"She was the key to delivering the big picture – multiple time travelers going to multiple destinations," Molly said. "Me and Tanner will take the point now. Since you're the only traveler we're worried about, it'll be as smooth as creamed corn."

"So no one else will be able to travel with my Watch?"

"Correct. We've already got your genetic profile hard-wired, so we just need to finish up the navigation. You're leaving Thursday, right?"

Gary nodded, his mind still spinning over Jenn's abrupt departure.

"Fantastic," Molly said. "It's close enough to the summer solstice to give us a power boost."

"Summer solstice? I think you've watched too many seasons of *Outlander*," he chuckled, breaking the tension. "I don't think there are any Standing Stones in Connecticut."

"But there's a ley line link to Independence Hall in

Philadelphia.”

“And my return trip? Lucie expects me to come home.”

“That’s the plan,” Molly said, a little too uncertainly for Gary’s liking. “I just want to stress test the route a few more times.”

“We might send a dog,” Tanner offered.

“A dog? Are you serious?” Gary asked, struggling to keep his voice steady.

“Sure. We could wire one up so we could track...”

“Stop right there. Who would look after the pup on the other end?”

“OK. You’ve got a point,” Tanner replied, retreating to the tech pack. “We’ll stick to computer simulations.”

Gary stood, spreading his arms to encompass the room. “I trust you guys. Just make sure you get me home.”

Tanner took another hit of the peace pipe.

CHAPTER 4

Sensing Gary's discomfort, Molly led him out of the conference room. Reaching her desk, the first one on the right, she swiveled her head, making sure no one was watching, then bent over and unlocked a drawer. She removed a jeweler's tray of black velvet, placing it on the desktop.

The Watch sparkled. Gary's blood pressure soared.

"The hardware's done, but, like I said, we're still finishing up the route tests," Molly said.

Gary couldn't take his eyes off the Watch. By design, it was an exact replica of a Daniel Quare design introduced in the eighteenth century. Quare, a famed watchmaker to British nobility, invented a clock "complication" that would chime each hour, enabling time to be told in the dark, a critical breakthrough in a world without electricity.

Gary picked up the Watch and notched it on his wrist. The case was silver, engraved with an intricate floral pattern. The band was distressed leather. Hour and minute hands pointed to bold Roman numerals on its face. An outer, faint ring of Arabic numerals delineated intervals of five, although there was no second hand. To his delight, the mechanism ticked distinctly as its mainspring uncoiled and powered the balance wheel.

Time had consumed the Johnson family for generations. Growing up in Poland, Gary's father, Bernard, had learned the horology craft from his father who, in turn, had learned from his father. Gary never met his grandparents, they were killed in the Holocaust, several years after shipping teen-aged Bernie off to relatives in England. Back then, Bernie was a Janousky, but he adopted the surname, Johnson, when he first arrived in the States in 1950. He never gave up his Jewish faith, however.

Sadly, the surge in post-World War II manufacturing put inexpensive watches on too many people's wrists, squeezing the profits at the Johnson family store, aptly named Time Travels, in Brooklyn. Accordingly, Bernie encouraged his son to study computers, the emerging technology in the 1960's.

Gary quickly learned that programming was a lot like watchmaking - the skillful artisan had to cram many moving parts into a fixed space. While most college men daydreamed of fast cars and faster girls, or vice-versa, his idle thoughts centered on the possibility of movement in the fourth dimension - time.

With Molly at his side, Gary tapped the Watch face three times. A digital display, built upon next-gen Bionic Advanced Risc Processors, replaced the eighteenth century façade. While maintaining some applications compatibility with Apple's latest i-Watch, Molly's team had custom-designed Cortex processors as well as quadrupled memory capability. They constructed TimeR's travel app with Apple's SWIFT programming language, plus a few of their own extensions and AI tools.

TimeR's most advanced accomplishment, however, was its proprietary gene-editing code, utilizing CRSPR tech. It enabled a specific individual, Gary would be first, to shape-shift from one century to another. His voice, reciting the proper password - "TimeR1776" to travel, "TimeR2026" to return - would activate the Launch button, the routing hard-wired between present-day

Connecticut and colonial Philadelphia.

While Gary ogled the Watch, Molly took both his hands in her own, squeezing them gently. "Close your eyes, chief. Feel the energy in the ground."

She bowed her head, waited for him to comply, then recited: "We are all thankful to our Mother, the Earth, for she gives us all that we need for life. She supports our feet as we walk about upon her. It gives us joy that she continues to care for us as she has from the beginning of time. Now our minds are one."

Gary blinked, swearing the ground had trembled.

"An old Iroquois prayer," Molly said, lifting her head.

"Can I wear it home tonight?" he asked, his gaze returning to the Watch.

"You're the boss," Molly replied. "Just bring it back in the morning."

CHAPTER 5

By the time Gary got home, the house was dark. Maribel and the kids were gone. Lucie must have gone to bed early. With Mangano's warning ringing in his ears and TimeR's incompletely tested Watch on his wrist, he knew he'd face a critical decision in the next twenty-four hours, if not sooner.

Gary retreated to his happy place, a windowless basement workshop crammed with shelves of pliers, screwdrivers, magnifiers, levers, and springs ranging in size from small to tiny. Framed Revolutionary-era flags, a coiled snake on a yellow field and a pine tree on a white background, hung on the wall. A well-thumbed hardcover, *The Time Machine* by HG Wells, lay closed on his worktable. The once futuristic novel had been his inspiration since his parents had gifted it to him for his thirteenth birthday. Initially piquing his interest in time travel, it later tantalized him with the possibility of combining digital power and horological craftsmanship.

Taking screwdriver and tweezers in hand, Gary lost himself trying to recreate Quare's revolutionary complication. A knock on the door interrupted his work.

"Can I come in?" Lucie asked. Wrapped in her robe, she meandered to Gary's side, resting a hand on his shoulder as she surveyed his handiwork. "Nervous about your upcoming journey, *mon cher*?"

"Yes, but it's more than that."

"Hmmm." A history major herself, albeit at the Sorbonne, Lucie first captured Gary's attention at a lecture on the Articles of Confederation at the New York Historical Society. He had weaved through a maze of fellow pocket-protecting nerds to make his pitch to the statuesque brunette who appeared way out of place. Perhaps, it was his Quixotic dream to journey to the past that sparked their unlikely romance. Of course, Gary didn't tell her that he was serious about time travel until they had slept together. Twice.

Gary put down his tools and took a deep breath. "Mangano said the government, our government, may try to discourage me from traveling to 1776."

"And why is that?"

He explained the government's reasoning as best he could.

"But you will not be easily discouraged, will you?" she asked, gently massaging his neck.

"I have to go. Not just for me," Gary said, turning towards his wife, taking her hand. "For us."

"For the money?"

"Yes."

"You've taken out another mortgage, haven't you?" Lucie dropped his hand and turned away.

Gary hung his head. "How did you find out?"

"You left the papers on the kitchen table."

"I'm sorry. I didn't mean to."

"Maybe you did." Lucie pivoted back to her husband. "You are under a great deal of stress, *mon cher*."

"We may have to sell the house."

"We'll survive."

"We will, I know that," Gary said, standing, hugging his wife close. "But I'll be a loser. The Chinese will beat me in the race back in time."

"*Un vaillant chevalier* - never a loser."

"Thank you."

Lucie broke away and paced about the workshop.

"But, you still shouldn't go."

"Not go?"

"You're not a young man anymore. Your shoulder aches, your knee barks, you passed a kidney stone last year, your blood pressure is high – do you want me to go on?" Lucie asked. "And you're the healthiest of all your friends."

"That's why I have to go now – before something happens."

"What if you fall, or *Mon Dieu*, have a heart attack in 1776? There will be no ambulance, no paramedic, no ER to save you."

"This is my last chance."

"Last chance at what? You should be a proud grandfather. Enjoy your watchmaking, your family, your golf."

"I'll think about it," Gary replied, sitting back down at his desk, busying himself with his plyers.

"I'll go with you."

"To 1776? You're..." Gary started but stopped before completing his thought. Referencing his wife's age was never a winning strategy.

He held up his wrist with TimeR's Watch ticking away. He had completely forgotten about it. "Look," he said, pressing the stem on the side of the Watch and holding it for three seconds. A photo of Lucie alone in her garden replaced the clock face. It faded away automatically before he could blink. "I'll be able to text when I'm away."

"*C'est magnifique*," Lucie said, unstrapping the Watch from Gary's wrist and rolling it over in her hands. "And why can't I travel with you?"

"The Watch is linked to a specific genetic profile. It's only programmed to transport me right now."

"And you're confident this Watch will work as planned?"

"It will - but it's not quite finished yet."

"Not quite finished?" Lucie returned the Watch.

"Molly and her team are still testing the return trip," he replied as nonchalantly as possible.

"*Merde.*" Lucie arched her brows, mumbling softly to herself.

"Don't worry. Molly won't let me leave until she's absolutely sure she can bring me home."

"What if the battery runs out?"

"The Watch is solar powered. I'm pretty sure the sun was shining in 1776."

"Backup?"

"Terahertz rays. Electromagnetic radiation," he replied, putting his tools away. "Anything that has a temperature, like a human body, produces T-rays. MIT did the research to convert them to electrical current."

"What could go wrong then?" Lucie asked, sarcasm leaking from her lips like Quincy's chocolate milk polka-dotting his pajamas. "It's late. Let's go to bed."

CHAPTER 6

Jennifer Tryon, thirty-five but still bicep-bulging fit, stalked back and forth in her one bedroom apartment on Riverside Drive in Manhattan. The Hudson River sparkled in the moonglow. Running a hand through her butterscotch blond hair, cropped short in an Ellen DeGeneres cut, she checked her phone one more time. It would be morning in Hong Kong.

Ding Yu, the forty-year old, superstar Chinese investor, should have called by now. His VC fund, HardCode, ranked up there with Kleiner, Benchmark and Andreeson, early investors in Amazon, eBay and Coinbase respectively. His seal of approval would open every door in the tech world for Jenn.

At last, her phone buzzed. She scurried away from the window, forcing herself to slow before accepting the FaceTime request. Yu, wrapped in a red changshan jacket embroidered with a gold dragon, was on the other end, sitting outside on a deck. The Victoria Peak tram line and the skyscrapers of the city were in the background. Jenn also noted a glass spire poking through the foliage. It was her childhood residence.

"I resigned from TimeR yesterday. Tryon Time is ready to launch," Jenn said.

"Good, good. I will wire ten million US to your account by the end of the day. That should enable you to start hiring engineers." Yu sipped from a porcelain tea cup. "Do you have the app code?"

Jenn nodded. Over the past year, she had maintained a personal copy of her work at TimeR. Yes, it was technically stealing, but...

"Your genetic-translation and geo-temporal location work is brilliant. You deserve to reap the rewards."

"I'm not looking to make money – like Gary. I want to foster time travel for good. Tryon Time will send travelers back to key points in history, so we can observe the movers and shakers. Then we can return and influence events in the twenty-first century. Imagine a world without exploitative colonialism, human oppression, or evil despots."

"All most worthy ideals, my dear. I am honored to be on your team."

"Thank you."

"And Tanner Mitchell?"

"She's pissed at me for dumping her, but we won't be needing her at Tryon Time."

"Can she cause a problem for us?"

"I don't think Tanner will want to note on her resume that she's gay and fucked her boss."

"Excellent. When do you think Tryon Time will be ready to launch its first traveler?"

"A year, maybe sooner," Jenn replied, suddenly feeling the weighty burden of running her own company. "We'll have to finalize both the traveler and the location and complete the appropriate programming."

"Let's target January 1," Yu said. "It would be an excellent way to usher in the new year."

"I'll do my best."

"Do better," Yu replied. He waited for a matronly house servant to clear his breakfast dishes, then added, "Where do you think your first traveler will go?"

"London, 1937. Have a sit-down with Prime Minister Chamberlain before he gives in to Hitler. Think about how many lives might be saved in our time if we learn to stand up to fascist dictators."

Before Yu could comment, Jenn heard a door slam in the background. Three dark suited men appeared behind Yu. Two reached under his arms and yanked him to his feet.

"You will come with us, comrade," the third, an older man with slick, salt-and-pepper hair and a black patch covering his right eye, said. "Your country needs your services."

Yu face exploded in panic. He had sworn to Jenn that his success insulated him from government intervention. "I need to call my lawyer... my wife."

"There is no time for personal calls."

Yu turned towards the screen. "Hide Jennifer," he hissed before the screen went dark.

Jennifer's stomach somersaulted. She doubled over, gasping for air. Ding Yu, her benefactor, had just been detained by the Chinese Ministry of State Security. How could she have trusted him?

His government, as autocratic as any in the world, was determined to win the race back to the past and would stop at nothing to squelch the competition. The MSS would be extremely disappointed to learn that Yu did not have the technical skills to help much. Jenn, however, did. And she still held a Chinese passport.

CHAPTER 7

Gary and Lucie awoke early on a too sunny to be Monday morning. They lingered for a few minutes, listening to the birds in the garden greet the new day. Rising, they shared a conspiratorial glance born of forty years of shared decisions – agreements, disagreements, compromises.

"Are you still planning to bring back a copy of the Declaration of Independence?" Lucie asked.

"Yes, but without any ceremony. Mangano says the White House doesn't want any hoopla over that document anymore," Gary replied.

"It's an American relic. We could always sell it privately."

"Privately?"

"I still have contacts at Sotheby's," Lucie said, recalling her days working at the famous auction house in New York. In fact, the night she first met Gary, she was evaluating a letter, purportedly written by Major General the Marquis de Lafayette, in the Historical Society archives. "I checked online last night. A Dunlap broadside sold privately in 2000 for $8.1 million. A printing by John Holt of

New York fetched $3.3 million in 2024.”

"Why did the price drop?" Maybe people *were* actually losing interest in the Declaration, Gary thought.

"Dunlap was in Philadelphia. He was first to press so his broadsides are the most valuable. Only twenty-six are still in existence."

"I'll bring back a Dunlap then."

"*Tres bonne.*"

"If I had a bankroll, I could make the trip even more worthwhile," Gary said as he dressed. White golf shirt, blue jeans, black sneakers.

"Bankroll?" Lucie replied, absentmindedly rearranging the perfume bottles on her dressing table. "I thought Captain Parsons was supplying you with Continental dollars."

"That's spending money – I'm talking about investing. In real estate," Gary said, turning. He stood still, hands on hips, waiting for Lucie to figure things out. At last, the light went on.

Lucie handed her diamond stud earrings, two carats each, to her husband. "Would these work?"

"I could probably buy half of Manhattan in 1776 with them," he said, silently realizing how greedy that sounded, but he was planning to risk his life. How much was that worth?

"Main Line Philadelphia... according to Zillow... the *average* home in Villanova goes for almost $4 million today," Lucie said, reading from her phone. She withdrew a gold link bracelet from her jewelry box.

"It will be our secret," Gary replied, adding the bracelet to his stash.

"*Viva la France,*" Lucie said as she led the way to the kitchen.

A buzz at the front door interrupted breakfast. Sam Parsons, captain of the Fifth Connecticut's Revolutionary War reenactment group, stood at attention on the porch, a battered whale-gray duffel in hand. At 6'2", square-shouldered and sharp-chinned, he cut an impressive figure, befitting his "day" job as an officer at the Navy's New London submarine base. "Paul Revere here – sounding a warning."

Gary looked quizzical as he ushered his friend, and coach, inside. Parson's namesake and direct ancestor had led the charge against the redcoats at the Old Stone House in Brooklyn on August 27, 1776, the bloodiest fighting of that long, sad day. Gary had grown up not far from the battlefield, the ghosts of the dead Continental Army soldiers haunting his youthful dreams and sparking his interest in all things Revolutionary.

"The FBI just paid me a visit. I bet they visit you or the good Professor next," Sam said. While the captain prepped Gary for everyday life in colonial America, Professor William Pilgrim, a noted Revolutionary War historian at Yale, schooled him in the intellectual context of the era. "I brought over your gear," he added, holding up the pack. "I'd hide it somewhere safe."

"Let's go downstairs," Gary replied, leading the way to his basement workroom. Lucie, carrying a cup of coffee, followed, closing the door behind them. Gary sorted through the pack: white shirt, breeches, boots as well as a dressier indigo-dyed shirt, checkered waistcoat and buckled, came-over-on-the-Mayflower, shoes.

"The ruffles are a nice touch," Lucie said, smiling as she held up the everyday shirt.

"What about underwear?" Gary asked.

"Most men went commando. That's why the shirts have long tails. They tucked them in to protect their pintles."

"Pintles?"

"Figure it out," Sam chortled.

"Better get used to the patois of the day," Lucie said, trying unsuccessfully to stifle a laugh.

"I thought I read somewhere about silk boxers coming into fashion in the late eighteenth century," Gary replied meekly as he reached underneath the clothes for his travel gear: palm-sized pistol, four packets of gunpowder, four lead balls, pocket knife, fork, flints, and waterproof document protection sleeve. He walked over to his desk, opened a drawer, and removed what looked like an old spoon. In James Bondian fashion, Molly's team had concealed a powerful flashlight in its horned handle. A battered tin snuff box with a false bottom concealing an array of modern drugs completed his kit.

Lucie stepped into the bathroom, returning with a roll of toilet paper. *"Pour les indigestions,"* she said, squashing it on top of Gary's colonial clothes.

"Did you bring the money?" Gary asked Parsons.

"Here's a hundred dollars in fake Continental currency, printed with modern technology so it's completely authentic looking," the captain said, handing over an envelope. "And here's another fifty in dealer-verified Continental paper and coins. You can pay me back when you return."

"Out of curiosity, how does that translate to today?" Lucie asked.

"A dollar in 1776 is roughly equal to thirty dollars in 2026."

"Will that be enough?" Gary asked.

Parsons nodded. "A private room and meals in a high class inn ran about ten dollars per night back then. So you should have a comfortable cushion for a short stay."

Gary's mobile buzzed, interrupting the conversation. "It's Pilgrim," he said, setting his iPhone on speaker.

"They just left," the professor said, his voice quavering. "I think they're driving down I-95. You're next."

Gary swallowed hard. "The FBI?"

"Yes. They tried to feed me a crock of bullshit about George Washington. Wanted to know how any man who voluntarily walked away from executive power – twice - could be a good example of American leadership."

"What did you tell them?" Gary said.

"I quoted the Declaration of Independence: a prince, whose character is thus marked by every act which may define a tyrant, is unfit to be the ruler of a free people."

"Wow. What did they say to that?"

"He who saves his country does not violate any law."

"Sounds like a pretty civilized conversation," Parsons said, looking somewhat relieved.

"Not really. Agent Gibson, the lead guy, there were three of them, threatened to revoke my research grant if I continued to teach subversive ideas. You're next Gary. They don't want you to go to 1776," Pilgrim replied, signing off.

"What are you going to do, *mon cher*?" Lucie asked.

"I'm an American – born and raised here. We'll work out a deal," Gary said, standing tall.

CHAPTER 8

A banging on the front door ended the discussion in the basement. Pack in hand, Gary walked up the stairs hesitantly. Lucie followed, but Parsons remained in the workroom.

Gary checked his Watch, almost noon, finding comfort in its heft and authenticity, as well as the high tech under the covers. Nevertheless, his safe journey was far from a sure thing. Jennifer Tryon's disappearance and the dope in the tech room didn't boost his confidence. While he had complete faith in Molly, Tanner Mitchell was less inspiring. All good reasons to delay.

Lucie was right. His life was really good here in 2026: a wife he adored, kids who still enjoyed his company, grandchildren who lit up his day, friends he could count on, a 17 handicap he could play to. And enough money, if they sold the house, to live modestly till the end.

Why bet the whole pot today? If he waited a week, maybe a month, the government might see the light and Molly's team could be certain he'd return.

Agent Gibson, a tall Black man sporting a neatly-trimmed,

goatee and hammerhead pecs a Greek god might envy, was inside the house before Gary could open the door. His two associates, both strapping, twenty-something, crewcut white men, bounded close behind. They all wore dark suits adorned with an American flag pin.

"We have a warrant to search your house," Gibson said, holding out a sheet of paper bearing the eagle-eyed Great Seal of the United States.

"Search for what?" Gary asked, taking the warrant, giving his pack to Lucie while he read it.

"We'll start with your Watch." The agent motioned for Gary to hand it over.

"I want to call my lawyer."

"You can do this the easy way or the hard way. If you want a lawyer – fine. We'll arrest you right now and he can come downtown to get you out of jail. Then he can check in with ICE to see if he can stop your wife from being deported."

"Deported?"

"She participated in the "No Kings" march in New York last year. Our facial recognition software nailed her. And she's French. Got her green card in 1983, if I remember correctly. We can revoke that privilege anytime."

"*Putain de cul*," Lucie muttered.

"Insulting a federal officer is not going to help your case, *madame*."

"My country, France, paid for the Revolution. We fought in it. General Lafayette was George Washington's favorite son. We gave America the Statue of Liberty," Lucie said. "Is that what you're trying to erase?"

"Look, Gary, can I call you Gary?" Gibson asked. "France is not our ally anymore – not since they signed a trade deal with China."

"What does trade have to do with the Declaration of Independence?" Gary asked.

"Everything, man," Gibson sighed as if talking to a child.

"The American people need to look forward. Great things are coming. Greenland. The Panama Canal. Canada. We'll be going to Mars. We're not going to let radicals like Professor William Pilgrim drag us back into the past."

"I'm the time traveler not Pilgrim," Gary said. "And I'm a capitalist through and through."

"Why are you being so difficult, bro?" Gibson asked, motioning for Gary to step off to the side, out of Lucie's hearing. "You must be listening to the wrong podcasts."

"I'd like to call my lawyer," Gary replied, not moving.

"Hand over the Watch first."

"No." Gary stuck his Watch hand in his pocket. Lucie stepped to his side.

"*Bravo*," she added, taking his free hand.

"So you're both going to be difficult?" Gibson said before turning to his team.

"Go now. Leave," Lucie whispered to her husband, placing the pack in his hand. "Mangano will look after me."

Gary stormed outside towards the porch. Lucie stepped in front of the FBI men.

"Out of our way, Granny," Gibson said as he shoved her aside.

Gary looked skyward as he raised his left hand to waist height. He tapped the Watch face three times. When the launch screen appeared, he enunciated the password, TimeR 1776, one syllable at a time.

A jolt, starting at the Watch, rolled up his left arm, across his neck and shoulders, and down all the way to the fingers of his right hand. He closed his eyes as the sensation plunged through his legs. The patio slates fractured, the pool water whitecapped, the wind howled like a ravenous wolf.

Gary squeezed his eyes shut as a jagged fissure rippled towards him. Sinking to one knee, he braced in the eye of the tornado for what seemed like minutes, his mind strangely calm.

At last, the wind sighed a dying breath. Gary opened his

eyes and willed himself to stand upright, clutching his precious backpack in his right hand.

Red brick Georgian homes, gaily painted clapboard storefronts, and tottering shanties lined the cobblestoned street in front of him. Ships' masts, he stopped counting at twelve, loomed to his rear. The stench of horseshit fouled the air.

No backyard. No Lucie. No FBI.

CHAPTER 9

Philadelphia July 1776

A bell pealed from a distant tower. As if on cue, people swirled about Gary, paying him little mind. Beards flaked with bread crumbs, five tattooed laborers marched away from the docks; three young women, fashionably attired in pastel day gowns and matching caps, strolled with linked arms; a barefoot urchin, smallpox scars cratering his face, begged for coins.

Gary shuddered, shaking the last of the fog from his brain, and assessed his physical state. His left shoulder felt like it had been yanked by a team of oxen, but he was still able to rotate his arm over his head. His right arm as well. He flexed his fingers, all ten responded as expected. His toes wiggled too. Tentatively, he took three steps forward, no problems here. So far, so good.

Now, the scariest part. He raised his left arm again, slowly, almost afraid to look at his wrist. A scarlet welt nested under the Watch, but the device itself appeared unblemished. And it was still ticking, its hands displaying the time as ten minutes after noon, consistent with the sun's position overhead as it peeked through a curtain of leaden clouds.

The Watch might be right, but his attire was not. Hurriedly, Gary reached into his pack for his blue jacket to cover the logo on his golf shirt. His jeans might pass muster if no one looked too closely, but his sneakers would have to go. He kicked them off and ducked into a dark alley separating a haberdasher from a tavern, to change.

After fastening the buckles on his shoes, Gary looked himself over. Tri-corn hat, jacket, ruffled shirt, breeches all looked appropriate. He took a deep breath and reentered the street.

A one horse carriage whisked by at a brisk trot, almost bowling him over. The driver, a Black, uniformed in burnt orange livery, tugged the reins hard, but the passenger, looking suspiciously familiar, waved him onward.

A stooped-shouldered man, austerely attired in a stiff black coat and matching hat, a Quaker possibly, reached out with a steadying hand. "Beelzebub Ash at your service, friend. Is thee well?" Gary nodded, relieved that his dress appeared to have passed its first test.

"Those Virginians have little respect for our fair city," Ash added. "Mr. Jefferson's a lawyer himself. He should know better than to allow his man to drive that fast in broad daylight."

Mr. Jefferson? Thomas Jefferson? "Which way to the State House?" Gary snapped, seeking confirmation that he, in fact, had landed in 1776.

"Take a left on Fifth Street. Four blocks up," the Quaker replied. "No hurry though, young man. Congress will be in session for several more weeks at least. The fribbles think we should break from England. Declare our independence, whatever that means. A bucket of mouse droppings if you ask me."

Young man? Was the Quaker blind? The Liberty Bell pealed again.

"What adorns your wrist, if I may ask?" Mr. Ash could clearly see quite well.

"A watch." Gary replied, unsure whether to show off his treasure or shove his hand into his pocket.

"A timepiece?" Ash's eyes widened.

"Yes."

"May I see?"

Gary lifted his wrist, allowing Mr. Ash to examine the Watch face.

"A Quare, I believe," Ash said, bending over the Watch. "I saw one several years ago at Milne's shop on Second Street."

"Yes, a Quare," Gary replied, shuffling his feet. While relieved that the Watch had passed inspection, he was anxious to leave.

"Quite expensive."

"A gift from my father." Gary doffed his hat in an effort to escape.

"But, on your wrist?" Ash straightened, crooking his finger at Gary like a schoolmaster lecturing a wayward pupil. "Ostentatious, isn't it?"

"It's the fashion in Connecticut." Gary was thinking fast but still headed for trouble.

"Ah, I see. I've never ventured to Connecticut."

"My apologies, sir, but I must be going."

"I've yet to see a gentleman in Philadelphia wear his watch so boldly."

"Perhaps the fashion here will change."

"Perhaps," Ash replied, nodding slowly as Gary jammed his left hand into his pocket. "I bid you farewell then."

"And you."

Before Gary had walked five steps, however, Ash called out. "Be wary, friend. Certain men here might think the fashion originated in London, not Hartford. And they might not take too kindly to it."

Gary slipped back into the alley, eying the Watch. Could it communicate with 2026? He pressed the stem and held it for three seconds. Lucie's photo appeared. He missed her already. He tapped the Watch face three times. The clock dissolved, replaced by the menu screen. "Safe in Philadelphia 1776," he whispered. A swish indicated his text was in route to Molly.

The Watch's map app pinpointed Gary's location as High Market between Front and Second streets. Jefferson's house should be on the next corner, Franklin's another block up the street. He shuddered with excitement. He had toiled his entire life to step back to this point.

Should he try to meet the great men? What reason would he have to interrupt their momentous work? Could they help him to achieve his own goals? Which were....? He leaned against a hitching post to think.

To prove that he had actually time traveled, he needed to retrieve a Dunlap broadside - after it was printed on July 5th of course. With Lucie's jewelry, he could also buy land, further cementing their finances. They might need the money for legal bills should the FBI press its case. But for now at least, he was safe from twenty-first century pursuit.

Eighteenth century justice was another matter however, Gary thought, as the acrid aroma of boiling tar drifted up from the docks. A bath in tar and feathers was the colonial equivalent of modern day social media trolling, only much more physically damaging. It's just the shipwrights at work, he told himself, quieting his nerves.

Gary squared his hat and set off for the City Tavern across from the State House, the Professor's first recommendation for lodging. With Congress back in session, it would probably be fully occupied, but silver usually talked.

Two minutes later, the Watch buzzed "Lucie is safe. Huzzah." Gary pumped his fist. Realizing he had displayed the Watch in public again, he slapped his hand back into his coat pocket. What a colossal screw-up. When did men start wearing watches on their wrists?

His Watch was solar powered, so it needed daylight to recharge; nevertheless, he needed to get it off immediately. A third mistake could prove fatal.

CHAPTER 10

Gary skirted around the State House, its yard milling with people on Monday July 1 anxious to hear news of Congress' closed door deliberations. Even from a distance he could hear a young man barking about "the Royal Brute of Great Britain," a quote from Thomas Paine's *Common Sense,* the best-selling pamphlet. Its direct, simple language hammered home the arguments that swayed the masses to break with England. Three blocks west on Cherry Street in the artisans' district, he found the shop of Philip Syng, Philadelphia's most acclaimed silversmith, rival to Paul Revere in Boston.

Gary rested outside the window displaying an array of candelabras, goblets, buttons, gorgets, and cutlery. He noticed his left knee, or rather didn't notice it despite the brisk hike from the waterfront. The sharp pain that had plagued him in 2026 was gone. He flexed the knee - then lifted his right foot, balancing solely on the left. No pain or crackling noises. His old, or rather his younger, knee was back. Obviously, time travel was easier on his body than he had feared.

He was about to enter the shop when curiosity got the better of him. Diverting into another alleyway, he removed his jacket and unfastened the top two buttons of his shirt. The jagged surgical scar from his rotator cuff surgery last year was gone too.

Didn't Ash address him as a "young man"? He removed his hat and ran his finger through his hair - lush, not stringy. Was it streaked with gray? What about his appendix? It had ruptured when he was twenty-five, six weeks before he met Lucie. He had to be ambulanced to the hospital for its removal. Had time travel altered his body? His mind? How old was he now?

Further speculation would have to wait until he found privacy and a mirror. First, however, Gary had to protect the Watch so he wouldn't attract unwanted attention. A bell jingled as he opened Syng's door.

While the Syng name still remained, the shop's proprietor was now Richard Humphreys who acquired the business in 1772. Humphreys had earned his fortune in the China trade, bringing porcelain, silk and spices, and likely opium as well, to North America. With the British now blockading ports, Humphreys was eager to deal with a well-dressed gentleman boasting a full purse of coins.

Thirty minutes later, Gary re-emerged on Cherry Street, having traded half his stash for a sturdy silver rope chain. With the Watch still buried deep in his pocket, he had decided not to show it to the shopkeeper, he hastened back towards the State House.

A drizzle peppered him as he walked. With his head down, he failed to notice the bald man, a jagged scar bisecting his left cheek, keeping a steady twenty steps to his rear, or the slightly older gentleman, sporting a checkered waistcoat and lightly powdered hair, trailing his pursuer.

City Tavern, a two story brick structure flying the red and white striped flag of the Sons of Liberty, was already packed when Gary arrived. Despite Professor Pilgrim's warnings, he was unprepared for the stench of unwashed men, horse flesh, and tobacco greeting him at the swinging door. Reeling, he removed his dripping hat and forced his way through the crowd to the bar and ordered a mug of flip, a concoction of rum, molasses and ale.

"Twenty pence," the barkeep, displaying the prodigious girth and fleshy jowls of a life without want, demanded as he splashed the beverage in front of Gary.

Assuming he should tip, Gary counted out twenty-five pence and laid it on the bar. The barkeep pushed a coin back. "Said twenty pence. You daft son?"

Gary mumbled an apology, content to sip his brew and listen to the swell of conversation surrounding him. Rather than try to bluster his way immediately into a room for the night, he decided to first get the feel for his surroundings, and perk his courage up as well.

As the Professor had explained, the Continental Congress debate on the draft of the Declaration of Independence had begun in earnest that morning, July 1. By late afternoon, enough of the details had leaked to spark a vibrant debate at the Tavern.

"Unanimous? We need the vote of all thirteen colonies. Why is New York dragging its heels?"

"Life, liberty and the pursuit of happiness. Darn straight, I'm entitled to all three. So is every other man here."

"Three? The Declaration lists twenty-seven abuses by that despot King George."

"The King has countenanced the slave trade - a cruel war against human nature."

"Hogwash. Nothing wrong with slavery. It's been the way of the world since biblical days. Where would my fair South Carolina be without it?" Edward Rutledge, who at twenty-six years old would become the youngest man to sign the Declaration, pounded his mug, spewing froth across the table.

"What do you think, son?" the barkeep asked Gary after he had wiped up the mess. Think? Gary was as starstruck as a groupie backstage at a rock concert.

"About slavery?" Gary replied, his mind working slowly to separate his opinion on the Declaration, which he had well-prepared, from the shock of the repeated reference to his age.

"Never would ask a customer about Negroes. Not good for business."

"The Declaration will make the world stand up and take notice of America. I wager it will become the most important document in our history."

"Here, here," the barkeep raised his own tankard in a toast. "If we win the war, that is. Otherwise, it will go in the rubbish heap and Jefferson, Franklin and the whole lot of men here will hang."

They won't hang, Gary thought, his knowledge of the future inflating his self-confidence. "I'll need a room for this evening, maybe longer," he said. "Where can I find the proprietor?"

"John Tralee, at your service," the barkeep replied. "And your name?"

"Gary Johnson."

"Pleased to meet you, Mr. Johnson. Where did you say you were traveling from?"

"Connecticut."

"And what brings you all the way to our City of Brotherly Love?"

"I'm looking to obtain a letter of marque from Congress." In conjunction with the Professor, he had settled on the cover story of a prosperous Connecticut shipowner.

"A most worthy goal." Tralee raised his glass again. "I've invested in several such privateering ventures myself."

Gary nodded, putting another coin on the bar. A letter of marque put a legal veneer on piracy, empowering armed American ships to attack and capture British merchantmen on the high seas, sail the prizes into port, and sell both the captured ships and their cargoes at auction. George Washington himself had financed a fleet in 1775.

Tralee's questioning had now officially started the clock ticking on his stay in Philadelphia. "Do you have a room available for tonight?" Gary asked.

"You may be in luck," Tralee replied. "By any chance, do you know Oliver Wolcott? Colonel Wolcott that is.”

Gary shook his head slowly, reviewing his lessons but drawing a blank.

“Surprising. He’s a Connecticut man too. Yale, I believe. Sheriff of Litchfield County.”

“I’m from the other end of the colony.”

“It’s a small colony, though, isn't it?”

Gary sipped his ale rather than risk exposing more of his fragile cover story.

“The Colonel was one of the colony’s delegates to Congress, but the Governor, Trumbull I believe, has appointed him to command the militia in New York City.”

A fracas erupted at the far end of the bar, the South Carolina slaver tussling with a Massachusetts man. Tralee stopped them from coming to blows.

“Wolcott’s room is available then?” Gary asked when Tralee returned.

“Up the stairs. Third room on the right. I’d show you myself but I’d dare not leave my post tonight.”

“I’m sure it will be satisfactory.”

“Will you be stabling your mount with us as well?”

“No.” Gary had decided to say little or nothing about his mode of transportation unless he absolutely had to.

“Supper’s at six then. My wife does the cooking. Don’t get many complaints,” Tralee chuckled.

Gary worked his way through the crowd, the fug somehow more tolerable. His room had all the basics except a lock on the door. Regardless, Gary had to protect the Watch. He fastened it to the newly purchased silver chain and looped it over his head. After tugging hard on the chain several times, he tucked it into his shirt.

Satisfied that his treasure was secure, he decided it was time to assess his appearance. First, he ventured a glance at his abdomen. The appendectomy scar was gone. Next, he tiptoed towards the looking glass hanging on the wall above the wash basin. He closed his eyes as he drew near, recalling a photo taken of him in the eighties outside a Bruce Springsteen concert at the Meadowlands. Wavy hair, prominent nose, dare-me eyes. More Elon Musk than Tom Brady. When he peeked, that same face stared back at him.

The realization that he might actually be twenty-five again thumped Gary like a Gerritt Cole fastball to the head. Suddenly exhausted, he lay down on the rather large rope bed, neatly appointed with blue checkered quilt, positioning his pack under his head for safekeeping.

He awoke an hour later staring at an older man in a checkered waistcoat and lightly powdered hair. "William Sands," the visitor announced, extending a hand. Gary sat up, still groggy, and shook hands.

"Tralee said there'd be plenty of room here," Sands continued as he shuffled to the far side of the bed. "I'll take this side, if you don't mind. Anyone else arrives, we'll put him in the middle."

CHAPTER 11

Gary bound down the stairs, his nemesis back in 2026. Having a youthful body again definitely had its advantages. The short nap had helped re-energize his mind as well.

City Tavern was packed for supper. A turkey roasted on a spit; turnips and carrots simmered in a pot; an apple pie baked in the Dutch oven tucked deep into the massive hearth. The aroma in the room had improved markedly since the afternoon.

Gary took a seat at a communal table. John Adams, sallow-skinned but thick-waisted, sat at the far end engrossed in conversation with two other gentlemen, a document lying between them. In addition to a plate heaped with victuals, each of the men had a quill and inkwell at hand.

Although uninvited, Mr. Sands pulled up a chair opposite Gary. "I gather the Declaration was well-received by many in Congress today," he said, stirring his vegetables with his knife. "But not all. South Carolina and our fair colony of Pennsylvania voted against it. Delaware and New York abstained."

"They'll all come round, I bet," Gary replied, gnawing at his drumstick, determined to say as little as possible.

"Perhaps, but the Committee will have to persuade Mr. Jefferson to eliminate his tirade against the trade in Negroes if he hopes to get Charleston's vote," Sands went on, tilting his head towards the three men huddled together.

Although Jefferson was clearly the primary author, a Committee of Five, including Franklin, Adams, Robert Livingston from New York, and Roger Sherman from Connecticut, shared responsibility for drafting the Declaration of Independence. "A bit hypocritical, don't you believe, for a Virginia plantation owner to blame King George for slavery," Sands said.

Gary nodded in agreement. "Why is Pennsylvania opposed?" he asked.

"The work of Dickenson and Morris. They're still hoping for reconciliation with the Crown," Sands said while stabbing a spindly carrot. "The war is bad for business."

John Dickenson had spearheaded the infamous "Olive Branch" peace petition in 1775 which King George had summarily rejected, electing instead to send more British troops and the feared Hessian mercenaries to the colonies, fanning the flames of rebellion rather than subduing them. Born in England, Robert Morris was a prominent shipowner and global trader, rumored to be the wealthiest man in America.

"Mr. Franklin will persuade them to support the Cause," Gary replied, wiping the grease from his mouth with a cloth.

"You appear quite confident. Are you a Pennsylvania man yourself?"

"No. Connecticut's my home. But I believe Franklin's word carries great weight." Gary immediately regretted his forcefulness. His knowledge of the future could prove dangerous, if unchecked.

"Quite possibly, if the old man can rise from his bed. His gout is acting up fiercely."

"Of course, Dickenson and Morris are men of principle so one can never be sure," Gary backtracked.

"Dickenson perhaps, but I've yet to hear a man accuse

Morris of standing on principle."

"Do you know if Franklin's receiving visitors?" Gary asked. If he was going to meet just one Founding Father, the fellow inventor and entrepreneur was his first choice.

"I've not personally conversed with Mr. Franklin in some time, but I have heard his mind is as sharp as ever," Sands replied, turning his attention to the slab of turkey on his plate. "Would this be a commercial meeting you're seeking, or more personal in nature?"

"Both." Having read several biographies of Franklin, as well as much of his correspondence, Gary was in awe of the man.

"Perhaps, I can be of assistance then. I have many contacts here in Philadelphia."

"What business are you in - if I may ask?" Gary swathed his bread in butter.

"I'm an agent for Robert Cary and Company. We specialize in tobacco trading." Sands sliced his meat and delicately lifted a piece towards his mouth. "In London," he added before chomping away.

Gary buried his head in his mug for several seconds. He would have to tread carefully now.

"General Washington has been a client of ours for many years," Sands continued. "Perhaps, I could arrange an audience for you."

"Perhaps."

"I would need to learn more of your business, of course."

Before Gary could reply, the serving girl, a freckle-faced redhead, swished her skirts over, depositing a plate of cherry pie topped with whipped cream in front of each man. "Another ale gentlemen?" she asked, leaning across Gary to clear their plates. Her plentiful bosom, coyly framed by a lace bodice, defied gravity.

"Yes, thank you," he said, enjoying the view.

"Tea please," Sands asked.

"We don't serve tea here no more," the girl retorted without looking up.

"Coffee then," Sands said, clearly surprised. "An impudent wench," he added once the waitress was out of hearing. Gary suppressed a smile, already looking forward to the wench's return.

"Your business? I believe we were discussing your business before we were interrupted," Sands said.

Gary spooned a large portion of pie before answering. "I'm a shipowner. Looking to expand the scope of my enterprise." No point in unveiling all so soon.

"You appear quite youthful to be a *shipowner*."

The pie was incredibly tasty, just the right amount of spice, Gary thought as the wench returned. In no rush to answer, he wiped a droplet of cream from his lips and dug in for another helping.

"But, of course, I admire boldness in a young man," Sands added hastily.

"I'm partial to bold young men as well," the wench said, flashing a black-toothed smile at Gary. He responded with a welcoming nod, her flattery more than sufficient to override her need for dental work.

"That will be all, woman," Sands said with a dismissive brush of his hand. "We have business to discuss."

"It's Erin, not woman," she tossed back. Gary's gaze followed her sashaying hips down the long table.

"A trull would never prattle like that to a gentleman in London," Sands said before lifting his steaming cup.

"I admire a woman with spunk," Gary replied, thinking of Lucie in her younger days. And older days as well.

"Well, I believe you can *rent* that spunk for the evening, if you so desire." Sands sipped his coffee, letting the proposition linger in the air. "Alternatively, I could provide an introduction to several of the finer single women in Philadelphia. I believe they would be most eager to meet an enterprising young bachelor such as yourself."

"I'm a married man - with children," Gary blurted, still far from getting a grip on his new youth. He was a grandfather, for god's sake. Wasn't he?

"Well, in that case, I hope that you conclude your business promptly and return home to your family." Sands pushed his chair back from the table. "I will be here until morning - if you seek my assistance," he added before stalking away.

"I know. We appear to be sharing a bed."

Adams, Sherman and Livingston had concluded their meal as well. Taking a deep breath, Gary approached Sherman, fifty-five years old but still spry. The Connecticut congressman was an isolationist, a staunch believer that his home colony, soon to become a state, needed little assistance from its neighbors. Connecticut had ample ports, inland waterways, cities and even its own college. "Mr. Sherman, could I have a word, sir?"

"Excuse me?"

Gary extended his hand, but Sherman did not take it. Accordingly, he decided to get right to the point. "I'm looking to acquire a letter of marque from Congress for my ship, the *Lucie*."

Sherman looked Gary over slowly, as if inspecting every button on his jacket. "A letter of marque, eh? And where is the *Lucie* domiciled?"

"New London, sir." The town was the largest deep water port on the Long Island Sound, and, more important, at least another full day's travel should anyone from Philadelphia want to check his cover story.

"And where do you worship?"

Connecticut was governed by a powerful theocracy for thirty-five years *after* the Revolutionary War had been won. "First Congregational, of course."

Sherman beamed, handing his card to Gary. "You may deliver your petition to my lodgings tomorrow morning at eight."

"Thank you, sir."

"I will not promise a prompt response, however. Congress has more important business to consider, as I'm sure you know."

"Of course." Congress usually considered the normal business of the day each morning, leaving a discussion of the Declaration of Independence until the afternoon. Pleased with his progress, Gary said good evening to Mr. Tralee, the proprietor, and headed upstairs to bed.

Sands was already buried under the coverlet despite the warmth of the room. Gary opened the lone window; there were no ceiling fans, let alone air conditioning, in 1776. He removed his jacket and checked the Watch, snug against his chest.

Before he could undress any further, there was a knock on the door. Erin greeted him with a low curtsy. "Would ye be wanting company this evening?"

"No, I think not," Gary stammered.

"Not a wee bit lonely?"

A loud snore interrupted their conversation. Gary opened the door and pointed to the sleeping lump. "Unfortunately, I already have company this evening."

"There's plenty of elbow room between those sheets," Erin said, peeking inside. She uncapped her cinnamon hair and let it tumble over her bony shoulders. Another sonorous blast from Mr. Sands rattled the candlesticks. "We couldn't wake that poof if we tried," she added, smiling wickedly.

Could she really be suggesting...? "I'm worn out from my travels," Gary managed. He had little practice rejecting any woman, let alone a willing *young* woman.

Erin retreated, but showed no sign of defeat. "Rest up then. I'll be here tomorrow."

CHAPTER 12

Sands left before dawn, but dreams of Erin stirred Gary for another hour. Nevertheless, he was downstairs by seven. The tavern was already half full, a matronly Black serving porridge, biscuits and coffee.

He struck up a brief conversation with a dripping wet gentleman still wearing boots and spurs who turned out to be Caesar Rodney, governor of Delaware. Rodney had ridden through the stormy night to cast the deciding vote for independence in the Delaware caucus. Fortunately, the clouds had cleared, a portent for the historic day: Tuesday July 2, 1776.

After breakfast, Gary set out to connect with Roger Sherman at the Indian Queen Hotel on Fourth and Market Streets. He freed the Watch from his shirt so it could start to recharge in the natural light. The battery indicator showed 90% full so he wasn't worried about running out of juice. Hopefully, T-ray power would kick in as well, despite Lucie's misgivings.

Approaching the hotel, he returned the Watch to its safe place. Sherman sent his valet down to the lobby to accept Gary's petition. Although disappointed not to connect with the Congressman personally, he understood the priorities of the morning ahead.

Gary also had business demanding his immediate attention. First, he reconnoitered Dunlap's print shop on Arch Street, a block off the docks on the Delaware River. He knew the printer wouldn't get the Declaration until it was signed on July 4, but he wanted to see the operation in person and hopefully establish a personal contact with John Dunlap, a twenty-nine year old Irishman.

The printing press, invented in the fifteenth century by Johannes Gutenberg, turbocharged the dissemination of news and ideas in colonial America much the same way that social media impacted America in the twenty-first century. By 1776, the colonies had only five cities with more than ten thousand inhabitants but boasted forty newspapers. For the 90% of the population that lived in the countryside, the newspaper was the primary source of information about the outside world, no matter how outdated the news might be when they read it.

Philadelphia, the largest city by far with a population over 40,000, had six newspapers. Benjamin Franklin founded one of the first, *The Pennsylvania Gazette*, and made his fortune selling papers as well as advertising, a colonial era Mark Zuckerberg.

As a hands-on engineer and entrepreneur in his own right, Gary was fascinated by colonial printing. The paper was made from linen and cloth, the ink from tannin, iron sulfate, gum and water. Standing outside Dunlap's window, plastered with pages from his primary money-maker, the *Pennsylvania Packet*, a weekly priced at two pennies, he watched the artisan at work.

The press itself was an imposing wooden frame taller than a man, housing a stone controlled by a metal handle, known as the Devil's Tail. The printer first set the type one letter at a time in a composition stick. Because the composition was situated both upside down and backwards from the way it would appear, type-setting was an art that required years of practice to perfect. It was also the most time-consuming part of the printing process.

Several lines of type would then be combined into a galley tray. Ink was spread evenly over the tray with inking balls. Paper was folded over the inked tray in a combination known as a "coffin." The printer would then slide the "coffin" under the stone, then crank the Tail to apply up to 200 pounds of pressure. Illustrations could be added to a page by pressing engraved wooden blocks or copper plates. When satisfied that a page was printed correctly, the printer would set it aside to dry and start on the next one.

Professor Pilgrim had explained that the first Dunlap broadside of the Declaration of Independence would have taken hours to print. Subsequent copies were likely cranked out in a few minutes.

Gary knocked briskly and stepped inside the shop. "I'd like to place an advertisement in the *Packet*," he said.

Dunlap, wearing an ink-stained apron, looked up from his work. "You've come to the right place then," he replied with a trace of a brogue. "Do you have the copy?"

Gary reached inside his pack, withdrawing a handwritten page. "I'm looking for investors for my ship, the *Lucie*. She'll sail as soon as I receive my Letter of Marque from Congress."

After wiping his hands on a rag, Dunlap scanned the text. "I can place it in my next edition. Won't go out much before next week though.   I'll likely be occupied printing the Declaration of Independence over the weekend."

"If it's ratified."

"It will be. Mr. Hancock stopped by this morning to provide his assurances."

"I understand Congress is still weighing in with comments."

"Aye. Seems every delegate has an opinion. Mr. Hancock was quite vexed." Dunlap swiveled to watch a muscular young man, his face pebbled with freckles and pox scars, work the press. He appeared to be lost, searching for the right letters to add to his composition stick. "Aiden, have you not yet memorized the type chest, lad?"

"Reckon not," Aiden replied, his head down staring at the

chest containing tiles for twenty-six letters, ten numerals, and assorted punctuation marks.

"Perhaps a caning will jog your memory," Dunlap said, reaching for the appropriate instrument leaning against the counter. Gary could see Aiden cower, obviously not the first time he had felt the lash. Aiden was likely indentured to Dunlap, a step up from slavery but just barely.

"I'm sure Mr. Jefferson is even more upset," Gary said, trying to distract Dunlap.

"Aye. The Virginian is not accustomed to such warm treatment."

"How many broadsides will you be printing?" Gary kept up his banter, while Aiden appeared to progress with his type setting.

"At least fifty, maybe more. Mr. Hancock plans to send them to every colony. Wants them read out loud to the citizenry."

Gary thought of offering to buy one hot off the press, but decided to wait and better establish his bonafides. "I'd like to stop by to see the page setup for my advertisement. After you've printed the Declaration, of course," he said before leaving the shop.

Gary skipped out of the print shop, suppressing a huge smile. He didn't see any obstacle to obtaining a Dunlap broadside. Although tempted to turn to check if Aiden had escaped unscathed, his happy feet propelled him forward. Accordingly, he failed to notice the bald, scar-faced man following him once again.

Gary's second stop was the Pennsylvania Land Office which managed the holdings of the Penn family. Since King Charles II had granted the entire colony to William Penn in 1681 in payment of royal debts, the Penn's owned a substantial amount of land. And much of it appeared to be for sale, Gary was pleased to learn.

He hoped to acquire a tract in Radnor Township, thirty miles west of the city, which would come to encompass both the town of Villanova and the university of the same name. The township was originally settled in 1663 by Quakers from Radnor, Wales. Although the land was the home of the Lenape Indians, Quakers had purchased five thousand acres from the Penn's and built a thriving settlement.

Located on the Lancaster Turnpike, the first toll road in America, opening in 1794, Villanova had remained a fixture on the Main Line ever since. The University opened its doors in 1842, further cementing the town's stature. An investment of Lucie's earrings would easily return a hundred times their value, maybe more.

The clerk in the Land Office asked a few cursory questions, but cut even those short when Gary indicated he could pay a fair price - immediately. He left with a map of the township outlining a country estate of 150 acres that was on the market. The Land Office would draw up the legal papers while Gary rode out to survey the property. He expected to return within the week to close the transaction.

Of course, Gary had no intention of riding anywhere. He would buy the property sight unseen.

CHAPTER 13

When Gary returned just after noon, revelers at the City Tavern were raucously toasting the newly proclaimed "free and independent" United States. The break from England had passed unanimously, 12-0, with only New York abstaining.

Congress, however, had not yet approved the Declaration of Independence. Delegates filed past Gary to return to the State House to register their comments on the document. Thomas Jefferson sat alone at a secluded window table, a well-marked document and half-empty glass of claret in front of him.

Determined to capitalize on this "once in ten lifetimes" opportunity, Gary wheedled a wedge of cheese and loaf of still-warm bread from the Black hostess and approached. "Hungry?" he asked, guessing that Jefferson had worked right through the mid-day meal.

"Why yes," the Virginian replied, eyeing the plate in Gary's hand. Jefferson was formally attired in a brown waistcoat, matching breeches and taupe knee length stockings. His hair was queued and powdered in the "American" style, not wigged. "Please join me."

"Gary Johnson - from Connecticut," Gary said, his nerves triggering a long-buried Brooklyn accent. He breathed deeply and spoke more slowly. "I don't want to disturb you."

"A welcome respite," Jefferson replied, slicing the cheese, offering the first piece to Gary. As Gary sat, Jefferson called for more wine. He waited for the waitress to fill their glasses before continuing. "I'm not accustomed to my words being so....so dissected."

"Dissected?"

"My fellow Congressmen tinker with every sentence, every paragraph." Jefferson tapped the black lines scrawled across the document.

"The price of compromise, I believe," Gary said, sipping his wine. "But I'm sure you'll be satisfied with the end result. Generations of Americans will recognize your singular contribution to the birth of our country."

"I certainly hope so. It's the future that most concerns me. I want this Declaration to serve as a blueprint for a new nation that will be a beacon of liberty to the world."

"Your words will stir Americans for centuries," Gary replied.

"Yes, well, they have already aroused my fellow Southerners." Jefferson stuffed a mound of cheese into his mouth and washed it down with a gulp of wine. "I must return to the State House or there will be nothing left of the Declaration but drivel."

After Jefferson left, Gary wandered up to his room, disappointed that Erin was nowhere in sight but pleased to find no other traveler had replaced Mr. Sands. Yet.

Alone, he was able to lay the Watch on the nightstand near the window to charge in the fading sunlight. He re-read Jefferson's original draft Declaration that the Professor had annotated, highlighting the redactions and edits, some completely trivial such as the substitution of "utterly neglected" for "neglected utterly." He could easily understand Jefferson's frustration.

At supper, Gary found a seat near John Adams at the long

table. The normally taciturn Massachusetts lawyer was quite vociferous this evening, alternating between excitement about the vote for independence, a goal he had worked tirelessly behind the scenes to effect, and trepidation that Jefferson would get all the credit.

Fortunately, Erin arrived bearing a heaping platter of roasted meat, greens and potatoes. Starving, Gary was first to dig in, drawing a reproachful glance from Mr. Adams who was not finished bloviating. Erin worked her way around the table, drawing greetings, ribald comments and a pinch on her ass. She handled them all with a light touch. Gary felt a twinge of jealousy, but had no regrets about rejecting her favors last night.

As supper ended, Adams stood and toasted: "July 2, 1776 - a date that Americans will celebrate forever." "Here, here," the men replied in unison, before breaking into smaller groups for port and tobacco.

Watching Erin clear the far end of the table, Gary slipped a coin under his plate despite Mr. Tralee's earlier admonition. While Tralee, the proprietor, might be insulted by his tip, he doubted a waitress would have such hesitation.

Passing on the after-dinner refreshments, Gary retired, pleased to find the bed unoccupied. The room still baked from the summer heat, so he opened the window and pulled back the curtains. A whispering breeze would do little to cool the air, he thought, longing for a return to air conditioning.

Gary was almost undressed when the door quivered with a loud thump. His new roommate, he presumed. Pulling on his shirt, leaving it unfastened, forgetting the Watch still dangling from his neck, he opened it halfway.

Erin barged in, her cheeks matching the color of her fiery hair, leaving an enchanting lavender scent in her wake. "Did ye forget this?" she asked, holding up his coin.

"No," he said, getting out of her way. "I thought to compensate you for your service. It's a custom back..."

"Compensate me? What service did I perform?" Ruby lips

pursed in defiance, bosom thrust forward, reeking of perfume, she overwhelmed his senses.

"Dinner. I mean supper. You served..."

"I served a meal to forty men. Not ye alone," she practically spit out the words. "This coin could feed me family for a month. What did I do to earn that?"

"I'm sorry," Gary mumbled as tucked the Watch against his chest. He fastened his shirt, relieved that Erin hadn't noticed his timepiece.

She tossed the coin on the bed. "Stuff that back in ye fat purse. Mr. Tralee will think I stole it anyway." Her gaze remained glued to the silver, however, belying her words.

"I want you to keep it." A detente settled between them like the Berlin Wall.

"Then I'll have to stay the night," she said. "Why do ye think Mr. Tralee failed to assign another traveler, or two, to this room?"

"I had no idea..." He closed the door to signal his acquiescence.

"I told him ye might be embarrassed," she said, shuffling her slippered feet. "He thought ye might prefer to fornicate with men."

"No, definitely not. I most certainly prefer women."

Erin pushed her dress off her shoulders, wiggling it down over her hips. Naked, she stepped out of the crumpled frock and planted her hands on her hips. "What about this woman, then?"

Gary stopped breathing. His heart hammered so violently it threatened to burst the chain dangling around his neck. Erin's emerald eyes sparkled; her chocolate-tipped nipples pointed at him like dueling pistols; her unruly bush was dense enough for a sparrow's nest; her bare feet crusted with grime.

He stood statue-still until Erin took his hand. "Let's go to bed," she said, breaking the spell.

"No, I can't." He croaked out the words, barely able to complete the brief sentence.

"I'm quite certain ye can," Erin replied, ogling the erection tent-poling his silks.

When was the last time he had gotten that hard that quickly? His mind raced to Lucie, their kids, their grandkids. The tent sagged. "I can't. I'm married. Happily married."

Erin's exuberance deflated as well. "Ye wife must be a special woman," she said, crawling into the bed, curling into a fetal position atop the coverlet. "I have to stay the night. Ye understand?"

Gary went to the window, failing to discover another option in the blackness. Erin rustled behind him. He lay down next to her, keeping his distance, but nevertheless raptured by the moon gleam reflecting off her bare ass.

"You said you had a family?" he asked.

"Two healthy boys," she said over her shoulder as she crossed herself. "John is five, wee Timmy is three."

"A husband?"

"Killed fighting the lobsterbacks on Bunker Hill last year."

"A brave man," Gary said, stifling the impulse to reach out.

"A fool," she replied, but nevertheless swiped away a tear. "Left me without a shilling. How did he expect me to feed our bairns?"

Gary said nothing, leaving Erin to her memories. After a ponderous minute, she half-turned, scooting her hips closer to him. A black-toothed grin peeked through strands of tousled hair. "Knock if ye change ye mind. It's already paid for."

CHAPTER 14

As Gary tossed in bed, counting to one hundred - in French – to keep from knocking on Erin's back door, Jennifer Tryon landed at the foot of High Market Street. She jumped to her feet, her Watch, sporting a rainbow colored band, strapped tightly to her wrist.

A cobblestoned boulevard, dimly illuminated by flickering street lamps, stretched before her. The smell of whale oil permeated the still summer evening. Light spilled from a rambling clapboard to her left, the twang of a fiddle and the guffaws of drunk men spilling into the street.

The realization slowly sunk in: her emergency escape from the twenty-first century had worked. She hadn't planned to travel to colonial America, but when the Ministry of State arrested Ding Yu, she had no choice. Philadelphia 1776 was the only destination programmed into the Watch. She barely had time to pack.

Jennifer removed the device and stuffed it into the left pocket of her skirt. A horse neighed somewhere in the darkness. Looking up, she marveled at the stars, the sheer number of them, their sparkle, their nearness, a light show unimaginable in the twenty-first century.

From the right pocket, she removed a print-out of the back page of yesterday's *Pennsylvania Gazette*, hastily downloaded from the Harvard library website. The Golden Goose, a reputable public house on 5th Street, advertised accommodations for travelers for $2 per night.

Dressed in her only Puritanical outfit, a knee-length black skirt and investment banker starched white blouse, she skirted around the soft glow emanating from the tavern. Windows were dark for two blocks, although smoke puffed from a chimney on First Street.

Jennifer stopped on the corner of Second, staring at the candle flickering in the upstairs window. It had to be the home of Jacob Graff, a prosperous stone mason. Thomas Jefferson, now thirty-three years old, boarded here, along with his slave Robert Hemings. Jefferson was likely putting the finishing touches on his masterpiece. She lingered, soaking in the history.

She had to knock five times on the door of the Golden Goose before anyone stirred inside. A stout gray-haired matron cracked open a side window. "Can I help you, Madam?" she asked in a German-stilted accent.

"Friend, I am in need of accommodations for the night." She jingled the coins in her purse.

"What brings you out at this hour?"

"My carriage broke a wheel. My man is attending to it but it won't be fixed until tomorrow at the earliest."

"Most unfortunate. Did you lose your cap in the accident?"

"Cap? Yes, yes, my cap," Jennifer replied, shaking her head. "It must have fallen off when we crashed."

"I see. And you were not harmed?"

"No. Just a bruise. On my shoulder." Jennifer had, in fact, taken a kick to her right shoulder in martial arts class last week.

"And why are you here? In Philadelphia?" The proprietress still made no move to open the door.

"Why?" Jennifer had not anticipated the interrogation. "I'm en route to...Brooklyn to visit relations."

"Brooklyn? And what is your surname?"

"Tryon. Jennifer Tryon." There was a pregnant pause.

"Governor Tryon's daughter?"

Jennifer blanched, then nodded hesitantly. Her father, Nigel Tryon, a pharma exec, was a direct descendant of William Tryon, the current and last Royal Governor of the colony of New York. Nigel had met her mother, Sun Li, daughter of a prominent Chinese businessman, during his tenure in his company's China office. To affirm her place in British society, Sun Li adopted the nickname, Sunny, and zealously documented the family tree from the reign of Queen Elizabeth the First. Jenn, however, saw no immediate need to detail the many generations separating her from the Royal Governor.

A bolt slid. The door opened wide. She was ushered inside hurriedly. "God save the King. You are welcome here for as long as you like, my dear."

The proprietress closed the door and re-bolted it. "I'll take you to your room. The Committee of Safety has eyes everywhere."

Sounds like the Chinese, Jenn thought ruefully as she climbed the stairs. Her room was furnished with a narrow bed, nightstand, chamber pot and wash basin. A looking-glass mounted on the near wall reflected the flicker of a lone candle on the windowsill. Before leaving, the proprietress looked Jennifer up and down. "Your clothes do not look like they were sewn here. English perhaps?"

"Italian actually," Jennifer replied, realizing instantly that she had slipped.

The proprietress' eyes flashed in surprise. She shook her head disapprovingly as she reached into her skirt for a simple muslin cap and handed it to Jennifer. "In America, a pious woman covers her hair."

"Yes. Thank you."

"My name is Sigrid Hauser, widowed three years now.

Please inform your father that I am a friend of the English."

"Of course. He will want to thank you in person. When the British...arrive in Philadelphia."

"Arrive here? Yes, I imagine the Crown will put this foolish rebellion down soon enough." Mrs. Hauser bowed and retreated down the stairs.

Alone, Jennifer quivered, realizing she had been incredibly fortunate to stumble into Mrs. Hauser's establishment. A rebel-leaning boarding house might not have been so welcoming.

Before going to bed, Jennifer needed to take stock of her appearance. Lifting the candlestick, she approached the mirror with trepidation. Her simulations had shown that travel back into the past might take years off the life of the traveler, the swing dependent upon the number of years traveled, the power of the underlying processing engine, and the genetic make-up of the traveler. Since she had left TimeR before checking and double-checking the data set, she had not informed anyone else, including Gary and Molly, of this possibility.

Jennifer breathed easier when she saw a hint of crow feet. Her stomach appeared taut, her tits firm. Maybe she was thirty now, but no younger. Even more important, she still looked Caucasian, like a Tryon. While her younger brother and sister resembled Sun Li with coal black hair and Oriental eyes, she had somehow inherited her father's British features. Even close friends struggled to believe they had the same parents.

CHAPTER 15

Jennifer couldn't have picked a worse morning in American history to wake up British in Philadelphia. On June 28th, four days before her arrival, Thomas Hickey, one of George Washington's most trusted, hand-picked Life Guards, was hanged on Bowery Field in New York City in front of twenty thousand spectators, the largest crowd ever assembled in North America. Hickey had been convicted of treason, part of a plot to assassinate the commander-in-chief.

The spymaster behind the plot? Royal Governor William Tryon, now quartering aboard the *Duchess*, a Royal Navy warship in New York harbor, his own life hardly worth a shilling on land. The news, trickling in by newspaper and word of mouth, whipped anti-Loyalist fervor to a frenzy. A rebel mob roamed the streets.

Since Widow Hauser's was a known haven for Tories, there were no other guests in the dining room for breakfast. The proprietress strongly suggested that Jenn remain indoors. Jennifer capitalized on the time alone in her room to bone up on her American history. Fortunately, she had stored several books on her phone.

It quickly became clear that George Washington was irreplaceable. The Americans had no one else who could rally the troops as well as the people in both the north and the south. He would become larger than life over the course of the Revolution.

Had Washington been assassinated in 1776, Jennifer realized, the Declaration of Independence would have crumbled into dust. Congress would have likely appointed General Horatio Gates, a pompous former British Army officer who had moved to Virginia, as the new commander-in-chief. Gates' failings became apparent in 1780 in South Carolina. After the troops under his command were routed at Camden, Gates was apprehended 170 miles north, galloping for his life.

Even with George Washington alive and well, however, the British were highly confident of a quick victory. An armada of more than four hundred ships arrived off the coast of New Jersey on June 29th, delivering British regulars, Scottish Highlanders and the dreaded Hessian mercenaries to North America. Led by two battle-hardened veterans, General William Howe and his older brother, Admiral Richard Howe, the redcoats planned to roll up Brooklyn, capture New York City, and then sail either south to take Philadelphia or north to seal the Hudson River, cutting off New England from the rest of the colonies. No one expected the Revolution to last past Christmas 1776.

Furthermore, after the British victory, any man who signed the Declaration would be branded a traitor, subject to forfeiture of life and property. Congressmen would solemnly note the document's closing words - "we mutually pledge to each other our lives, our fortunes and our sacred honor" - before inscribing their names.

Taking a study break, Jenn gazed out her bedroom window at the red brick manse across the street housing a family of five and their servants. The domestic scene ignited memories of her own privileged childhood. Her family lived in a spacious apartment in Hong Kong until she was seven. When their father was recalled to the UK, they moved to the Tryon estate on the moors of Cornwall.

Jenn knew she was gay before she graduated boarding school. Since the US appeared much more welcoming to lesbians than the UK, she was determined to attend college there. As an all-England fencing champion, she had scholarship offers from every Ivy, choosing Harvard because of its computer science department and cosmopolitan location.

While Jenn ditched competitive fencing midway through college, she never tired of the thrill of one-on-one combat. Several years later, when she was working for Microsoft in Seattle, she launched into martial arts. Her lover at the time, Naomi, a full-blooded Duwamish Native American, would battle her in the octagon, then share her bed afterwards.

Thoughts of cage-fighting sparked a surge of adrenaline. Jenn propped two pillows on a chair and attacked them with an intricate series of chops, kicks and punches, sweating profusely in the humid summer heat. Of course, there was no shower so she had to wash herself with a damp cloth before returning to her research.

The beat of drums and trill of fifes snapped her back to her window perch. A ragtag procession of workingmen - leather-aproned artisans, beanied stevedores, and ink-smudged printers – marched up the street. Several carried the red and white striped flag of the Sons of Liberty. A coterie of un-capped, ill-dressed women shouted encouragement from the periphery. Jenn strained to hear the lyrics of their Liberty Song:

> *Then join hand in hand, brave Americans all,*
> *By uniting we stand, by dividing we fall;*
> *In so righteous a cause let us hope to succeed,*
> *For heaven approves of each generous deed.*

The mob stopped directly in front of Widow Hauser's entrance. A wigged gentleman, dressed in a scarlet jacket, appeared to be held captive in its center. He struggled in vain to free himself from the spiderweb.

"Will you denounce King George?" a pony-tailed butcher shouted. His slaughter-house stink wafted up to Jenn's window.

"God save the King," the gentleman replied, his wig slipping off as he struggled to keep his head defiantly high. Jenn wanted to applaud the patriotism of her fellow Englishman.

"Tar the Tory," the crowd chanted. "Tar the Tory."

Obligingly, four men emerged lugging a cauldron of boiling, viscous brew. The mob ripped the gentlemen's clothes off, leaving him stark naked on all fours in the street. He screamed as hot tar slathered over his bald head, face and torso. Two of the women broke through the ring, not to aid the victim but to cover him with chicken feathers. Two more rebels appeared carrying a fence post between them. The Tory, wailing in agony, was tossed atop the rail and strapped down so his genitals would chafe against the rough wood. After a final rendition of their anthem, the mob marched away, its message to the Widow and her guests starkly clear.

Swallowing down a gob of vomit, Jenn pulled the shade closed as the sun set in a blaze of pink and orange. In the twenty-first century, she had participated in many protests - the Women's March, Me Too, Black Lives Matter, Pro-Palestine - but they were minor league compared to the American Revolution. She had little doubt the Sons of Liberty would come calling again, particularly if they got word that the Widow harbored a Tryon.

The smart call might be to escape back to the twenty-first century immediately. Dissent in her time was punished by nasty posts on X, not tar and feathers. But...she was actually here in the eighteenth century, a key milestone for her start-up. She wasn't quite ready to cut short her journey.

Could she get to New York and the protection of her great ancestor? Perhaps he would have advice on diverting a rebellion before it turned violent. Idealistic? Definitely. Time travel for good. That's why she founded Tryon Time.

CHAPTER 16

Philadelphia was quiet on Wednesday morning July 3rd, the celebration of yesterday's vote for independence giving way to the realization that the Declaration needed more editing to insure its unanimous approval. Jenn helped the widow clean up after breakfast, then slipped out the back door.

With her head enveloped in a broad-brimmed bonnet, Jennifer wandered down to the docks on the Delaware River, hoping to book passage to New York City. Unfortunately, the slips were full of vessels with their sails stowed. Few sailors, or even stevedores, were in sight. With the British navy, and its massive men-of war nearby, no ships flying American colors dared venture to open waters.

Jennifer walked back up Market Street, perusing the open-air stalls sheltered under a sprawling canopy. Gunsmiths, wheelwrights, haberdashers, and potters hawked their wares. A blacksmith's forge glared a fiery red. Butchers, bakers, beekeepers and chicken farmers maintained a steady chatter. She stopped in front of a fishmonger, the salty stink of his catch luring a crowd.

Fresh fish implied a boat and crew that had left the safety of Philadelphia's pier.

Jennifer waited patiently until the fishmonger's cutting table was empty and the shoppers dispersed. "Will you have a new catch again tomorrow?" she asked.

"God willing," the thickly bearded proprietor, apron dripping with entrails, answered. "If the rain holds off."

"Rain?" Jennifer replied, searching the cloudless sky.

"Rain or redcoats - only things that can keep my Flying Franny in port."

"I'm looking to sail, not fly," she said, edging closer. "...to New York. To visit my grandfather. He's gravely ill."

"No chance you'll get to the City, dear. The bloody lobsterbacks have it sealed tighter than my granny's cunny."

"Yes, well, how close could you get?"

"Depends on the price you're willing to pay."

Jennifer had only a handful of coins in her purse, but she was not going to walk away without closing the deal. She untied her cap and unfastened one of her gold hoop earrings. "How close will this get me?"

The fishmonger took the jewelry in his briny hand and bit down on it. "Both of them?"

Jennifer nodded. "Second one payable on arrival."

"Staten Island. I'll drop you on Great Kills Beach. You'll have to make your own way from there."

"When do we leave?"

"Tomorrow. On the morning tide."

Flush with success, Jennifer recapped her hair and set off towards her boardinghouse. She had just reached Third Street when a moist hand gripped her elbow.

"We'd like a word with you, Mistress Tryon," a bald, scar-faced man said in a flat, hanging judge tone that brooked no disagreement. "In private."

"We? Who?"

"Nathaniel Knight, secretary of the secrets committee of the

Pennsylvania Committee of Safety," he replied, steering her around the corner away from the mid-day bustle of Market Street. "We don't take well to British spies in our city, ma'am."

"I am not a spy," Jennifer replied in a steady, steely tone as she wrenched her elbow free. How did Knight find out who she was? Unfortunately, it was too late to matter.

The commotion attracted a handful of bystanders. One, a young man in a blue jacket, looked vaguely familiar, but Jenn couldn't place him. She crouched, setting her weight on the balls of her feet, eyeing the distance to her captor's groin. She could level him with a kick, but where would she run?

"The Crown prefers its spies to be of the female persuasion," another man, belly spilling over breeches, said as he appeared out of the shadows.

"Spying is low work. Not fit for an honest man," a third Safetyman, hat off, pistol lurking behind it, added as he completed the circle surrounding Jennifer. "Now come with us, woman."

CHAPTER 17

Although his bed was empty, the heat from Erin's curled body still lingered, teasing Gary as he awoke on July 3rd. Taking advantage of the empty room, he texted Molly, indicating that he could return to 2026 next week. Hopefully Tuesday, he thought, but didn't want to set a date and get anyone's hopes up, let alone his own or Lucie's.

The hot topic at breakfast was slavery. Gary wanted to complete his business, not get mired in a controversial debate, but the only seat available was next to Rutledge, the vitriolic, young Congressman from South Carolina.

"How can Mr. Jefferson, a Virginian, write that Negroes deserve the same 'sacred rights of life and liberty' as a white man?" Rutledge asked, holding up a sheet of paper. "I for one will never sign this document." He again pounded his cup on the table, this time splashing hot coffee.

"Here, here," Button Gwinnett, a Georgia man, seconded as he successfully dodged the scalding brew. "My slaves are my property. I shall do with them as I please."

Professor Pilgrim had explained that because Gwinnett had died in a duel only a year after he signed the Declaration, his autograph was the rarest of all fifty-six signatories, selling for $722,000 in a Sotheby's auction. Gary buried his head in his porridge, trying to think of a way to get Gwinnett to sign his napkin.

"Now, now, calm down gentlemen," Thomas McKean of Delaware said between mouthfuls of a muffin smothered in strawberry jam. "We cannot do as we please if we remain subjects of King George. Independence must be our goal and we must rise above our petty differences to attain it."

While McKean was the Delaware delegate who persuaded his governor, Rodney, to mount his midnight ride, he personally did not stay in Philadelphia long enough to sign the Declaration in 1776. He left on July 5th to command a Pennsylvania militia unit in the defense of New York City. McKean did not affix his name until sometime between 1777-81, becoming the last signatory on the document.

"Petty differences, my arse," Rutledge said, leaping from his seat. "General Washington now allows Negroes to serve in the Continental Army. Side by side with white boys. What's next? Shall Blacks manage our plantations? Attend our schools? Serve in our legislatures? Marry our daughters?"

"Heaven forbid," Gwinnett choked on his words, spitting up a slab of bacon.

"Then suggest some edits," McKean said evenly. "We have all day to reach a compromise."

While Gary stayed glued to the conversation, he was relieved that his opinion was not sought. In fact, none of the congressmen seemed to notice him, let alone object to his presence. Tilting his tricorn hat at a jaunty angle, Gary left the City Tavern fifteen minutes after the congressmen departed for their morning session at the State House. He needed to trade Lucie's jewelry, at least some of it, for the cash to purchase the Villanova estate.

It was only a three block walk to Milne's shop on Second Street, but Gary arrived soaked in sweat. How did colonials wear wool in the summer? He longed for a pair of shorts and a moisture-wicking polo.

He removed his blue jacket and opened the top button on his ruffled shirt, but it did little to cool his body. Good thing Molly had built the Watch to be waterproof, or at least water resistant. He juggled Lucie's diamond earrings in his right hand. If Milne dealt in fine Quare watches, as noted by Beelzebub Ash, then he should offer a good price for them. He'd buy Lucie a bigger pair when he got home.

Wanting to be viewed as a serious and successful businessman, Gary put his damp jacket back on, re-set his hat, and entered the store. Like Syng's, Milne's displayed a gallimaufry of tableware and cutlery, but Gary's eyes were drawn to the gold-hilted sword on display behind the counter.

"You've got a fine eye, lad," Edmond Milne, a gaunt man with a lazy left eye, said, meandering out of the back room. "Would you be interested in one just like it?"

"Possibly," Gary said, imagining how the weapon would look over the mantle in Connecticut. A fine souvenir of his journey back in time. "How much is this one?"

"It's already spoken for," Milne answered, lifting the sword to show the engraving. "General Washington purchased it when he visited last month. Ordered these as well." He pointed the sword to a dozen shot glasses. "I cast them from His Excellency's silver dollars."

Royal habits die hard, Gary thought. Most Americans in 1776 were still comfortable with a monarch, and saluted George Washington appropriately. "Perhaps," he said. "I'd like to look around a bit."

"Of course. Can I offer you an Adam's Ale? Or would you prefer something with a bit more kick?"

"Adam's Ale would be most appreciated." Gary wasn't ready for alcohol before lunch, although it was commonplace at this time.

He pretended to examine an ornate candelabra, letting Milne's curiosity build. "Actually, I'm here to sell a pair of earrings," he said, returning to the counter. "We're looking to invest, I mean purchase, an estate west of here."

Milne's good eye nearly burst from its socket when he saw Lucie's diamonds, but he quickly squelched any display of enthusiasm. After examining the stone carefully with the aid of a magnifying monocle, he said, "I might be interested."

Gary extended his hand to take the earring back, but Milne held on. "Five hundred Continentals, or the equivalent in sterling," the jeweler said.

Fifteen thousand in 2026 dollars, Gary quickly calculated. "Do I look like a cat's paw?" he asked, trying out his colonial slang.

"Six hundred." Milne raised his bid.

"Six fifty."

"Sold. Sterling or dollars?"

"Sterling," Gary replied. "Can you deliver a draft from your banker by midday tomorrow?" While Robert Morris would not establish the Bank of North America, the first national bank, until 1781, wealthy individuals had private financial arrangements to facilitate commerce in 1776.

Milne nodded. He dipped his quill in the inkwell and wrote out a bill of sale. "Your seal here," he said, pointing to the bottom of the document.

"I'd prefer to sign," Gary replied. In fact, he had no personal seal, a mark against him he realized as Milne wrinkled his nose.

"As you wish."

"Perhaps you could design a seal for me?"

"Most certainly. Befitting a proper gentleman." Milne rolled up the bill of sale and tucked it into his desk. "Do you have a family crest?"

Gary shook his head. "I came from humble beginnings."

"Not a problem. We can get started next week."

"Perfect." Gary hoped he wouldn't be here, but it would be to his advantage to have Milne, and possibly others, believe he would.

"And the watch around your neck?" Milne asked. "Might

you be interested in selling that as well?"

Gary clutched his treasure. "It's not for sale."

He re-wrapped the diamonds and buried them in his pack. He would be relieved to transfer them to Milne when he received payment.

Walking back to the tavern, Gary stopped at a commotion just off Market Street. A woman of slender build, her back to him, was surrounded by three somber men.

"I am not a spy," she said, cold and confident despite the serious charge. The voice, hinting of London posh, sounded familiar but the woman was bonneted. He couldn't see her face even as the men marched her off in a tight formation like a Spartan phalanx. None of the other passers-by moved to intervene.

"Looks like a witch, if you ask me," a stooped woman, clutching a basket overflowing with greens, remarked. "Our Sons of Liberty will teach her a lesson, I wager," she added before shuffling off.

CHAPTER 18

City Tavern was swathed in success when Gary returned. Congress had hammered out a compromise. The delegates were exhausted.

The southerners gathered in one corner, ale and bourbon flowing to celebrate the elimination of all anti-slavery language. The New Englanders conversed in hushed tones and solemn nods, seemingly thunderstruck at what they had accomplished. Only a year ago, they feared even to mention the word "independence." Tomorrow, July 4, 1776, the United States of America would begin to circulate its Declaration to the world not only announcing its severance from England but also enumerating the self-evident truths the newly formed country would represent.

Thomas Jefferson sat alone at his corner table, despair etched into his aquiline features. "They dismembered my draft," he said, pointing his goblet at his fellow congressmen. "Fully a quarter of it is gone."

"Yes, but weren't the congressmen simply reflecting the opinions of their constituents?"

"Perhaps," Jefferson said, sipping his claret, motioning Gary to take the empty chair.

"It is still a monumental work," Gary replied, sitting. "You should be quite proud."

"Mr. Franklin employed those same words."

"Mr. Franklin is a wise man."

"A persuasive one as well."

"What is the essence of the Declaration? In your opinion, of course," Gary asked as Erin approached their table, wine bottle in hand. "What message should I take back home to twenty-twenty - I mean Connecticut?"

Jefferson paused, oblivious to Gary's slip-up, as Erin filled their glasses, silent in the presence of the famous Virginian. "A new nation is born, founded on three principles," he said, holding up the requisite number of fingers. "One - all men are created equal. Two - every man is entitled to certain inalienable rights. Three - the role of our government is to implement and defend those rights."

"What if our new government oversteps its bounds – one day in the future, I mean?"

"An excellent question. America must devise a government with checks and balances. The time to guard against corruption and tyranny is before they shall have gotten hold of us. It is better to keep the wolf out of the fold, than to trust to drawing his teeth and talons after he shall have entered."

"Here, here," Gary toasted. He sipped his wine before asking his final question. "And slavery? How does our Declaration reconcile with that institution?"

"It doesn't at all. Rather ignores it now."

Gary sat silently, luxuriating in the atmosphere of the room. He was...in Philadelphia...in 1776...talking to Thomas Jefferson.

After a minute of rumination, the Virginian continued: "As I originally wrote, before my fellow Southerners had their say, 'slavery is a cruel war against human nature itself.' But it is a necessary evil today." He raised his glass, signaling for more wine. "We need unity to win our war with Britain. And we need slavery to achieve unity. It's that simple."

"Won't it be hypocritical for people to read that 'all men are created equal' while Black men are still enslaved?" Gary pressed.

"Those words will certainly stir people to consider that question, as I have," Jefferson said.

"Do you think America will ever abolish slavery?" Gary had to ask.

"Yes, but not in my lifetime," Jefferson said, now gazing out the window at the setting sun, blood red against the wan blue sky. "Future generations will have to fight that battle."

Did Jefferson have any idea how many hundreds of thousands of lives that battle would claim, Gary wondered. He looked again at the fissures creasing Jefferson's forehead. Yes, he probably did.

Could the Founding Fathers have done more here in 1776 to prevent the Civil War? Scanning the dining room at the City Tavern, he thought not. They had no hope of abolishing slavery and uniting the thirteen colonies.

Had the Founders pushed abolition, the colonies would have likely splintered into small nation/states, barely able to defend themselves, powerless on the global stage. New England and Pennsylvania had the economic resources to proceed independently; New York and other mid-Atlantic states had influential Tory factions that might have advocated for a return to the British Empire; and, the South might have aligned with France or Spain who still controlled neighboring territories in Louisiana and Florida, respectively. Slavery would have continued unless another version of the Civil War erupted.

"Supper gentlemen?" Erin approached with a tray of meats, lightening the mood.

Jefferson retired before dessert, leaving Gary, stuffed and slightly inebriated, alone. John Adams and the Massachusetts men also headed to bed early, but the Southerners were still loud and proud.

Button Gwinnett, swilling port, led his entourage in several verses of "Yankee Doodle" that Gary had never heard. The song, originally written by the British in 1755 as a slight against the backwards colonials, the Yankee doodle dandies, had evidently been reversed to tout George Washington and the success of his Continental Army.

"And there was Cap'n Washington, upon a slapping stallion…" Gwinnett sung off-key, a colonial karaoke star.

Gary approached as the Georgian finished. "Well done, Mr. Gwinnett," he said, a sheet of paper and quill in hand. "Did you write those last couplets yourself? Never heard them before."

"Most certainly not. But I do love tweaking my nose at the redcoats."

"As do I, as do I," Gary said, dipping his quill in ink. "I've jotted the lyrics down here and was hoping you could sign. I'd like to tell my friends back in Connecticut that I met Georgia's most talented delegate."

"Most talented…" Gwinnett muttered to himself as he scratched out his name. "Here you go."

Elated, Gary retired quickly to the Tavern's cozy library. He still wanted to soak in the atmosphere of colonial times but thought it best to remain out of sight right now. The Tavern had a copy of several of the bestselling novels of the day, *Gulliver's Travels, Robinson Crusoe* and *Candide*, on its shelves. He thumbed through them, savoring the feel of the coarse leather covers and well-worn pages.

Eyelids drooping, Gary forced himself up. The tavern had grown still. Erin was not in sight. Nor was William Sands. Disregarding his exhaustion, he took the stairs two at a time, delighting in his youthful agility. The door to his room was closed.

CHAPTER 19

Erin sat at the window, uncapped, combing her hair in the moonlight. She still wore her work clothes, a once-white, gravy-stained gown with low-cut bodice and an indigo-checked apron around her waist. A bottle of whiskey and Gary's tin snuff box lay open on the sill in front of her.

She turned her head as he entered, nodding briefly before proceeding to snort a pinch of scented tobacco into each nostril. "Bonny good stuff," she giggled, snapping her head up. "I mean snuff."

Gary realized he had left the box and his toiletries in the room, but kept his pack, containing Lucie's precious jewels, with him at all times. "You're drunk," he said as he closed the door.

"Why do ye care?" she slurred.

"Because I assume we're sharing a bed together."

"Ye won't sleep with a drunk woman?"

"I didn't say that," Gary replied, walking towards Erin. "It's been quite a while since I've had that pleasure."

"Ye will not be getting any pleasure tonight, remember,"

Erin said, swigging another gulp of liquor, wiping her mouth with her sleeve. "...unless of course ye have changed ye mind. It's already..."

"Paid for. I know." Gary held out a hand for the bottle. Erin gave it to him. Ugh, she was not wearing any perfume tonight. "Will anyone else be joining us?"

"No. Ye coin bought us one more night alone."

"Then you might want to wash up." He put the whiskey on the night table, out of Erin's reach.

"With this?" She asked, displaying Gary's roll of toilet paper.

"No, that's for...never mind." He filled the wash basin with lukewarm water from the pitcher on his nightstand, and carried it over to her, along with his washcloth. "Use this."

She rubbed the cloth under each armpit. "Where are ye from?" she asked, snapping to sobriety as if switching on a lamp.

"Connecticut," he replied, aware that the tenor of the conversation had grown more serious - and more dangerous.

"How did ye get here?"

"Hmmm..."

"By boat?" Erin pressed. "A British boat?"

"I'm not a spy." By instinct, he echoed the woman's response from earlier in the day, realizing he probably sounded just as guilty as she did.

"Then how did ye get to Philadelphia?"

"Why do you want to know?"

"Because I'm sleeping with ye." She tossed the washcloth at his feet.

"Why are you sleeping with me?" Gary was still stalling, but his vanity sought an answer as well.

"Because I need the money and ye appear to have plenty of it."

"What makes you think that?" He hoped his face didn't betray his disappointment.

"Ye silver chain, the watch dangling from it. The pack ye won't let out of sight. They all smell of money."

"I'm a successful businessman. A married successful businessman. And I don't have to explain myself to you."

"Why? Because I'm a tart?"

"No," he replied with little conviction.

"Ye still haven't told me how ye got here?" Erin stood and wandered towards the bed without taking her eyes off him. "Did ye fly to Philadelphia like a bird?" she asked, flapping her arms.

"Let's go to sleep," he replied, turning the coverlet.

"This is the last night." She made no move to climb into bed.

"I know."

"No, ye don't know," she said, as she slipped around the bed towards him. "This is the last night I can protect ye."

"Protect me? From whom?" Erin's freckles danced in the sputtering candlelight as she drew close.

"Do ye think I'm the only one who knows ye are a rich man with a big secret?" She was close enough to whisper now. "People have been following ye. They know."

"Which people?" Gary stepped back. "William Sands?"

"Among others."

"The Committee of Safety?" He continued his retreat, banging into the candleholder, catching it before it could fall and start a fire. "Why haven't they arrested me then?"

"Mr. Tralee has vouched for ye." Erin said, sitting down on the bed. "On my word. But, if I were ye, I'd leave in the morning."

"Thank you." Gary finally gathered his wits. "I am here on business, you can tell that to Mr. Tralee. Personal business. Not British business or patriot business, for that matter. And I rode my horse, Yankee, from Connecticut. Rode him hard. So hard he collapsed right after we crossed the Delaware. Had to shoot him and walk the rest of the way."

"If ye say so." Erin lay down, not even bothering to undress.

Gary stood by the window as she fell fast asleep. Her rhythmic snores punctuated the countdown on his stay in 1776.

CHAPTER 20

Gary rolled awake on Thursday July 4th filled with anticipation and dread. Erin was gone. Sadly, no lavender fragrance lingered, her sleeping space marked only by a smear of gravy.

Last night's roast sat heavily in his stomach, so he raced downstairs to use the thunderbox, a two seater conveniently located just outside the rear of the tavern. Shortly after he dropped his breeches, John Adams joined him, doing the same. In between bursts of flatulence, Adams appeared to be reading over a document.

"A letter," Adams said. "To my wife."

"Abigail," Gary replied instinctively.

"Are you acquainted with her?"

"By reputation only."

"Reputation?"

Gary shifted uncomfortably, realizing he was digging himself into a hole. "Only as the learned wife of a greatly respected lawyer and legislator."

"Yes, well, I do try to keep her informed," Adams said, rustling his letter. "Her disposition turns quite frosty if I do not write frequently."

"As does mine."

"I am surprised at the Suddenness, as well as Greatness of this Revolution. Britain has been filled with Folly, and America with Wisdom, at least this is my Judgment. Time must determine. It is the Will of Heaven, that the two Countries should be sundered forever," Adams read his missive aloud to his captive audience.

"Well said."

Adams checked his pocket watch and bounced up. "I must be off or I'll miss the Express Post. The rider leaves promptly at eight."

As Gary climbed the stairs, he tried to imagine recounting this conversation to his golfing buddies back home. Sharing an outhouse with a future President of the United States. Discussing their wives. Which modern day President would he want to shit next to?

Closing the door to his room, he texted home. He remained optimistic about his imminent return but vague about the date, omitting any mention of the threats Erin had enumerated last night.

Congress opened early this morning so Gary breakfasted alone. Before signing the Declaration, the delegates first had to approve General Washington's flying camp, a mobile reserve which he could launch into battle anywhere on the eastern seaboard, and finalize Tom McKean's command of the militia units heading to New York.

The matronly hostess nodded in recognition as she delivered Gary's coffee and porridge. He scanned the *Evening Post*, skimming the coverage of the Declaration, which contained no surprises. The advertisements and announcements contained more relevant news:

- A brigantine, *Two Friends*, and a schooner, *Mary Ann*, were for sale.

- Hogsheads of hay, coffee, brandy, tea, chocolate, pimento, madeira, indigo and cinnamon were available.
- Joseph Cartwright's wife eloped again; he did not want anyone to trail her and would not pay any debts she contracted.
- A watch, made by James Gerard in London, was missing and presumed stolen by a person in company with two others. Joseph Steward offered a reward.

The last item snapped Gary to attention. Because writers of the time often substituted the letter "f" for "s," he had to read the announcement several times to be sure he got it right. Was William Sands linked to the thieves? He said he was a tobacco agent but maybe that was just his cover story, enabling him to meet wealthy, watch-owning men.

Gary looked up, scanning the room to see if he was under surveillance. John Tralee popped out of the kitchen, but there was no sign of Mr. Sands or the Committee of Safety men. He rubbed his Watch, secure under his shirt and jacket. If all went well, he would conclude his business tomorrow, July 5th, and be home for supper.

Would he be safe without Erin's protection for the next thirty-six hours? How did she know William Sands? What about the Committee of Safety? Was she working both ends for her own gain?

To survive and succeed, Gary knew he would have to be his best. The last time he had concentrated this hard was on the golf course with his "boys" – all in their early seventies. They still carried their clubs, despite the wear and tear on their bodies. Gary wore a brace on his left knee; his partner, Tom, had a wrap on his right elbow. Alex's vest hid the corset supporting his back; Marty's joints still purred like a vintage Ferrari, but his nose was heavily gauzed after skin cancer surgery.

Their match was even on the eighteenth green. Gary faced a five foot curling downhill putt for the win...and ten dollars...and, most importantly, bragging rights for the week. He did his best Tiger Woods, stalking around the green, reading the line from all sides. Three deep breaths, putter aligned, shoulders square, head down...until he heard his ball plunk into the bottom of the cup. Nothing but net.

Gary sought out John Tralee. To maintain his cover story, he asked him to book a seat on the July 6th stagecoach to New York, a trip he did not intend to make.

CHAPTER 21

City Tavern started to fill by 10AM. The imminent signing of the Declaration was on every man's tongue. Ale and whisky flowed freely, but Gary stuck to coffee. His head swiveled like a windshield wiper but no threats emerged from the growing crowd.

Fortunately, Mr. Milne showed up an hour early. They went outside, standing in the shade of an ancient oak, to exchange Milne's bank draft for Lucie's earrings. Gary was relieved to be rid of the earrings, although he still had Lucie's bracelet, as well as Gwinnett's autograph, worth far more than the bracelet. Both were in his pack, secure on the floor between his feet.

Next stop was the Pennsylvania Land Office. The clerk practically jumped from his bench when Gary entered. Yes, the Penn estate in Villanova was still available. Had Gary visited it yet? No mind. Milne's bank draft would do nicely. The office's attorney had already drafted the legal documents. Gary could take title immediately, if he so desired.

The clerk's eagerness to complete the transaction aroused suspicion, but the prestigious Penn family name soothed Gary's doubts. He signed over the draft and pocketed the deed to the land, adding it to the waterproof sleeve for safekeeping.

Gary walked briskly to Dunlap's print shop, his final destination of the morning. While the day was sunny, the temperature had dropped into the seventies. For the first time during his stay in 1776, Gary was comfortable in his blue jacket and tricorn hat.

Dunlap attended another customer, a squat, dumpling-faced man, while Aiden diligently worked the press, ignoring the conversation which appeared to grow heated.

"Mr. Hancock needs two hundred, by tomorrow," the customer said, pounding the table.

"Two hundred? Impossible," Dunlap replied, looking as if he had swallowed a bad oyster. He gestured towards Aiden. "My apprentice is not the swiftest."

"There are other accomplished printers in Philadelphia. They would most welcome this assignment."

"But Mr. Hancock said…"

"Mr. Hancock has decided that every man in every corner of every colony must hear the clarion call for independence."

"By tomorrow evening?"

"By sundown."

"All right then. I will do it myself." Dunlap rolled up his sleeves as his customer pounded out the door.

"I'll not have time for your *Lucie* until next week," the printer said, brandishing the Declaration. "Mr. Thomson will brook no delays."

Charles Thomson was the Secretary to the Continental Congress, but not an elected delegate. After negotiating a treaty with the Delaware tribe in 1757, he earned the nickname "the man who tells the truth." Thomson was the only official present at every meeting of the Continental Congress from the first session in 1774 until it disbanded in 1788. For a brief period after the Revolution, he was the sole attendee and effectively ran the US government. In 1788, he had the honor to inform George Washington that he had been elected President and accompany him from Mount Vernon to New York, the new nation's temporary capital.

"Understood," Gary replied. "Would you need some assistance proofing and collating the finished copies? I have no skills as a printer but am quite adept at reading."

Dunlap looked over at Aiden who had just fumbled a type. "Yes, that would be most helpful. But I wouldn't be able to pay you until I received my stipend from Congress. Could take weeks."

"No matter. It would be my privilege to help with such a historic document," Gary said, flicking his hand. "But I would ask one small favor."

"Yes?"

"I'd like the honor of being the first to deliver a copy to my home in Connecticut."

"That could be arranged. I'm sure Mr. Hancock wouldn't mind."

"I'll return after supper then."

"Be prepared to stay the night," Dunlap called after him.

Perfect, Gary thought, as he headed back to City Tavern. If Sands or anyone else was after him, they would never think of looking at the print shop. And he would have his official Dunlap broadside by the end of the next day, if not sooner. He practically skipped along High Market Street, weaving in and out of the pedestrians and carriage traffic.

Church bells rang all afternoon in celebration. A band of fiddlers entertained on Fifth Street. At twilight, fireworks blasted into the sky, culminating in the launch of thirteen rockets. The United States of America was born. The people now had a country to fight for. To die for, if God willed.

Two burly men bearing a sedan chair across their shoulders pulled up in front of the Tavern at seven. They gently placed their load on the cobblestones and helped their charge down from his perch. The crowd parted as if Moses had reached the Dead Sea. Dr. Benjamin Franklin, America's most accomplished man, had arrived.

CHAPTER 22

Franklin was born in Boston in 1706, the tenth son of a candlemaker who would eventually sire seventeen children with two wives. At twelve, Ben's father apprenticed him to an older brother, James, a printer and founder of the *New England Courant*. Ben learned the trade but chafed at his brother's discipline, made worse by Ben's belief that he was the better typesetter and writer. He wrote his first columns under the pseudonym, Silence Dogood, supposedly a middle-aged widow. The popularity of these columns widened the sibling rift.

In 1723, Ben broke his bond and ran away to Philadelphia. Although suffering several setbacks over the years, he eventually made his fortune in the printing business, publishing the *Pennsylvania Gazette* and *Poor Richard's Almanac.*

Once his financial future was secure, Franklin turned his focus to public service and science, earning the honorary title of "Doctor." He founded libraries, schools, and hospitals. He improved Philadelphia's fire brigade and organized its militia. He became a justice of the peace, head of the Pennsylvania legislature, and Postmaster General. The latter position enabled his paper to gain access to news from all thirteen colonies well ahead of his competitors. From 1755-75, he served almost continuously as Pennsylvania's representative in London, first disputing the Penn family's control of the colony and then arguing against British taxation.

Franklin's scientific discoveries in vision, he invented bifocals, electricity, and oceanography earned him global fame, while his theories on health, particularly the benefits of fresh air, and a vegetarian diet would not be well-recognized until after his death.

Franklin was a much better public servant than family man. Shortly after marrying Deborah Read in 1730, he introduced her to his infant son, William, born by another woman, and asked her to raise him as her own. While in London, he boarded at the home of Margaret Stevenson, a widow. Their friendship grew closer and more public over the years. Deborah refused to sail to London, instead imploring her husband to come home. He stalled for a full decade. She died in December 1774, six months before her husband returned to Philadelphia to champion independence.

Nattily dressed in a brown velvet suit, Franklin stood taller than most men in the tavern. Wisps of platinum hair flowed to his shoulders, framing a pudding-plump face. Although gout had weakened his legs, requiring him to clutch a cane in each hand for support, his shoulders remained broad from his early years setting type and swimming.

Erin rushed to Franklin's table to refill his claret glass before it was even empty. Across the room, Gary watched them engage. Erin tossed her hair, Franklin's gaze drifted down her bodice. They appeared comfortable in conversation, as if old friends - or lovers. A twinge of jealousy rattled Gary's otherwise ebullient mood.

The Georgia men called him to sit at their table in the rear, a difficult offer to refuse since he might likely earn almost a million dollars from Gwinnett's autograph. The Black hostess served them while Erin handled Franklin and the other dignitaries at the head table.

"Blackie, this meat is far too rare. Tell your master to cook it properly," Gwinnett called out, pushing away the tray of beef.

"My name is Adeline and I am a free woman," she replied, cooly pivoting to the next diner. "I am beholden to no master except Jesus."

"Praise the Lord," Thomas McKean added. Delaware and Georgia men were again sharing the same table.

"Woman, I demand my meat well-done," Gwinnett said, standing.

"I will relay your request to Mistress Tralee," Adeline said, slowly working her way down the table.

"Be quick about it." The Georgian pounded his mug, splashing brew on McKean's boots.

McKean stood, looking down at his soggy feet before facing Gwinnett. "I believe an apology is in order."

Not hard to see how Gwinnett could make enemies, Gary thought. And ultimately end up on the wrong end of a duel. Before this disagreement could proceed any further, John Hancock called out, "Gentlemen, we must all hang together."

With the two men still locked in an icy glare, Franklin forced himself to his feet. "Yes, we must all hang together or, most assuredly, we will all hang separately."

The import of the Doctor's words took a moment to register. Governor Rodney took Franklin's cue, raising his goblet in a toast: "To our lives, our fortunes and our sacred honor."

"Here, here," the delegates, and Gary, stood one by one until the entire room had glasses raised. Gwinnett and McKean cast a final daggered look at each other before taking their seats. The remainder of the meal was uneventful.

Immediately after dessert, a peach pie, mollifying any leftover resentment in the Georgia crowd, Gary took his leave. Erin was busy at the head table, but she turned her head in time to watch him approach. She shook her head, as if to say why are you still here, before turning her attention back to Jefferson and Franklin.

He left City Tavern without saying goodbye.

At Dunlap's, Gary's hands trembled with excitement as he read the broadside. "When in the course of human events...," he could recite the introduction and the preamble, "we hold these truths to be self-evident..." by heart, but reading them now crystallized Jefferson's genius. He clearly distinguished the dispute between the Americans and the British as much more than simple political differences.

To emphasize the point, Jefferson specified twenty-seven grievances against King George, including "refused his assent to laws...obstruction of justice...made judges dependent on his will alone...sending swarms of officers to harass the people...cutting off trade with all parts of the world...imposing taxes without consent...inciting domestic insurrection." Could these same grievances stir readers in 2026 to revolt against authority?

Gary was surprised to see only two signatures on the Declaration, Hancock and Thomson. There were supposedly forty-nine delegates in Philadelphia that day.

"What happened?" he asked Thomson, who remained at Dunlap's to watch the first copies come off the press. "Didn't the other delegates sign?"

"They signed a private copy for President Hancock," he replied. "However, the president has chosen not to release their names to the public at this time." For their own safety, Gary surmised.

The Declaration of Independence that currently resides in the National Archives was "engrossed," written in a clear hand, on parchment in late July and signed by fifty-six men, forty-two on August 2, 1776 with fourteen added later. Hancock again kept the document under wraps, not releasing the names until January 1777 after George Washington and his army had won significant victories at Trenton and Princeton.

Gary, Dunlap and Aiden watched the sun come up on July 5th, their fingertips black with ink. By six that evening, they were finished. Two hundred copies printed.

"Well done, Mr. Johnson," Dunlap said, ceremoniously awarding the last copy to Gary. "See that it is read to the good people of Connecticut as soon as possible."

"I will leave for home at daybreak," Gary replied, although secretly he planned to leave before midnight. He would return to the City Tavern only to pay his bill - and wish Erin farewell.

CHAPTER 23

Jennifer Tryon awoke just after dawn on Friday July 5th with a throbbing headache. She lay on a straw pallet, locked in a windowless closet, wearing only a shift due to the stifling heat. Instinctively, she checked her left wrist for the time, but her Watch was gone. Smashed beyond repair. All she had left was the rainbow wristband.

Panic lanced her gut. While Jenn left no life partner behind in 2026, she was still close to her family. Nigel and Sunny, now in their seventies, were retired comfortably in Cornwall, while her siblings, and their respective broods, lived in the London suburbs. She feared she would never see any of them again.

Jennifer gently massaged the golf ball sized swelling on the back of her skull where Nathaniel Knight had hit her with the butt of his pistol. Right after she had kicked his compatriot in the balls, knocking him to the floor squealing like a pig. Which he fully deserved for trying to rip the Watch off her wrist.

Jennifer's prison was located in the bowels of the barracks of the Pennsylvania militia. She had listened to the men stomp about, curse, gamble, and snore for the past two nights, terrified that they would smash through her door. She vowed to go down fighting, but no one bothered her. It was silent outside now, as if the men had left. Or was she hallucinating?

Rising to her feet, she washed her face with the tepid water remaining in her cracked basin. She pushed the door. It rattled but was still bolted. Sitting up against the wall, she nibbled on the last of her hard tack.

Jennifer replayed her interrogation for the umpteenth time. Knight had tried to entrap her into an admission of espionage but she had nothing to admit. And no incriminating papers, code books or disappearing inks anywhere on her person. They had searched thoroughly, uncomfortably thoroughly, she thought, crossing her legs. So far, so good.

Nevertheless, Knight did not relent. She was obviously British, had no travel documents, and had chosen to stay in Widow Hauser's boarding house. Why was the daughter of a Royal Governor visiting Philadelphia if not to gather information? She had no acceptable answer.

To admit she wasn't Governor Tryon's daughter would have only lead to even more vigorous questioning, as well as remove the only shred of protection that she had. And the Governor did, in fact, have a daughter around her own age, so no one in Philadelphia could quickly dispute her claim.

The Committee men were about to lock her up for the night when Knight asked about the totem on her wrist. "Where did you get it?"

"It was a gift from a friend."

"An Indian?" he asked, pointing at the rainbow band.

"Yes, an Iroquois," she had answered honestly but without thought. Molly Brant hadn't exactly given her the Watch.

"The Iroquois are aligned with the British," he said, grabbing at her wrist. Then, all mayhem broke loose, Jennifer recalled, rubbing her sore skull again. She had regained consciousness briefly, just in time to see Knight stomp maniacally on her Watch, before drifting back into blackness.

A crisp rap on the door of her cell grabbed Jennifer's attention. She sprung to one knee but had nowhere to run.

"Mistress Tryon?" a gruff male voice called out.

"Yes."

Hearing hands fumbling with the bolt, Jennifer gouged a shallow hole in the dirt, burying her wristband and covering its grave with a cairn of small pebbles. If she were to die here, she wanted the rainbow symbol to live forever. When the door slid open, she sat innocently on the pallet.

"Major Robert Rogers, ma'am," a block-shouldered, gray-bearded man said, bowing with the glint of a smile illuminating his battle-scarred face. "At your service."

Robert Rogers? A hero of the French and Indian war. Founder of Rogers' Rangers, America's first special forces unit. Died a derelict in England. Jennifer started to fill in Rogers' biography, at least what little she could remember. Whose side was he on? What was he doing here? Could he help her?

Jennifer stood, reaching out her hand. Rogers shook it, maintaining an air of formality. "I was told a deranged British female was quartered here. Quite deadly with her feet and hands."

"God save the King," she replied, curtsying with a light smile.

"You might want to get dressed then," he said, handing Jennifer her frock. "I'll wait outside."

Jennifer wriggled into a peasant dress she had found in a twenty-first century thrift shop and made a vain swipe at her hair. Surprisingly, Knight and his men had not taken her lone earring, still fastened to her right lobe. The thought that they were spycatchers, not thieves, provided some comfort. She stepped out of her cell into an empty barracks.

"Now, you look more like the daughter of a Royal Governor," Rogers said.

"You know Governor Tryon?"

"Too well. He is the cause of my current misfortunes."

Rogers motioned for her to sit at one of the long tables. "Tried to enlist me in his scheme to assassinate George Washington. I turned him down. Last October mind you. Nevertheless, the good general got wind of my meeting with the Governor and had me arrested in New Jersey last week."

"So you're a prisoner too?" Jennifer asked, somewhat relieved to have a partner in crime.

"Awaiting trial for treason."

"As am I."

"I don't like either of our chances," Rogers said. Noiselessly, he rose from the table and paced briskly the length of the long room, about fifty yards she guessed, and back again. Five times. Then ten. Ignoring her.

He still moved well for a man in his forties, Jennifer thought, flexing her fingers as she studied him. When she was sure he was watching, she splintered the wooden table with a single karate chop.

"Do you have Indian blood?" he asked, clearly unnerved by her display.

She shook her head. Just British. And Chinese.

"Only seen one woman in my life who could fight like that. An Indian princess. Wielded a war club better than any man."

Jennifer could see his eyes soften. "Tell me about her."

"She's dead," Rogers said. "At least I left her to die in the Adirondacks last month."

"You left her to die?"

"The law of the wilderness. She took a ball to her chest. Wounded so badly she couldn't move," Rogers said, gazing out the window. "I had to leave or I would have met the same fate. She died a warrior's death. All she ever asked for."

"I'm hoping for more than a good death," Jennifer said.

"As am I," Rogers said. He walked over to the main entrance, an archway tall enough for a horseman to ride through, shuttered by two barn doors. There was a smaller, man-sized door off to the side. He pushed. It opened easily. Rogers peered outside, then returned to Jennifer.

"It appears our captors are off celebrating their grand Declaration," he said. "I suggest we capitalize on our good fortune and leave."

"Run away? Where to?"

"New York. I believe we both have contacts that will welcome us there."

"Won't the Committee of Safety come after us?" she asked.

"Undoubtedly. But I believe I still possess skills that will enable us to evade capture. As do you."

Gary Johnson was supposed to travel to 1776 on July 4th. He was now her only chance at a ticket home...if he came...if they connected... if he would help her. Rogers was right. The odds were not in her favor. "Let's go."

CHAPTER 24

Mission accomplished, Gary thought as he strolled down Market Street. Twilight had settled over the city. Candles flickered in every open window. The town wardens bustled about, lighting the street lamps. A goat scavenged in a trash pile.

He tossed his hat in the air, catching it neatly before it hit the cobblestones. Two frugally-attired Quakers leaving their meetinghouse interrupted a heated conversation to stare at his public display. He smiled goofily at them, feeling no need to apologize. If only his golfing buddies could see him now, it would be high fives all around.

The Watch rested securely under his shirt. He thought of texting but decided to wait until he had completed his business and was really ready to launch his homeward journey.

How will it feel to be seventy years old again? Muscles creaky. Looking the Grim Reaper squarely in the eye. A decade of reasonable health left - if he was lucky. But he would be with Lucie and his family. Back where he belonged.

Could he return to 2026 as a twenty-five year old? He was

certain the science behind time travel would never let that happen. A traveler could not be biologically younger than his children.

What would he remember of his time in the past? Everything, he assumed. His trip back in time hadn't wiped out any memories of his life in the twentieth and twenty-first centuries, so why would his return trip be any different. And he would have the physical documents to prove he had made the journey.

Would he be welcomed home as a hero or a criminal? He had once daydreamed of a ticker tape parade up Broadway; but, after his visit from the FBI, he'd now settle for an anonymous retirement.

The dining room at City Tavern had the exhausted aura of an arena the morning after a big game. Gary already missed the chatter and clatter of the Congressmen. He had born witness to the founding of America. The FBI could never take that away.

The Georgia delegation congregated in their corner but appeared unusually subdued. John Adams nodded in recognition to Gary before returning to conversation with his cousin, Sam. Both men wielded spoons like swords to emphasize their talking points. Erin emerged from the kitchen carrying a tray of meats, heading towards the patrons in the back without looking Gary's way.

"Mr. Johnson?" Congressman Sherman approached but Gary's mind was elsewhere. "Mr. Johnson?"

"Yes," he replied, gathering his wits at last. "A pleasure to see you, sir."

"About your letter of marque."

"Has it been approved?" Gary asked. In fact, he had forgotten all about his official reason for visiting Philadelphia.

"Approved? Hardly. Congress has had more important matters on its plate this week."

"Yes, of course. Now that the Declaration has been signed..."

"We will get to your application soon enough. I've sent a message via express to New London to confirm the particulars of your ship."

"The *Lucie*," Gary squirmed. Erin headed in his direction,

her tray significantly lighter.

"I've queried the other Connecticut delegates, but none can vouch for you or your family."

"Disappointing news, sir. I was not planning to stay in Philadelphia much longer."

"Well, it should be no more than a week. Ten days if the Post Road washes out again." Sherman straightened his hat. "I will stay in touch."

Gary breathed a sigh of relief as the Congressman left. He would be back on the golf course before Sherman learned that his ship did not exist. Safe from both the Committee of Safety and William Sands.

"Will you be joining us for supper tonight, Mr. Johnson?" Erin asked, her expression blank.

"No. I'll be taking my leave." Gary thought that's what Erin wanted to hear, but her pouting lips indicated otherwise.

"As you wish," she said, starting for the kitchen.

"Wait." He knew he was stepping onto thin ice. "I believe I have time for a last meal. Mrs. Tralee's cooking is too good to pass up."

"I'll put an extra dollop of sweets on your pie then."

Gary dined alone. Erin served him but didn't linger. John Tralee pulled up a chair as she cleared his plate. He held two envelopes in his hand. "Your bill, sir."

Gary scanned the page, handwritten in a loopy script. He had more than enough Continental dollars to cover the total. Before he could reach into his pack, however, Tralee handed him the second envelope. Red bordered and sealed with red wax. "A messenger delivered this a few minutes ago," he said. "That's Mr. Jefferson's signet."

"Thomas Jefferson?"

"Yes, sir. An invitation from the esteemed Virginian is rare indeed."

Perhaps Jefferson wanted to continue our conversation on slavery, Gary thought as he broke the seal and read the single page, an invitation to breakfast tomorrow morning at seven at Jefferson's residence. Of course, he would attend.

"I'll adjust your bill accordingly," Tralee said.

CHAPTER 25

The port went down too smoothly, Gary thought, his head throbbing as he trudged up the stairs to his old room. Jefferson, *the* Thomas Jefferson, had reached out; Tralee had doted; Erin had smiled. It was his last night in 1776. How could he NOT celebrate?

Fortunately, his room was empty - he was too old for a roommate, let alone a bedmate. He stripped to his shorts and washed up as much as possible at the basin. Four consecutive days without a shower, hot or cold. Even Lucie wouldn't go near him when he got home.

Although the daytime temperature had moderated, his room still was too warm for comfort. What was the weather in Connecticut 2026? Did Lucie have the AC on? What would she serve for dinner? She made a delicious *boeuf bourguignon*. Would the kids still be there? His mind wandered ahead to his return home. With anticipation, he noted contentedly, not regret.

He checked the Watch, secure around his neck. By sleeping with it on, the T-Rays from his body had fully charged it every night. Kudos to the scientists at MIT.

He pressed the stem, recalling Lucie's photo. One more night.

"All good. Coming home tomorrow afternoon," he texted with the Watch cradled in his hand.

Three minutes went by with no reply. Then five. Molly was probably asleep already. She'd get his missive to Lucie in the morning. With plenty of time to prepare whatever welcome she had in mind. Not too much, he hoped. He would be exhausted. And seventy years old again.

A knock on the door brought Gary back to 1776. He pulled on his shirt, buttoned it to conceal the Watch, and opened the door.

Erin. Dressed in her work gown. Cinnamon hair demurely bundled up above her neck. "I wanted to say good-bye," she said, looking both ways down the hall, clearly nervous.

"Come in," Gary said, closing the door behind her. He tried to keep his distance but Erin's lavender perfume drew him within touching distance. If only he could be twenty-five and single again. Unfortunately, one out of two wasn't good enough.

Locking his gaze on Erin's freckled forehead, Gary fought back the recollection of her stark naked body, hands on hips, breasts thrust tauntingly forward. It was a losing battle. Erin's bodice was too revealing. He stepped towards the window to break the spell.

"Ye will be leaving in the morning?" she asked.

"Yes. Immediately after my breakfast with Mr. Jefferson."

"A most flattering invitation to be sure. But are ye certain it came from Jefferson?"

"What do you mean?"

"It could be a ruse to lure ye away from here."

"A ruse? The envelope had Jefferson's personal seal. Mr. Tralee himself vouched for it." Gary pivoted away, separating the curtains, staring up at the full moon. The seal and the border of the envelope were blood red; Jefferson's man driving the whiskey wore a burnt orange livery.

"Be careful." Erin stepped towards him.

Gary turned. He reached into his pack, feeling past Lucie's

bracelet wrapped snugly in a sock, and withdrew his tiny pistol. "I'll keep this in my pocket."

Erin's eyes widened. "Do ye know how to use it?"

A fair question. Gary remembered his shooting lesson with Captain Parsons. He needed twenty shots to hit the chest of a human-sized target at thirty yards. Parsons consoled him with the factoid that the British Army fired 4 million musket balls to kill eight thousand enemy soldiers in a Napoleonic War battle. Little wonder the Founding Fathers so readily endorsed the second amendment. No chance of a mass murder in their day.

"Why do you care?" Gary had to ask.

"Ye are a good man," she said, taking his hand. "Not too many of them around here. I don't want to see ye hurt. Or worse."

"I can take care of myself."

She placed her hands on his shoulders, her touch searingly hot. Gary froze, intoxicated by her scent.

Erin levered up on her tiptoes and kissed his cheek. "Good night, then."

His hands somehow rested on her hips, fingertips tracing the curve of her body. She inched closer, but Gary made no further advance. She nodded and stalked out the door.

CHAPTER 26

"Off to meet Mr. Jefferson?" John Tralee asked, beaming, at breakfast on Saturday.

"Yes," Gary replied, stifling a yawn after another night tossing with torrid dreams of Erin. "Then back to Connecticut."

"I've confirmed your place on the Boston coach. The driver will pick you up here at ten. Promptly."

"Most appreciated." Gary scanned his updated bill, opened his wallet and counted out the appropriate Continental currency. While Tralee checked each note carefully, crumpling the paper to be sure of its authenticity, Gary reached into his pack for his purse. He handed Tralee a weighty silver coin. "Can you give this to Erin for me? She's too proud to accept it directly."

"I'm pleased she could be of service," Tralee replied, nodding his approval. He hesitated, as if debating his next words. "Erin's a good woman. She does what's necessary to care for her bairns."

No response was the best response, Gary decided. "I'll be off then."

"Your letter of marque? Have you received it?"

The letter had slipped Gary's mind again. He shook his head, hoping his negligence hadn't set off any alarms. "Can you forward it to Connecticut?"

"Of course. I pray your venture proves successful."

Gary breathed a sigh of relief. "I look forward to returning to Philadelphia bearing the spoils of war."

The sun, rising in a cerulean blue sky, shone in Gary's eyes as he walked towards Jefferson's quarters on Second Street. He ducked into a still shaded alley next to a tanner's shop. The stench from curing animal hides was overwhelming.

Molly had not replied to his message last night, so he wanted to try again. He pulled out the Watch, tapped the face, and spoke clearly: "All good. Coming home today. Love to Lucie." The swish indicated his text was on the way.

He couldn't escape the tannery fast enough. He took a deep breath, put his head down and barged towards Fourth Street.

William Sands, pistol in hand, blocked his path. "Conversing with your watch. It must be particularly special."

"It is," Gary replied, scared for the first time in 1776. Erin's warning flashed red as he fumbled in his jacket pocket for his pistol.

Sands shook his head sadly as he smacked it skittering along the cobblestones. "The watch, please." He pointed his pistol, gold-plated and fully cocked, directly at Gary's chest. "Don't be a macaroni."

"I'll give you cash. Jewelry. But please don't take the Watch," Gary realized he sounded pathetic, but didn't care. "It's a gift from my wife."

"I will give her a gift in return, then. Your life."

Gary shakily unbuttoned his shirt and reached for the Watch. If he could distract Sands, he could launch himself home to safety. "Can I show you something? Why it's so special?"

Sands nodded, but his pistol hand didn't flinch. Gary tapped the face three times. The launch screen appeared. Sands leaned over to look, his eyebrows and lips scrunching in consternation as he tried to make sense of the device.

Gary's mind raced to remember the password. TimeR 1776? Sands reached for the Watch. Gary yanked it away. TimeR 2026. That's it.

Before Gary could launch, a whiskey, pulled by a statuesque gray stallion, squeezed into the alley, and clattered to a stop. Erin was at the front, her hands bound behind her back, a purple bruise despoiling her left cheek.

The driver, hatless but densely bearded with a black patch covering his right eye, dropped the reins and wrapped his right arm around Erin's waist. His left hand held a knife, at least a foot long, to her throat.

"The watch, please. And your whore will go free," Sands said, icicles dripping from every word.

"Run," Erin shouted. "There's a back way out..." Her captor ratcheted his grip, stifling her voice, draining the color from her face.

Gary cradled the Watch in his hand, the launch screen still visible. One word would send him to safety. Sands kept a two-step distance, clearly bewildered. Gary pointed the Watch at him. "It will cast a spell over you. You'll die in agony."

Erin's captor drew his blade lightly across her forehead, a bloody trickle appearing in its wake. Sands crossed himself with his free hand. "The watch, now," he said.

"Release her first." Gary replied. He couldn't let Erin die - not here, not now.

Sands nodded and his man complied, tossing Erin off the whiskey. She stumbled, righted herself, but then fell. Within reach of Gary's pistol.

With Sands' gun still in his face, Gary groped behind his neck, unfastening the latch that held the Watch. "Trouble," he said loudly, hearing the swish indicating his message was in route.

Sands grabbed at the Watch with his free hand, but got tangled in the chain. Gary spun away, the precious Watch sliding off his neck. Sands reached with his gun hand to corral it, momentarily taking his eyes off Gary.

Gary dropped to one knee. Erin pushed his pistol towards him. He picked the weapon up, aiming at Sands' head.

The recoil from the trigger knocked Gary back on his haunches. Sands whipped around as the ball whizzed by his ear. The whiskey driver, however, keeled over, a scarlet stream spouting from his neck.

Sands looked wildly about as he stuffed the Watch and chain into his waistcoat pocket. The blast had quickly attracted a gaping bystander. Then another.

Sands jumped onto the whiskey, kicking his dying henchman into the alley. He snapped the reins. The stallion lurched forward. Gary could only watch as the carriage, Sands and his transport back to 2026 disappeared into the morning light.

"A fine shot," Erin said, helping Gary to his feet.

CHAPTER 27

"Thief! Stop him!" Gary screamed at the slack-jawed bystanders as Sands' whiskey raced away. "He stole my Watch!"

"We have to leave," Erin said, tugging Gary's sleeve. "This way."

"But Sands went…"

"No matter." She pointed at the punctured, lifeless body of his henchman. "We have to leave."

"Leave? Why? I shot in self-defense." Gary still held his smoking pistol.

"Did ye?" Erin massaged her throat, confirming her windpipe was still intact. "What if Sands says otherwise?"

"Otherwise?" Gary jerked his arm free, bewildered.

"Sands is a scoundrel," she said, coughing up a blob of mucus, spitting it into the dirt. "He'll claim that ye stole the Watch from him. Or he loaned it to ye and.."

"Lies. Damn lies."

"Ye are a foreigner. And I'm a whore," she said, drawing whisper-close as she wiped the blood leaking down her forehead with the sleeve of her dress. "Who will believe either one of us?"

"But..."

"Go," Erin pleaded, pushing Gary away. The crowd, now numbering a dozen, was starting to inch down the alleyway towards them. Fortunately, the stink from the tannery slowed their advance. She positioned her body to shield Gary's retreat from view.

"Make way for the constable," a distant voice shouted.

Pocketing his pistol, Gary bustled towards the sunlight at the far side of the alley. Erin waited, tensed, prepared to block any pursuers. When no one emerged from the pack, she hiked her skirt and hastened after him.

She caught up on Second Street, when Gary stopped to stare at Jefferson's window. He would be safely at home with Lucie in 2026 right now if not for his desire to breakfast with the great Virginian. How could Sands have duped him so easily?

"This way," Erin said, taking Gary's hand, yanking him out of his self-flagellating trance. "Sands may head to the docks."

They fast-walked down High Market Street towards the Delaware River, lost among the swarm of Saturday morning shoppers and shopkeepers. A shirtless Black pushed a wagon load of manure; a seamstress waved a swath of lush beige wool; a butcher brandished a pork chop. Expecting to hear the wail of a police siren, Gary snatched a glance over his shoulder every ten seconds, but then he remembered that he was in 1776. Information traveled slowly here.

Reaching Front Street, they looked frantically in both directions. No sign of Sands. "The ferry's this way," Erin said, pointing to their left. A ferryman, poling a raft holding three travelers, glided into a slip.

"Why would he go south?" Gary asked, swiveling his head in the opposite direction. Lashed to the quay, several multi-masted schooners, sails furled, buzzed with seamen unloading hogsheads of rum.

"He'd more likely try to reach the British camps outside New York," Gary added, pulling Erin to their right. She swept a lock of hair out of her eyes and followed.

A well-muscled stevedore, tattoos snaking down both arms, slow-eyed Erin as if he knew her. She ducked her head, grasping Gary's elbow as they passed. He paid no mind, his eyes scouring the waterfront for Sands or his whiskey.

The *Flying Franny*, sprouting lines and nets on every side, glided from her berth, heading towards the Delaware Bay and the Atlantic Ocean. Odd that a fisherman would be heading out to sea this late in the morning, Gary thought briefly before returning his attention to the task at hand.

"There," he shouted. The formidable gray stallion was tethered to a rail outside a row of warehouses and counting rooms.

Gary burst through the nearest door, ignoring Erin's pleas to wait. He tripped on a loose floorboard but quickly regained his balance. The room was large and airy; double height windows framed a view of the river; four rows of clerks toiled heads down entering figures into ledger books. Gary's entrance caused a great shuffling of feet which, in turn, led a mule-faced man, neatly attired in a slate gray jacket and matching waistcoat, to arise from a massive oak desk.

"Yes?" he asked, arching his overgrown eyebrows. "For what reason, may I ask, have you invaded Willig, Morris this fine morning?"

"Sands? William Sands?" Gary stammered as he caught his breath. Erin lingered in his shadow. "I'm looking for William Sands. On an urgent matter."

"Cary and Company reside two doors down."

CHAPTER 28

William Sands, powdered wig slightly askew, stood behind a tattered table, dipping his quill into an inkwell when Gary and Erin entered. The windowless counting room was dark and smoky. Two clerks, both men in their twenties, looked up briefly then returned to their labors.

Sands set down his quill and straightened his waistcoat, withdrawing an ivory Meerschaum pipe sporting an intricately carved floral pattern. "Yes?" he asked.

"I want my Watch back," Gary said, planting his feet firmly in front of Sands.

"*Your* watch?" Sands tamped a wad of tobacco into his pipe.

"And what about my footman, poor Owen, whom you brutally murdered?"

"Murdered? 'Poor' Owen held a knife to Erin's throat." Gary pointed to Erin's face, bloodied and beaten. "I shot him to save her life."

"We can let the constable decide that."

"Call him then. I'll wait." Gary needed a second to

remember that there were no phones, portable or otherwise, in 1776. But, Sands, his bluff called, seemed in no hurry to summon anyone. "I want my Watch," Gary declared again.

"And what proof of ownership do you have?"

"Proof?"

"Bill of sale? Family provenance?" Sands took another slow drag on his Meerschaum.

"That Watch has been in my family for generations," Gary replied.

"Your family? The Johnsons if I remember correctly. From Connecticut."

"Correct."

"Our firm, Cary and Company, has quite extensive commercial contacts in New York and New England, yet we've never done business with any Johnsons in Connecticut."

"That proves nothing."

"Fair enough. But our office in New York can find no record of your family or its holdings. On land or sea." Sands rearranged the papers on his desk apparently looking for Johnson family deeds. After finding none, he looked up with a pirate's grin.

"But you stole my Watch." Gary fingered the pistol buried in his jacket pocket. Its barrel was still warm but it wasn't loaded. And he wasn't planning to shoot anyone else this morning.

"I did not *steal* it. I reclaimed it for one of our clients. It was stolen from him several years ago."

"That's bullshit."

"Excuse me? Bullshit?" Sands blew a cloud of smoke in Gary's direction. "I'm not familiar with that term although I can guess its meaning."

"You're a liar," Gary said. Erin's eyes flared, as if Gary had slapped her rather than insulted Sands. She tried to tug him away, but Gary stood his ground.

"That's quite a serious allegation." Sands rang a bell on his desk. A hulking, bulbous-beaked man, resembling an overstuffed penguin in poorly fitted black and white livery, emerged from the back room.

"Mr. Williams, did you just hear Mr. Johnson impugn my integrity?"

"Most certainly did."

Sands set his lips, barely containing a leer. He reached into his desk and withdrew a white glove. He contemplated it for a second, as if counting the fingers, then tossed it at Gary's feet. "I regret that I must seek proper redress for your libelous insult."

"What the...?" Gary stared at the glove on the floor.

"He just challenged ye to a duel." Erin said.

"A duel?"

"It's a matter of honor now. There's no turning back."

"But I don't want to duel him. I just want my Watch back." Sands and Williams smugly watched the conversation, waiting for Gary's response.

"If ye refuse Sands' challenge, ye will be labeled a coward," Erin said, letting go of Gary's arm. She placed her hands on her hips and puffed out her chest, the sparkle in her eyes willing him to pick up the glove.

"Who cares?" Gary said.

"Who cares? Are ye daft, man? Is there no code of honor in Connecticut?" Erin spit out the questions. "Ye will never be accepted in society again. Anywhere in the colonies."

Gary was flabbergasted by Erin's indignation.

"Well then?" Sands asked, his impatience obvious. "Shall we say tomorrow at dawn? On Windmill Island?" Windmill Island, twenty-five acres, sat in the Delaware River between Philadelphia and Camden, New Jersey.

Gary stared at the glove on the floor. He knew he should walk away but a glance at Erin, petulant and unyielding, juiced his courage. He picked up the glove and flipped it back towards Sands. "If I win, your man Williams will return my Watch. Immediately."

Sands nodded. "Tomorrow at dawn then. Williams will row us out."

"Tomorrow is the Sabbath," Gary replied, stalling. "And I'll have to find a second."

"Monday then," Sands said, tucking the glove into his pocket. "Pistols or sabers?"

"Pistols." Gary instinctively rotated his right arm up and over his head, waiting for the pain to jab his shoulder, but he was twenty-five now. No shoulder pain. He had not felt so alive in fifty years.

Beaming with pride, Erin clasped his arm.

CHAPTER 29

Gary and Erin fairytaled out of the counting house. Having accepted Sands' challenge, he rode the high of youthful braggadocio, while she luxuriated in the timeless fantasy that her man would fight to the death to defend her honor. He blinked in the sunlight as the golden orb burst from its hiding spot behind a pillowy cloud.

"The beach is bonny," Erin said, pointing out past the docked ships to Windmill Island, lurking in the mid-river mist.

"You've been there?" Gary asked.

"Aye. Many times," she replied.

"For a duel?"

Erin laughed, taking Gary's hand. "We come out to Windmill to escape the heat and swim in the river."

Gary couldn't help picturing Erin, knee deep in the current, flaunting a cherry red bikini. Like the one Lucie had worn on their honeymoon in St. Tropez. The thought of his wife chilled his exuberance. He had to *win* the duel with Sands, not merely survive it, if he hoped to regain his Watch and return home. And he had less than forty-eight hours to prepare.

"I'll need to find a second. A good one," he said, dropping Erin's hand.

"John Tralee is keen on ye."

"I'm not sure how keen he'll be when he learns I shot Sands' man." Gary quickened his pace back towards High Market Street, although he really had no place to go.

"Do ye know anyone else?" Erin caught up with Gary but didn't try to reclaim his grip. "It's a grand responsibility."

"John Dunlap, the printer. I spent all night helping him produce his broadsides of the Declaration of Independence."

"So that's where ye were. Ye had us all baffled." Erin smiled softly.

"I didn't know you missed me."

"A wee bit."

They walked the rest of the way to Dunlap's print shop in silence. Gary went inside alone while Erin returned to City Tavern to check the lay of the land. They agreed to meet in State House Square in an hour.

"Mr. Johnson, I didn't expect to see you back in Philadelphia for quite some time," John Dunlap boomed upon Gary's entrance.

"Unfortunately, I've run into a problem. A temporary one, I hope."

"Aye.   I've heard," Dunlap said, dropping his head, appearing to study his type. "Word circulates fast in this town."

"Can I ask what you've heard?"

Dunlap looked up, gazed out the window, then shooed Aiden, his apprentice, into the back room. "That you had a run-in with William Sands. A murderous run-in," he said at last.

"That's true. He tried to steal my Watch. Held a pistol to my chest. And I defended myself."

"I understand you also defended a wench who was employed at the City Tavern."

The fact that Dunlap, and likely others, had heard about the shooting was good news, Gary thought. There must have been at least one witness who saw Erin's sorry state. "I did," he replied. "Sands' man beat her. And held her hostage."

"Hostage you say?"

"Knife to her throat."

"So you shot him?"

Gary nodded. No point announcing he was actually aiming at Sands, not his henchman.

"Have you met with the constable yet?" Dunlap tore a page off the press, scanned it briefly, and tossed it on the floor. "Too many monks," he said, pointing out several smudges to Gary.

"I'll see the constable this afternoon," Gary replied, steering the conversation back on track.

"I believe you'll find he's sympathetic to your cause. Sands is a well-known blackguard."

"Then why is he allowed to live here?"

"Many gentlemen trade with Cary and Company." With a grapefruit-sized leather ball in each hand, Dunlap laid a new coat of ink over the type. "On credit," he added.

"Sands blackmails them?" Gary inched closer to the press, wincing at the smell of urine which was used to soften the inking balls. He'd sniffed enough animal odors in the past week to last the rest of his life.

"I wouldn't quite phrase it that way," Dunlap replied as he swiped his inky fingers on his apron. "Where is your Watch now?"

"Sands has it. Claims it belongs to a client of his in New York City." Gary could see that Dunlap was producing this week's edition of the *Gazette*.

"And you have proof of your ownership?"

"Back in Connecticut." A true statement, albeit in the twenty-first century.

"Then you have another reason to hasten home."

"Definitely, but there is an important matter I must see to first." Gary explained the duel. "Would you be my second?"

Dunlap's entire frame jolted as if shocked by an electrical current, but he recovered quickly. "I have little experience with pistols."

Neither do I, Gary thought. "But you're a well-respected businessman."

"I do my best."

"What if I pay you?" Gary lifted his pack, letting the jingle of his coins do the talking.

"Money has no place in an affair of honor." Dunlap reached for the Devil's Tail with both hands, his taciturn expression signaling this conversation was drawing to a close.

"Sands is not an honorable man," Gary replied in a last, likely futile, attempt to win Dunlap over.

"But he is quite a good shot," Dunlap said as he inspected the page.

That's it, Gary thought bleakly. Dunlap doesn't want to have to cart my dead body back across the river and deal with the funeral details. Hard to blame him.

"Aiden," Dunlap shouted. "You're needed."

Gary took the cue and left.

CHAPTER 30

Gary walked slowly towards the rendezvous with Erin, his mind rollercoasting over plans and counter-plans for the upcoming duel. He nodded absentmindedly to a peg-legged man hopping along in the brown jacket and green waistcoat of the First Pennsylvania militia, side-stepped an elegant ebony carriage, its giant rear wheels twice the diameter of its front ones, and exchanged pleasantries with a pox-scarred woman in an auburn taffeta hoop skirt and high-necked lace bodice. As Gary approached State House Square, he realized that he hadn't thought twice about any of these encounters, an uncomfortable indication that he was growing too comfortable in the eighteenth century.

On the green, a street urchin hawked copies of the *Pennsylvania Evening Post*, the primary competitor to Dunlap's *Gazette*. Gary tossed him a coin, sat on a bench and scanned the cover page, featuring the complete text of the Declaration of Independence. While Dunlap inked broadsides for John Hancock, his newspaper had been scooped. That helped to explain the printer's foul mood.

Gary had just started reading the advertisements on the fourth and final page of the *Post,* hoping to find a notice of his Watch for sale, when Erin sat down next to him.

"Any luck with Mr. Dunlap?"

Gary shook his head. "He did inform me that Sands is quite the marksman."

"As are ye," she said, taking his hand.

"I'll have to find a spot to practice tomorrow."

"We can take the ferry out to the island for a look-see."

"Good idea."

"Where will ye spend the night?"

"I thought I'd try for my old room at the tavern."

"Mr. Tralee said he was fully booked." Erin dropped her gaze to the ground, the meaning of Tralee's rejection clear. "But, he did give me this," she added, holding up a weighty coin. "Said it was from ye."

Gary squeezed her hand and smiled. "To feed your boys."

"Thank ye kindly."

Hands clasped, they sat in silence for several minutes. A horseman rode up to the City Tavern, jumped off his frothing mount, tied it to the hitching post and strode inside. He returned quickly toting a sack of mail and galloped off.

"Ye hoped to be home in Connecticut by now, didn't ye?" Erin asked.

"Yes."

"Never to see me again."

"Most likely," Gary replied, frowning at the hard truth, but still holding Erin's gaze.

"Ye could leave right now."

"And forfeit my honor?"

"Ye might forfeit ye life."

"I'll win the duel."

"Ye will have to shoot straighter than ye did this morning," Erin said, looking away.

"True," Gary chuckled. She obviously knew he had missed

his target, but had tried to pump up his confidence anyway. "But at least I didn't choke under pressure."

"Choke?"

"It's a Connecticut term."

"It will be easier the second time."

"Hopefully."

Erin shifted on the bench, turning her face up to look directly into Gary's eyes. "Why do ye care so much about your watch?"

"What do you mean?"

"It's obvious that ye are staying here in Philadelphia, and risking ye life, to get that watch back, not for me," she said, folding her hands in her lap. "Can't ye buy another one? You've got buckets of money."

Gary stared at Erin's hands, noticing for the first time how chapped and nicked they were. She led a hard life, but never complained. He wanted to help, but he didn't see how confiding the secret of his time travel would accomplish anything. At least right now.

"Mr. Johnson?" A raspy male voice interrupted their conversation.

"Yes," Gary replied, looking up, warning lights flashing in his brain.

"I'm Chief Constable Huckleberry and these are my deputies, Heydrich and Gunther." The chief was a barrel-bellied, round-faced man, droll if not for his lupine gray eyes. "We'd like a word with you, sir," he continued in a high-pitched whine.

The deputies, tall, muscular men with tightly cropped blond hair visible under their tricorns, were obviously Hessian. They towered behind their chief, arms dangling loosely within easy reach of the blackjacks visible beneath their scarlet jackets.

"Of course," Gary replied, as if he had a choice. "I was planning to find you this afternoon."

"Do you have any proof of your residency - in Connecticut, I believe?" Huckleberry asked.

Erin glanced sharply at Gary, her pinched expression saying, "I told you so," even if she didn't voice the words.

Gary stood, squaring up to Huckleberry. "Connecticut and Pennsylvania are all part of the same United States now, aren't they?"

"I do believe so."

"If I'm no longer a foreigner, why would proof of residency be required?"

"A fair question. We'll have to ask Justice Chew," the chief constable answered, scratching the whiskers on his ample chin. "If he still holds his exalted office next week."

Although a fifth generation American who had served Pennsylvania with great distinction as Attorney General and Chief Justice for over twenty years, Benjamin Chew was now in extremely hot water. As a wealthy Quaker and slave owner, he opposed the Revolution and supported the British government. While never charged with a crime, he would be removed from the bench in 1777 and kept in preventive detention in New Jersey for over a year until the British Army retreated from Pennsylvania.

"Let's see the Judge on Monday morning. First thing," Gary said.

"And where will you be staying till then?"

"He's staying with me," Erin interjected, jumping to her feet.

"With you? Where do you reside, young *lady*?" Huckleberry spat out the last word as if it was a foul fruit.

"In Southwark. With me mother."

"Too many darkies and Irish in Southwark. Catholics too, I understand. I can't ask my men to surveil Mr. Johnson there."

"I give my word I won't flee," Gary said. "I've committed no crime and want to see my name cleared." He decided not to mention his imminent duel with Sands, unsure of its legality.

"I'd prefer you stay in the Barracks," Huckleberry replied, shaking his head. "All the able-bodied men in the First Pennsylvania just marched off to New York. There'll be plenty of room."

The deputies stepped in front of their chief, emphasizing the urgency of this request. One reached for Gary's pack, but he slapped his hand away. "This stays with me."

"We'll have to search it then," Huckleberry said.

"Let me have it," Erin said, clutching the pack to her chest, smothering the jingle of coins and jewelry. "I'll guard it with me life."

CHAPTER 31

The Barracks were cavernous and deserted, although the air was ripe with the smell of men and horses. Gary paced back and forth, tracking a black cat prowl the perimeter. Hungry, he hadn't eaten since breakfast, a lifetime ago. He thought of calling Uber Eats, but quickly remembered that was not an option. Fortunately, Heydrich appeared with a plate of bread, cheese and jerky. A flagon of beer as well.

Sitting on a bench at a long table nicked by knives and truncheon blows, Gary capitalized on the dregs of daylight to devour his meager feast. The reality of his predicament set in before the beer lost its froth. He was in jail in 1776, possibly facing a murder charge, with no way to return to 2026 unless he could recover his Watch. To regain it, he'd have to win a duel with William Sands, a far superior marksman although that was not a particularly high bar.

While Gary knew he had to stay focused on the present, or rather the past, his mind wandered back, or was it forward, to Lucie, their children, and grandchildren. He slammed his fist on the table.

The duel was scheduled for dawn on Monday, if he could get out of jail. Would Justice Chew release him? What if he didn't? The possibilities spun like a roulette wheel, and appeared just as random.

As the Hessian did not provide any candles, the Barracks quickly grew pitch black. Gary remembered his spoon with its concealed flashlight, but it was in his pack. His pacings had revealed a back room, little more than a closet, with a straw pallet. He stumbled in that direction, banging his knee before reaching the open door.

Gary awoke at first light, rolling over reluctantly, luxuriating in a dream, slow-dancing with Lucie at Maribel's wedding. Her perfume lingered as he shook off the cobwebs of sleep. Strands of straw clung to his face. He swiped them away, but the familiar floral notes didn't evaporate as he gained consciousness. Rolling to his stomach, he reached under the sheet and plunged his hands into the straw, tossing it like a salad. While the linen had likely not been washed in months, if ever, he was quite certain a woman had slept here recently.

Heydrich dutifully brought him breakfast, porridge, a biscuit, and cold tea. Before he left, Gary asked, "Who else has been locked up here this summer?"

The deputy pondered, as if deciding whether the answer might be a state secret. "Major Rogers, Robert Rogers," he said in thickly accented English.

"What happened to him?"

"He escaped. But not for long. There's a bounty on his head."

"No women?"

Heydrich shook his head.

Gary spent the rest of the morning pacing. Despite what Heydrich said, he was certain a female had slept in the closet. But, what did it matter? One of the soldiers could have literally rolled in the hay with his wife, or girlfriend, or whore. The sticking point, however, was the fragrance. Its notes were complex, more twenty-first century than the simple jasmine that Erin splashed on.

Regardless, he needed a strategy for the duel with Sands, whenever it took place, not a new cologne. More pistol practice was definitely required, so any delay imposed by Justice Chew would be helpful - provided he could get out of jail.

He had never witnessed a duel, at least not in person. But on television or in a movie? Gary's mind rifled through shows - *Gladiator*? No pistols there. *The Sopranos?* Tony preferred delivering a bullet to the back of the head. *Yellowstone?* Yes! In season three or four, John Dutton gave a bad guy a chance to draw against him, rather than just murder the bastard in cold blood. Dutton, however, set up the fight so he had an edge.

Gary was on his ninety-fourth lap when Heydrich re-entered with Erin, carrying his backpack. The guard stepped away to give them a modicum of privacy. After an appropriately chaste hug, Erin handed Gary a cloth encasing two sausages. "Figured ye would be hungry."

"I have a utensil in my pack. Can I get it?" Gary asked, looking over at Heydrich.

"No sharp points."

"It's a spoon," Erin said, clearly bewildered.

"To eat sausage?" Heydrich was just as confused, but nodded his assent.

"It's a Connecticut custom," Gary said, placing the spoon in his pocket. Erin rolled her eyes. After she left, Gary returned to his exercise, a plan finally taking shape.

As daylight waned, the weather turned nasty. Thunder boomed, lightning sizzled, and rain fell in torrents, drumming a steady beat on the Barracks roof. Gary retreated to the closet, hoping to lose himself in the pallet's lingering residue of home.

Laying down, he noticed what appeared to be a purposeful assemblage of pebbles within easy reach. Dismissing it, his mind drifted to 2026. He was in good hands there. Lucie was safe and would make sure he was not abandoned. Rob Mangano would do all in his power to appease the FBI if necessary to speed his return. Molly and her team would work 24/7 to build another Watch and send a rescuer, maybe Lucie herself, back to 1776.

A blinding flash jolted Gary awake. Lightning was the scourge of colonial cities, a hodgepodge of highly flammable structures leaning on each other like wobbly drunks. He jumped up, racing to the window. Flames nipped at the stable across the narrow street. The trapped equine inhabitants wailed in fear.

He banged the Barracks door to no avail. Heydrich must have disappeared.

No! Gary saw his guard lead a sorrel mare to safety, then head back to rescue another victim. He screamed for attention but the crash of the storm drowned out his pleas. He tried to lift a bench to break the window but it was too heavy.

Church bells called Philadelphia's fire brigade, organized by Benjamin Franklin in 1736, into action. Within minutes, Gary saw five citizens, then ten, then twenty, men and women, form a line, passing buckets of water from hand to hand. The flames, however, would not recede without a fight. Gary could only pray they wouldn't jump to his prison.

Another flash and a bone-jarring rattle. He frantically checked the ceiling and walls of the Barracks. A faint burning smell, like dying charcoal on the grill back home, drifted down from the roof.

Gary was defenseless, armed only with flagons of beer and water. The dank odor grew more intense as the temperature in the Barracks soared. Sweat clouded his vision. He hurled his body against the door but couldn't budge it. He shrunk back into the closet to make his final stand.

A rush of moist, cool air swept into the closet. "Hello? Mr. Johnson?" Heydrich clamored as he burst through the door. "Follow me."

Gary didn't need a second invitation. On his way out, he kicked over the cairn of pebbles, revealing a rainbow-colored wrist band. He didn't stop to pick it up.

"Dr. Franklin's lightning rod saved us," Heydrich said, once they were safely outside. While the rod itself had gnarled, it had conducted the electrical charge into the ground, leaving the Barracks' roof smoldering but intact.

Another squall augmented the bucket brigade's effort to subdue the flames across the street. Gary and Heydrich joined the stable hands to lead the terrified horses to safety. Only one, a chestnut filly, was too badly burned to save. The stablemaster put her out of her misery with a single shot.

The sky cleared, revealing a sparkling swath of stars that appeared to stretch all the way to Connecticut. Constable Huckleberry and Erin arrived at the scene almost simultaneously. The constable gave Gary permission to leave under the condition he would remain in Philadelphia pending his meeting with Justice Chew.

"Ye will stay with us," Erin insisted. "I'll see that ye get some hot food and rest before ye meet Mr. Sands in the morning."

CHAPTER 32

Southwark at night reminded Gary of hell scenes in *Hadestown*. Clapboard buildings leaned this way and that; tents dotted an empty lot; goats, pigs, dogs and cats roamed freely; smoke spiraled skyward from chimneys and bonfires, a particularly unwelcome sight after his escape from the flames at the Barracks. A couple appeared to be copulating in the shadows.

Squeezing his hand, Erin guided him around two drunks passed out in the mud in front of a saloon. "Almost home," she said, as they rounded a corner and appeared to enter a better part of town - at least from what he could see in the darkness.

Halfway down a block of weather-beaten brick row houses, Erin opened the gate on a freshly painted white picket fence and ushered Gary into her front yard. Although pocket-sized, vegetables sprouted on both sides of a well-trod path. She pointed towards the portico which contained entrances for two apartments. Candles flickered in the windows flanking both doors, only one of which was open.

"Mum," a thumb-sucking toddler called as he trundled to

greet them. A trio of chickens followed, clucking happily in his wake.

"Timmy, ye shouldn't be outside by yourself," Erin replied, sweeping him up in her arms. "Where's Mamo?"

Before he could answer, his five year old brother, John, bounded into the garden and attached himself to his mother's skirts. She reached down to tousle his hair.

"Don't ye worry. I've got me eye on the wee rascals," Mamo, a short, spry woman, called as she hastened towards her daughter. She tucked an errant strand of graying hair underneath her cap and looked Gary over like he was a prize-winning hog. "Ain't he a handsome one," she added, curtsying with an exaggerated flourish.

"This is me mum, Mary," Erin said as she fussed over her boys. "She can still dance a jig with the best of them at the Tin Whistle."

"Not like I used to though," Mary replied. Her dancing green eyes, eerily similar to her daughter's, belied the hollowness of her cheeks. "I'm pushing forty now."

Gary didn't know what to say, so he just smiled and followed Erin through the open door. The brick was just a façade, the flooring, stairway and supporting beams inside were all wood, warped and rotting in places. A kettle rested in the crane in the hearth simmering over the still-crackling embers. The table, resting on a threadbare rug, was piled with balls of yarn, a basket of potatoes, and laundry. A rocking chair sat empty in the corner next to a neat stack of children's blocks and the whittled figure of a soldier. The aroma of a leftover stew warmed the room.

"The necessary's out the back door," Erin said, handing Timmy off to her mother. She opened the cupboard and removed two plates, utensils and a cleaver. "I'll fix ye supper."

"There's turnips and carrots left in the pot, but we finished the chicken," Mary said. She hesitated for a second before nodding to Gary and adding, "Thank ye. We haven't had fresh meat on our table for some time."

While Gary headed to the outhouse, Erin, knife in hand,

stomped outside. When he returned, a chicken carcass filled the pot. Erin wiped her bloody hands on her apron. Mary and the boys were upstairs. The clock on the mantle chimed nine times.

Erin carried two mugs of beer to the table and sat next to him. "Supper will be ready shortly," she said, patting his thigh. "Are ye ready for tomorrow morning?"

Gary nodded. He stared at the flames of the candles on the table, debating how to enlist Erin's aid without revealing too much. "Yes," he replied at last. "But I'm going to need your help. I want you to be my second."

"Me? I'm a woman."

"I'm well aware. But you know Windmill Island."

Erin nodded. Now it was her turn to contemplate the flames. "Ye could just apologize to Sands...," she said without shifting her gaze. "...and walk away from the duel."

"Apologize? For what? He stole my Watch."

"The Watch? That's it, isn't it?" She brushed away a tear. "He'll kill ye and not think twice about it."

"He won't kill me," Gary replied, reaching for Erin's chin and gently turning her head. "You won't let him."

"Sands won't miss. He wants that Watch just as bad as ye do...," she rambled on as if she hadn't heard Gary's last words. "...though I don't know why."

"You'll make him miss," he said, taking the Connecticut spoon from his jacket pocket.

"And how am I supposed to do that? Flash my tits?"

Gary laughed, breaking the tension between them. "Shoot first. Fight dirty. Run fast."

"Shoot first. Fight dirty. Run fast," Erin slowly repeated. "Where did ye come up with that lard-brained plan?"

"My friend, Tom, was a Green Beret in Vietnam."

"Viet where?" Erin asked, grunting the 'Viet' in a pseudo-Germanic accent. "Is that where the Hessians were born?"

"No. Vietnam. It's a country in Asia." Gary pointed the butt end of the spoon at the clock, now cloaked in darkness. He hesitated, then dropped his aim. Should he apologize to Sands and find another way to get the Watch back? "Never mind."

"Shoot first?" Erin asked, reaching for the spoon. "But ye must wait for the count before you shoot. As must William Sands."

"I'll wait," Gary replied, his hesitation forgotten as he demonstrated the spoon's secret. "But you won't."

CHAPTER 33

The thump on the front door woke Gary from a damp, restless sleep in the humid upstairs room. He was sharing a straw-tick mattress with the boys while Erin and her mother slept together on the other pallet. Both beds faced the fireplace, mercifully dormant.

"Five o'clock and all's well," a man's voice boomed from the front porch.

"Thank ye, sir. We're awake," Erin called down. She pulled her sleeping gown over her head without hesitation, scrubbed her torso with a washcloth, and began to dress. "Mamo, you'll watch the boys till we return."

Her mother mumbled a reply and rolled over. John rose, pissed into the communal chamber pot, then flopped back into bed. Timmy never budged.

The glimpse of Erin's nakedness shook the cobwebs from Gary's brain. "Who was that?" he asked, pulling his breeches up.

"The knocker-upper. I paid him to wake us."

"What about the clock on the mantel?"

"It tells the time," Erin replied as she smoothed her day frock and capped her hair.

"No alarm?"

"We're not fancy folk - if ye haven't noticed." A frown flitted across Erin's face, but it disappeared just as quickly.

Downstairs, she lit a candle and laid out a breakfast of bread and cheese. A pot of coffee simmered over a low flame. While Gary ate, she fiddled with his spoon, aiming the flashlight beam first at the clock, then the children's toys.

"You'll burn out the battery if you keep that up," Gary said between bites.

"Battery? I know – another Connecticut invention," Erin replied, tucking the spoon into her skirt pocket. She handed Gary his pack, now bulging with balls of yarn. "To stop the jingling," she explained.

He wondered if she had seen Lucie's gold bracelet, but didn't ask. If his plan worked, he would reclaim his Watch and be back in 2026 for lunch. He would give all his coins to Erin before he left. As well as a full explanation, he had decided. She deserved to know the whole truth. If his plan didn't work...he banished the thought.

The Windmill Island ferry was only five blocks from Southwark. They walked slowly along the waterfront, savoring the first tinge of daylight as if it might be their last. The sky was cloudless, only a zephyr stirred the pennants of the ships at anchor. A solitary seaman, blond hair flowing over his shoulders, hastened across the street and disappeared up a gangway. Erin took Gary's hand as the landing came into sight.

"Mr. Sands said he'll meet you in the meadow," the ferret-faced ferryman announced as he poled off. The ferry was really a glorified raft of timber poles lashed together, surrounded by a flimsy handrail.

"How do you know Sands?" Gary asked, balancing himself as a ripple rocked the craft. The breeze picked up once they cleared the docks, a welcome respite from the rising sun.

"He goes out to the Island every now and then."

"For duels?"

The ferryman didn't reply, staring into the morning mist as if it cloaked a pot of gold. An unpleasant realization struck Gary: if Sands had ventured to Windmill Island for other contests of honor, and returned unharmed, then his opponents had not fared too well.

The island was triangular shaped and densely covered with trees. Unsurprisingly, the spokes of a windmill were visible at its northern tip. The ferryman navigated around a sand bar to deposit them on the shore.

"We'll be back shortly," Gary said, as confidently as possible, before stepping off. *At least Erin will,* the grim thought slipping unbidden into his consciousness.

"Follow me," Erin said, pointing to a path leading into the brush. The compact meadow, maybe fifty yards long and thirty across, was just below the ridge, conveniently shielding its occupants from prying eyes.

Sands, suited formally in a black coat and hat despite the heat, stood at ease when they emerged from the tree line. Williams, his second, was pacing out the dueling ground. "All is ready," he announced, returning to his master's side.

Sands eyed Gary and Erin with suspicion. "Where is your second, Mr. Johnson?"

"Here," Erin replied, boldly stepping towards Williams.

Sands gaped as if Erin had drawn a pistol and shot him. "But, she's a …"

"Female," Gary said. "I salute your powers of observation."

"That is completely unacceptable," Sands replied. "An affront to the gentlemen's code of honor."

"I didn't notice any gentlemen here."

"Williams. Pack up. We leave at once."

Gary stuck out his hand. "My Watch then."

"Pardon me?"

"If ye withdraw from ye duel with Mr. Johnson, I believe the code of honor requires ye to forfeit the stakes," Erin chipped in.

Sands stuttered, but swallowed his response. He stared at

the sky for several seconds, as if fixing on a distant star. "Williams, the pistols," he said at last.

Williams brought out a mahogany box and lifted its gold handle, displaying a brace of pistols, burnished to high gloss. He turned to Erin. "To your liking, ma'am?"

Erin lifted one of the pistols, fingering its trigger gently, then the other. She sighted down the barrel which had been matted to reduce glare. "Unrifled?" she asked. A rifled barrel imparts spin to the bullet, improving accuracy, unlike a smooth bore.

"Of course," Williams replied. "No gentleman duels with a rifled barrel."

Erin handed the weapon to Gary. "It's heavy," she warned. Dueling pistols were custom made with added weight to steady aim and reduce recoil.

"The bullets?" Erin asked, turning back to Williams.

He produced another cask, revealing four polished bullets. ".56 caliber."

Erin sighed, high caliber bullets did more damage, but nodded her approval. She retrieved the pistol from Gary and returned it to Williams. "We choose the other one," she said, pointing to the weapon still in the box.

"As you wish," Williams said, handing it to her along with two bullets. "British or French rules?"

"French," Erin replied without hesitation. In British rules, the duelists stood ten paces apart, facing each other, and fired on the count of three. The probability of at least one bullet striking its target was quite high. In French rules, the duelists started back to back, then paced ten steps, whirled and fired. The probability of death or injury was much lower.

"Why...?" Gary started the question but Erin cut him off.

"Shush."

"The sun is almost above the tree line. We must commence at once," Sands said, stepping forward, his impatience evident. "Since Mr. Johnson's second has chosen French rules, my second will adjudicate the proceedings."

"We will draw lots for the side," Williams said. Erin nodded. The meadow was situated so that the early morning sun would not be a factor for either participant.

"Wait," Gary said. "I want to see my Watch."

"You do not trust me to live up to the terms of our duel?" Sands said, has face contorting as if Gary had insulted his mother.

Gary almost laughed out loud. The man had stolen his most prized possession at gunpoint. "I do not."

"Very well, then. Here it is," Sands replied, withdrawing a silver-cased watch dangling on a sturdy silver rope chain from his pocket and handing it to Williams. "Your second can inspect it."

Erin dutifully stepped up, turned the watch over, wound the stem between her thumb and forefinger, opened the case, and snapped it shut. "It's ye Quare," she said, handing the timepiece back to Williams.

Gary wanted to handle the watch himself, at least to see if Lucie's photo appeared, but knew he couldn't. The duel was on. While he had never been a particularly religious man, he closed his eyes and offered a brief prayer to whichever God might be listening this morning.

Williams primed and loaded Sands' pistol, then handed it to his master. Erin did the same for Gary. The duelists placed the second bullet in their pockets. Both seconds stepped away from the line of fire. Erin slipped two steps behind Williams, so he couldn't see her.

"Gentlemen, take your places," Williams said, pointing to the center of the meadow, still shaded from sunlight and damp with morning dew. The patter of longshoremen loading ships whispered across the river.

Sands approached first, his steely eyes boring straight through Gary to the tree line beyond, before he turned his back. Gary glanced at Erin, her hand lost in her skirts. He would be walking away from her, so he would not see her again until after, if then.

Gary settled slowly, his back inches from Sands, his pistol

down. He again recalled that last putt back home as he fingered the trigger. Nothing but net.

"Present arms," Williams said. Both combatants raised their pistols. "On my count."

Sands farted loudly. He was nervous too, Gary thought. A good sign.

"One," Williams announced. Both men stepped smartly in opposite directions.

"Two, three, four, five." Gary made sure to breathe with each step.

"Six, seven." He focused on a forked branch in the tree line to force his head upright.

Erin withdrew the spoon from her pocket. Williams, completely absorbed by the drama he alone commanded, was oblivious to her movement. She flashed the beam on the ground as a test.

"Eight." Gary almost tripped on a baseball-sized stone, but steadied himself. Erin sighted the back of Sands' head.

"Nine." Sands pivoted - a full second too early. Damn the scoundrel. Erin pressed the trigger.

The beam caught Sands directly in his right eye. He jerked his right arm up, firing his pistol. Gary, back still turned, winced, but the bullet sailed harmlessly into the forest, thudding into a tree trunk.

"Ten," Williams said, his voice trailing off as he realized the calamity unfolding in front of him.

Gary whirled, pistol aimed squarely at Sands, only twenty paces away.

"Fire when ready, Mr. Johnson," Erin said, returning the spoon to her skirt pocket.

CHAPTER 34

Gary was mentally unprepared for a free shot. Did Sands actually fire and miss? Should he step closer? Shoot to kill? What if he only wounded Sands? Or missed completely? He knew from golf that a racing mind rarely produced a quality shot.

"That was unfair. A bolt of lightning...," Williams sputtered.

"Shut your bone box," Sands cut him off, pointing his smoking pistol into the sky. "Go ahead, Mr. Johnson, take your shot."

Gary gripped his weapon with both hands, lowering the aim to Sands' mid-section. Sands fidgeted as he realized Gary had just significantly improved his chances of a direct hit.

"Kill him," Erin said calmly.

Gary inhaled deeply and exhaled slowly, his pistol never wavering. Sands fidgeted, shifting his weight from right foot to left, but didn't retreat a single step. He still had a shred of honor left.

"My Watch," Gary said.

"Pardon?" Sands asked, slowly returning to the world of the living.

"Return my Watch, and I will consider our duel complete."

"Do it," Sands instructed Williams. The second dutifully handed the watch to Erin.

The tension drained from the meadow like the flush of a twenty-first century toilet. Williams retrieved both pistols and packed them up. Erin flashed the watch and a huge grin to Gary. He stood stock still, only his head swiveling as his gaze wandered over the treetops to the emerging sun. He was alive - and going home. Sands pivoted and stomped towards the ferry, closely followed by a scurrying Williams.

"We did it," Erin said as she roped her arms around Gary's neck, his watch looped around her wrist.

"You did it," he replied, making no attempt to untangle.

Erin reared back her head, then kissed him, plunging her tongue deep into his mouth. The passion was inevitable, particularly here, alone in the meadow, and now, the duel concluded successfully, his life secure, the watch won. He ached to tumble with her down into the beckoning grass, but...he was married and it was time to return to his wife and family. Erin retreated reluctantly, eyes downcast.

"I owe you my life," he said, lifting up her chin, reaching for her hand.

"And now ye will leave me," she replied, her free thumb circling the timepiece, as if debating whether to cast it away.

"But I will never forget you."

"Go then," she said, handing over the watch.

Gary put the chain over his head and tucked the watch underneath his shirt, savoring its coolness on his chest, unable to contain his excitement despite the dark cloud that shrouded Erin's face. He reached down for his pack, thrashed through the balls of yarn, and handed his purse to Erin. "For you and the boys," he said.

She shook her head, a tear streaming down her cheek. "I don't want ye money."

"But you earned it – this time."

"Aye, I suppose I did," she replied, wiping away the

moisture, clutching the purse. "Godspeed."

Gary needed to leave before he changed his mind. His explanation of time travel would have to wait. Slinging his pack, considerably lighter now, over his shoulder, he traipsed towards the trees.

"Wait," Erin called, rushing after him. "Ye spoon."

Gary didn't look back again, stopping only when he was deep enough in the forest that he couldn't see the meadow. Sunlight filtered through the canopy of leaves. A squirrel darted across his path. He sat on a moss-smeared boulder to calm his nerves and mentally prepare to return home. Assuming the routing worked...he had left before it was thoroughly tested.

He stood. Time to go. Thoughts of Lucie flooded his mind. How had she weathered his disappearance? Had the FBI left her alone? What would happen to her if he didn't make it?

Gary looked around, confirming he was still alone, before taking the watch out from under his shirt. It felt solid, comforting in its heft. He flicked open the case. The hands showed seven-thirty. About right. Silently rehearsing the password, TimeR 2026, he tapped three times on the watch face, waiting for the launch screen to appear.

CHAPTER 35

Nothing, except a steady monotone tick-tock. Gary waited, tracking the flight of a hawk against the parched blue sky. Maybe he tapped wrong. He tried again, softer this time. Then again, harder. He shook the watch. Scratched it, confirming the silver was real. Swung it over his head.

The hawk swooped downward, hovered briefly, then soared back to the heavens. He rapped his knuckles on the watch face. Shouted the password out loud. Still nothing.

The watch might well be an original Quare, worth millions in 2026, but it wasn't *his* Quare. It couldn't take him home. Sands, the bastard, had switched watches.

Gary belted a rib-rattling war whoop. The realization that he might never return to 2026 sucked the air out of his lungs.

Erin crashed through the underbrush, wheeled in a full circle, and scoured the trees for signs of an enemy. Seeing none, she brushed the leaves from her hair and approached Gary. "Are ye well?"

He nodded, the color gradually returning to his cheeks.

Returning to his seat on the boulder, he beckoned Erin to join him.

"Indians?" she asked, taking her place, leaning in to comfort him.

"No."

"Bandits?"

"No."

"What ails ye then?"

He held up the watch, shaking his head as if mourning a lost loved one.

"Banjaxed?" she asked.

Gary's expression went blank.

"Broken?"

"No, it works. It's just not *my* watch."

"Are ye sure?"

Gary nodded.

"A counterfeit? I wouldn't put it past Sands to..."

He shook his head, cutting her off. "It's a Quare. Just not mine."

"Ye watch had an inscription?" she asked, taking both his hands in hers.

"No."

"Then?"

Gary stood, walked several paces away, searched the sky for the hawk. Should he tell Erin the truth?

"A gift? From ye wife?" Erin stood, holding her head high, fiddling with an errant strand of hair. "I'm sorry...for before," she said, looking back towards the meadow. "I'll mind me place from now on."

"No," he said. Hope brightened Erin's face as he strode towards her. Now, it was Gary's turn to take her hands.

"I've told you I come from Connecticut," he said. "That's true. But what I haven't told you is that I traveled here from another time."

"Another time?" Erin's brow furrowed.

"The twenty-first century. The year 2026, to be precise."

"Two thousand and twenty-six? The future?" Her eyes widened as big as buttermilk pancakes.

"Two hundred and fifty years in the future."

"How...? Why...?" The questions stuck in Erin's mouth, refusing to spill out.

"I came to Philadelphia to witness the signing of the Declaration of Independence. *My* watch guided me here." He looked down his shirt and shook his head in despair.

"Not ye horse? The one that died by the river?"

"I never had a horse."

"Ye lied to me?" Erin yanked her hands free, spinning around to look away from Gary.

He grabbed her hand and tugged her back. "Yes, I lied. But I didn't know if I could trust you. Or anybody else for that matter."

"Why should I believe ye now?" she asked, but made no move to disentangle her hand.

"Only two men, Hancock and Thomson, signed the Declaration last week. Fifty more will sign next month. The British will rout Washington and the Continentals in August on Long Island. They'll occupy Philadelphia next year."

"We're going to lose the war? And stay British colonies?"

"No. We're going to win our independence. But not for seven more years."

"Hogwash," Erin said, freeing her hand, tucking it into her skirt pocket. "The seer who visits the tavern could have foretold all that."

"What about the light in my spoon? Could she have done that?"

"A trick. A witch's trick." Erin hunched, shriveling as she made the sign of the cross.

"People will fly in airplanes, drive in cars. America will have fifty states, not thirteen. They'll stretch all the way to the Pacific Ocean," he said, grabbing her shoulders. "You have to believe me."

"Fly? Like a bird? Have ye gone daft?" Erin broke free, shook her head, started to run.

"Why would I lie to you? I've only tried to help you. And your family," Gary shouted, chasing after her. "I've never tried to take advantage of you."

"Aye, that's true," Erin said, slowing, but not yielding.

"You don't have to believe me. But please help me."

"To get ye watch back? So it can take ye back to ye own time?"

"Yes."

"And if we can't get it back?"

"Then I'm stuck here in 1776."

CHAPTER 36

By the time Gary and Erin reached the river, flushed from the hike, the ferry had returned, its pilot sitting on the bank whittling an animal figure. "Took your sweet time, didn't you," he said, looking them up, down and sideways. "In the morning, no less."

Gary wanted to smack the leer off his face, but knew that would accomplish nothing. "Where did you take Sands?"

"Where do you think?"

"Which way did he go when he left ye boat?" Erin cut in. The ferryman resumed his whittling without a reply.

"Did he say anything to Williams?" Erin asked, handing over a coin from Gary's purse.

"They was pretty quiet. Mr. Sands didn't look too pleased though."

"Nothing at all?" Gary pressed.

If Sands had switched watches on purpose, he might have bragged to Williams, Gary thought. On the other hand, Sands might have made the switch accidentally. Could his real Watch still be at the Cary counting house? He needed to confront Sands as soon as possible.

"He muttered that you were a lucky man," the ferryman said. "Something about lightning catching his eye."

Gary jumped off before the ferry had even docked, heading north on Front Street towards Sands' office. When Erin started to follow, the ferryman grabbed her wrist. "They went the other way," he said, pointing towards High Market Street. Erin shouted for Gary to turn around.

By the time they arrived, High Market Street was already swamped with morning shoppers. A gray-haired Indian squaw displaying an armful of brightly colored beaded bracelets grabbed at Erin's wrist. Gary nearly knocked over a vegetable stand when a wigged head bobbed in the next aisle, but it wasn't Sands.

"Where next?" she asked when they reached Second Street.

Before Gary could reply, a somberly dressed Quaker, mouth agape, stepped from behind a wagon stacked with watermelons. "Mr. Johnson?" he asked, barely able to complete the simple question.

"Mr. Ash? A pleasure to see you again, sir." Gary smiled as he tipped his hat.

"But...you're alive..." Beelzebub continued to stammer.

"I do believe so." Gary's expression turned quizzical. "You look surprised."

"No, no. I was just..." Beelzebub shook his head. "I must be going. Good day, sir."

"That was quite odd," Erin said, as Ash hurried up the street.

"If the Quaker thought I was dead, he must have known about my duel with Sands," Gary said. "In advance."

"And expected Sands to kill ye," Erin added. "How would he...?"

"Because he was in cahoots with Sands." Gary recalled their first meeting mere minutes after his arrival in 1776. He had narrowly avoided Jefferson's carriage. Ash had been suspicious of his Watch. "He set me up."

"The Quaker? Are ye sure?"

"There's only one way to find out," Gary replied, pointing in the direction Ash had taken.

Fortunately, Ash was not a fast walker. They caught sight of him on Fourth Street and followed him into State House Square. The Quaker stopped under the majestic oak that had shaded Gary's jewelry sale to Mr. Milne. He shifted nervously from foot to foot, his head swiveling, obviously searching for someone.

Gary and Erin ducked behind a stall selling fresh Chesapeake Bay oysters, the oysterman eyeing them suspiciously as he shucked. Gary ordered a dozen, buying time as well as sustenance after the trying morning. He and Erin slurped while they waited, keeping their heads down and out of Ash's sight. They devoured the oysters so quickly that he had to buy a second helping.

Their vigilance was rewarded before their hunger was sated. A bald, scar-faced man approached Ash, leading him into a copse of leafy trees.

"That's Nathaniel Knight, chief spycatcher for the Committee of Safety," Erin said. "A regular at City Tavern."

"Is he after Sands?"

"Possibly..." Erin let the rest of her response dangle like bait on the end of a fishing line.

"He's after me?"

"More likely." She was proved correct when William Sands bustled into the square and ducked into the gossamer branches.

Gary linked Erin's hand to his elbow. "Let's go for a stroll."

He stopped, ostensibly to adjust the buckle on his shoe, within earshot of the incongruous trio.

"Johnson's alive. I just saw him on..." Ash said.

"I know, now stop driveling," Sands cut him off.

"Does he know that you switched watches?"

"He should by now."

"Where's his watch?"

"In the saddle bag of a trusted captain." Knight joined the conversation. "Riding hard to General Washington's headquarters in New York."

"Did you examine it?" Ash asked.

"No. I will leave that to the general's spycatchers."

"I'm quite certain Mr. Johnson is a British spy," Ash said. Erin dropped her head as if she didn't want to hear any more.

"I would agree," Knight said. "Mistress Tryon had a unique timepiece as well, but, unfortunately, it was destroyed in our little melee at the barracks."

Mistress Tryon? Jennifer Tryon? From TimeR? Gary quickly put the pieces in place. The arrest in the street, the perfume in the hay, the rainbow band buried in his cell.

Why did Jennifer Tryon travel to 1776? More important, could she help him get home? Not if her Watch was destroyed, he realized. If he didn't retrieve his own Watch, they both might be marooned forever.

"So, I've completed my part of the bargain - even though Johnson has survived," Sands interrupted.

"Yes," Knight replied, disdain spitting from his mouth like dragon fire. "If you haven't departed the colony, I mean the state, of Pennsylvania within twenty-four hours Mr. Sands, you'll be incarcerated for espionage and theft. Both punishable by death."

Gary had heard enough. Ash must have approached Knight who made the bargain with Sands. No one expected him to survive the duel. But, now that he had, would they let him leave? What about Constable Huckleberry and the meeting with Justice Chew? He had to get out of Philadelphia immediately.

He checked his watch, not the one he hoped to have but it still told time - 9:20 AM. He had forty minutes to catch the coach heading east to New York and beyond. "Let's go," he said, grabbing Erin's hand.

"Are ye going to New York?"

"Yes."

"I'm going with ye."

"No you're not," Gary said, shouldering his pack. "You have two boys at home."

"Mamo will care for them."

"I'll be fine on my own."

"Ye will stand out like a virgin in a bawdy house," Erin said, flashing a flirtatious smile as she took his hand. "We can travel as husband and wife."

"Cousins might be more appropriate," Gary replied, disengaging, but nodding his approval nonetheless.

"Whatever suits ye fancy."

CHAPTER 37

The stagecoach from Philadelphia to New York was advertised as the new nation's first "flying machine" because of its promise to complete the hundred mile journey in just three days. Departing from City Tavern, Gary had been fearful he would run into John Tralee or other acquaintances, but the entire city had congregated on State House Square this Monday morning, July 8, 1776, to hear the first ever public reading of the Declaration of Independence. While the crowd huzzahed, he approached the coachman, paying a few extra coins to insure what he hoped would be first class treatment.

Three middle-aged sisters, the Wishingwells, already ensconced in their forward-facing seats, looked askance when the driver ushered Gary and Erin inside, but the fourth passenger, a stocky young man, well-dressed in a steel gray jacket and matching waistcoat, generously slid over to make room. Gary got nauseous facing rearward for an hour-long ride on a twenty-first century commuter train, let alone a jaunt in a rickety, springless coach pulled by four galloping horses. Unfortunately, he had little choice if he hoped to leave Philadelphia this morning and retrieve his Watch.

Unsurprisingly, he puked up his oyster breakfast just outside of the city as the stage bounced across the Pennypack Creek bridge, a three-span stone structure built in 1697, currently the oldest roadway crossing in America. Fortunately for his fellow passengers, he had the window seat.

Clara, the eldest, wide-bottomed and fleshy-necked, offered a drink from a jug nestled on the floor between her legs. He took a swig, then vomited out the open window again.

"Clara likes her whiskey strong," Hannah, the middle sister, noted from the far side of the cabin. Her face, neatly sculptured like a porcelain doll, complemented her petite bosom. Betsy, once blond but still rosy cheeked, took the jug from Gary's helpless hands. "Helps pass away the hours," she said, sipping twice before handing the jug over to the gentleman. "Mr....?"

"Fairfax, Henry Fairfax," he replied, taking his turn, albeit more modestly. His face was classically handsome, highlighted by frost blue eyes set so close together they appeared to have a single focus. He offered the jug to Erin, taking the opportunity to squint down her bodice.

She hesitated, but then shrugged and lifted the jug to her lips. Leaning back, she savored the warmth seeping through her torso.

"Seems to agree with you more than your husband," Hannah said, patting her chest as she nodded towards Gary whose head lolled like a rag doll.

"He's my cousin, not my husband," Erin replied, curious to see the reaction of her fellow travelers.

"Well, he's not your responsibility then, is he?" Betsy asked, masking her flushed face with a silk fan printed with a kimono-clad figure. Oriental goods were a status symbol among the upper class. Her two sisters nodded in agreement. Henry scrutinized Erin as if seeing her in a new light as the jug made another round trip before everyone drifted into a rum-fueled haze.

Three hours later, the stage stopped at a fast-running creek to give the horses a brief respite. "Halfway to Bensalem," the coachman announced.

"Quite a comfortable inn there," Henry announced as he helped the sisters down. Erin nursed Gary, who had just awoken, for several minutes before he had the fortitude to leave the coach. Once comfortable that he could stand unaided, she hastened along the path the other women had taken into the brush.

Gary joined Henry and the coachman at the water's edge, the three men urinating into the gurgling depths. The driver finished first and hurried off to tend to the horses. "Your first trip to New York?" Henry asked as he buttoned up.

"No, but my first by flying machine," Gary replied. "And you?"

"I travel regularly up and down the coast on business."

"What line of work are you in?"

"I'm an agent for the Philipse family in New York. Handle their Negro trade mostly."

"A profitable business, I'm told," Gary said, turning away from the bank. He was in no mood, or physical state, to start an argument over civil rights, particularly on the first day of the trip.

"Most profitable," Henry said as he led the way back to the coach. "The plantations in the West Indies are enormous. They have an insatiable demand for blacks as well as the goods to feed and clothe them."

"And the war?"

"An inconvenience currently," Henry replied, a shadow falling over his countenance. "But money always talks. The Philipse's, the Brown's of Rhode Island, and Mr. Morris here in Philadelphia are among the wealthiest, and most influential, men in the colonies. They'll not be denied their profits. Nor will I."

"Here, here," the coachman said. "And you, Mr. Johnson? What brought you to Philadelphia?"

"I came to petition Congress for a Letter of Marque," Gary replied, instantly fearing he had said too much.

"You're a shipowner then?" Henry asked, his interest clearly piqued. "Perhaps we can talk more later."

"Here come the women," the coachman said. "I'd best be checking the horses."

Relieved to end the conversation before it proceeded any further, Gary helped each of the sisters up into their seats before sliding across the bench to his perch at the far window. He turned to watch Henry take Erin's hand and help her back into her middle seat.

"You're fortunate to have Mr. Johnson to look after you," the slave trader said, patting Erin's forearm, another excuse to peruse her cleavage.

"Most fortunate," Gary replied, scowling at Erin as she appeared to soak up the attention. The lurching coach cut short the conversation.

They arrived at the Horny Goat in Bensalem after three more hours of bone-jarring travel. Gary thumped off the ceiling twice en route, but kept whatever was left of his morning meal down. He and Henry lugged Clara, dead-to-the-world drunk, all the way up to her room, shared with her sisters, while Erin negotiated their lodgings with the innkeeper.

"I got a good price," she noted when he returned to the tap room, housing a half dozen roughhewn tables and benches. The Sons of Liberty flag hung over the hearth. "And, we'll only have to share our bed with Henry, no one else."

"I don't share well," Gary replied, realizing he had little choice in colonial America.

"Don't worry, I'll take the middle again."

The tap room was more than half full for supper, chicken stew and fresh bread, hearty but not up to the culinary excellence of the City Tavern. The red wine was sour, but the ale both passable and plentiful. Dessert, a blueberry pie, was the highlight of the meal. Betsy and Hannah retired early to see to Clara.

While the staff cleared the plates, a fiddler, accompanied by a dwarf playing the tambourine, emerged. "Dance?" Erin asked, sloshing down her beer as the fiddler picked up the beat.

Gary shook his head, his stomach had endured enough today, but realized his error when Henry quickly volunteered to take his place. Although heavyset, the New Yorker was nimble on his feet and apparently well-versed in the latest jigs. He spun Erin right and left, urged on by the rhythmic clapping of the other guests. Erin twirled off to dance with two other travelers, who had patiently waited their turn, but finished the final number wrapped in Henry's arms, albeit only for a second.

When Henry excused himself to find the necessary, Erin slid next to Gary on the bench. "Will you take me up to bed, *cousin*?" she asked playfully, dipping her index finger in the cream and licking it clean.

"Wouldn't that look somewhat incestuous, *cousin*?"

Erin loosened the strings on her cap, letting her red locks fall, framing her full, cream-flecked lips. Her gaze swept the room. "Do ye think anyone here gives a donkey's ass?"

Henry returned, carrying a broadsheet, before Gary could answer. "Those bastards in the Pennsylvania Assembly are going to seize all of the Penn family lands because of their support for the Crown," he muttered, tossing the paper on the table. "Without any compensation."

"This is not the time to talk business," Erin said, crumpling the tabloid in her hands.

"Penn lands?" Gary croaked as he wrestled the paper from Erin and unfolded it. He held the title to a Penn estate in his backpack. Was it worthless now? Was that why his transaction had moved so quickly? He scanned the article while Erin signaled to the tavern girl to refill her mug.

"Have we swapped the rule of a benevolent monarch for the rule of a mob of ruffians?" Henry bellowed. "If the state of Pennsylvania no longer respects a man's rights, I'll have to take my trade elsewhere."

"Henry trades in Negroes," Gary said to Erin. She shrugged, wiping the beer foam from her lips, her carefree smile replaced by a wanton smirk.

"I trade in property. Bought and sold. Pure and simple." Henry pounded his fist, knocking over a flagon, red wine sweeping across the table like a bloody plague.

"I feel sick again," Gary said, wobbling as he stood. "I'm going to bed."

"Go then," Erin said through clenched teeth, smoke figuratively steaming from her ears. She reached for her beer, draining it in a single motion as the fiddler started up again.

"I believe this is our dance," Henry said, offering his hand. "I'm sure your cousin won't mind."

Gary had painted himself into a corner. He slunk up the stairs, turning only once to see Erin, intertwined in Henry's arms, her angry eyes following his retreat.

Gary's head spun from the wine and the news. He had no Watch to return to 2026 and minimal prospects here in 1776: no home, no family, no land, and no career. And now no Erin. She was a woman, with womanly needs. And he had scorned her.

He stripped to his boxers, threw back the coverlet and crawled into his corner of the bed, the Quare nestling against his chest. Thoughts of Lucie flitted at the edge of his consciousness, but they were overwhelmed by despair over the events of the evening. He vowed to stay awake until Erin and Henry retired, but exhaustion finally overcame his jealousy.

CHAPTER 38

The rat-tat-tat of raindrops on the roof woke Gary around midnight. Although the candles had gutted, he could feel the sag of the mattress and the warmth of nearby bodies.

Dreading what he would find, he refused to roll over until the steady drip of water on the sill became unbearable. With his vision acclimated to the darkness, Gary rose, slipped out from under the coverlet, and closed the window, keeping his back to the bed all the while. At last, he gathered the courage to turn, relieved to discern two distinct humps in the bed - Erin, fully clothed, snoring on her back, and Henry, shirtless, curled away from her.

Gary lay back down facing Erin, resting his hand on her shoulder, her face inches from his own. He had almost drifted off when Erin quieted. Her body twitched; her skirts rustled. He sensed that Henry had rolled over but couldn't be sure.

Gary lay still as Erin spread her thighs, her breaths quickening. He gently squeezed her shoulder but she appeared lost in a drunken haze. Her leg nudged him as her hips rose and fell, their rhythm slow but steady. Fully alert now, he watched her fingers brush across a nipple, taut against the fabric of her bodice.

As Erin's thrusts grew more urgent, Henry's bulk rose, silhouetted in the darkness. He fumbled on the clasp of his fly with one hand while the other fumbled between her legs. Erin's head tossed but she offered no resistance - or words of encouragement.

He couldn't tell if she was still asleep or a willing partner. Should he defend her honor? Or leave her to her new lover? Gary rose to one forearm and shook Erin awake.

Her eyes flashed open. Her legs snapped shut, scissoring Henry in their grasp. She looked first to her side at Gary, then at Henry hovering over her. "No!" she screamed, clawing at Henry's eyes.

Henry swatted away Erin's hands and slapped her across the cheek, drawing blood from the corner of her lip. She recoiled, involuntarily opening her legs.

Henry dropped his weight, pinning her beneath him. He twisted towards Gary as he wriggled his trousers down, his bare ass glimmering like a half-moon.

Gary dove at Henry but could barely budge him. He rolled off Henry's hairy back as Erin bucked like an unbroken pony. She freed up one leg, kneeing her assailant squarely in his unprotected loins. Henry squealed, clutching at air as he doubled up in agony. Erin drove her knee into him one more time for good measure before crawling free.

Gary bolted to his feet and grabbed the pistol from his jacket pocket. "You'll leave the lady alone," he said, aiming at Henry's curled form. Erin scuttled off the bed to Gary's side.

Henry could barely squeak out a reply. He lay still for several seconds before rising to his knees, covering his sagging manhood with the coverlet. "She's no lady," he muttered as he dressed.

"Out," Gary said quietly, adding emphasis with the business end of his pistol. Henry packed and left, slamming the door in his wake. Erin hugged him, licking the blood from her lip but shedding no tears. They stayed entwined for several minutes until Gary finally broke the trance. "Let's go to bed," he said.

They spooned in the center of the bed, Erin cinching Gary's arm snugly to her bosom. His mind flipped through images like an Instagram post, Erin at the City Tavern, at her home, on the ferry, at the duel. They fell asleep to the peal of thunder and crash of lightning.

A knock on the door came just before dawn. "No need to rise," the coachman called. "The roads ain't' fit for travel."

Erin clambered up first, parting the curtain to look out the window. "We're not going anywhere today," she said, slipping off her frock and undergarments. Her nakedness glistened in the wane light.

Returning to bed, she cupped Gary's chin. "Henry was right, ye know."

"Right...?" he asked, sleep-addled but aroused enough to realize this was no time for questions.

"I'm no lady..." Erin rolled Gary to his back and peeled down his shorts. "...and I've waited long enough." She mounted him, her breasts raking his chest. The bed rocked with her pent-up fury.

When they awoke again just before noon, the storm still raged, pelting an ardent beat overhead. After another bout of spirited lovemaking, Gary stole downstairs for bread, cheese and beer. The three sisters sat knitting by the dormant fireplace, refusing to dignify him with even a glance in his direction. The innkeeper's leer confirmed that he too had heard the racket. Henry was not in sight.

The lovers shared the feast in the privacy of their room. Afterwards, Erin crawled back into bed. Sitting by the window, Gary watched her doze as the sun broke through the cotton ball clouds, lighting their meager surroundings in a golden glow.

CHAPTER 39

In the twenty-first century, Jennifer had gazed over the Hudson River every day from the living room windows of her apartment, never realizing New Jersey was so hilly, if not downright mountainous, and densely forested. Accordingly, her experience traversing that very same terrain in the eighteenth century, clothed only in her frock, was eye-opening.

For the past seventy-two hours, she and Rogers had hiked at night along barely visible Indian paths and napped during daylight in the wilderness. Fortunately, before leaving the Barracks in Philadelphia, she had swapped her colonial-era clogs for garish lime-green Hoka trainers, enabling her to keep up with the seemingly indefatigable Ranger.

"That should be Princeton," Rogers said, pointing ahead to the sleeping village barely visible in the hushed moonlight. "Perhaps, your boots can light the way."

"Will we be safe there?" Jenn had visited the town several years ago, but didn't actually see much of it, rarely leaving the dorm room of a thong-twisting Women's Studies major she had hooked up with on Grindr.

"Should be garrisoned by Regulars," he replied, sitting on a fallen tree trunk, reaching into his pack for a handful of dried peas. Although map-less, Rogers seemed to know every hamlet, avoiding them all until this morning. "If they're not off foraging the countryside."

"The redcoats are welcome here?"

"If they behave." Rogers fingered his beard, scruffed by imprisonment and hard travel. He snagged a louse, tossing it casually to the ground, then another, and a third. "Pesky little devils," he said, scratching his crotch. "Get in the nastiest places."

Jennifer ran her hand through her own hair, uncapped, relieved to find no visitors. Short hair had its blessings in the wild.

She joined him on the trunk, sipping from her black, water-purifying bottle, a "nice-to-have" on twenty-first century outdoor adventures, but an essential here in the eighteenth century. Its rechargeable power source was advertised to last a month, but she had never pushed it more than a long weekend.

"Does that turn water into rum?" Rogers asked, looking quizzically at the bottle for the umpteenth time on the journey.

"A good thought, but no. Just water." She offered him a draught.

"I prefer rum," he replied, swigging from his own canteen instead, a slight slur seeping into his voice.

Jennifer marveled at her companion's constitution. Her bare legs goose-bumped as a cool breeze rustled through the trees.

"I can warm you up," Rogers said, resting his hand on her knee.

"I prefer women," she replied, removing his hand.

"So do I," he said, returning his hand, slurring more noticeably.

"I'm gay," she said, removing it again, and, for the first time, questioning his sobriety.

"Gay? I haven't seen you smile once since I met you."

"Not that kind of gay," Jennifer said, chuckling. "I'm a

lesbian. I prefer female...companionship."

"You rut with women?" Rogers asked, the teapot coming to a slow boil.

"Yes."

"Not men?"

"Correct."

"Well, then," he said, standing, fingering his beard again. "Can't say I've had a brush with your kind before."

Nevertheless, he extended his hand to help her up. "Let's get to Princeton and rustle up a hot breakfast. Maybe find a seamstress who can fix you a proper pair of breeches."

Founded by Quakers late in the seventeenth century, the town of Princeton became a regular stop for post riders and stagecoaches on the King's Highway, the main artery of the thirteen colonies, connecting South Carolina to Massachusetts. Princeton University, formerly the College of New Jersey, moved to the town from Newark in 1756. Three Princetonians, Richard Stockton, John Witherspoon, and Joseph Hewes, signed the Declaration of Independence. Immediately after the Revolution, the town jumped into the spotlight for a brief period, hosting the Continental Congress for six months.

Their walk, less than a mile, mostly downhill, was not strenuous. The scent of fresh pine lingered in the morning dew. The forest thinned, the path riddled with stumps, the remains of the trees Princetonians had chopped down to build their village. A carpet of stars twinkled farewell as darkness slowly yielded to dawn.

Birds chirped, greeting the daylight. Rogers stopped several times, listening to sounds beyond Jennifer's comprehension. As they drew closer, she could see smoke curling from a chimney, candles flickering in windows, a bonneted woman tacking laundry to a clothesline. Her stomach grumbled from hunger.

"Wait," Rogers whispered, holding up his hand. He shook his head, cocking an ear to the ground. They were only thirty yards from the end of the tree line bordering the highway, a dirt road two wagons wide.

"What...?" Jennifer started to ask, but he cut her off with a hand signal.

They inched forward now, Rogers' head swiveling, his pistol at the ready. He halted again at the forest's edge, waiting several seconds to be sure the road was clear. Satisfied, he holstered his firearm and stepped out.

Jennifer followed, relieved that Rogers, although marginally inebriated, had led them to safety. She put on her cap, tying it under her chin, a pious woman once again.

A church bell tolled five times. To their rear, a horse whinnied as it tugged a farmer's wagon towards them. Rogers stepped aside, waving to the driver.

Too late, Jennifer noticed the wagon was conspicuously empty of produce, particularly for an early morning run *into* town. The driver, wearing a blue jacket, tugged hard on the reins, grinding his load to a stop. Two men, clothed in filthy buckskin, jumped out, muskets at the ready.

"Major Rogers, we've been expecting you," the driver, now brandishing a pistol, said. "I'm Captain Jeremiah Hawthorne of the First New Jersey regiment of the Continental Army, the proud Jersey Blues. We plan to return you and your lady friend to Philadelphia to face the justice you both so richly deserve."

Rogers turned, looking to escape back into the forest, but three more militia men emerged. Slowly, he raised his hands in surrender, as did Jennifer. She scanned the village, praying to see a troop of redcoats marching to their rescue, but all she saw was a lone goat wandering out of its yard.

"Tie them up," Hawthorne commanded. "Be careful though. I've heard that woman's as ornery as a she-wolf."

CHAPTER 40

The room was still dark when the coachman knocked. "We leave at dawn. Next stop Trenton."

Gary and Erin looked at each other in a new light as they dressed. He started to speak, but swallowed his words unspoken. They had crossed the Rubicon; there was no turning back.

"I could eat a horse," she sighed, lacing up her boots.

They were the first downstairs to breakfast. The innkeeper greeted them with a schoolmarm's smirk as he poured steaming coffee into two mugs. Erin paid him no mind, smearing an extra-large dollop of raspberry jam across a biscuit, downing it in two swallows before reaching for another. Gary had his spoon in the honey pot when the three sisters ambled in.

"Good day, cousins," Hannah offered as she sat at the far end of the table.

"We're..." Gary started to reply.

"...distant cousins," Erin interjected with a sly grin.

"Kissing cousins, I would say," Hannah harrumphed, looking up at the ceiling.

"Nothing wrong with that," Clara added, washing down her breakfast with a hearty swallow from her jug.

"Mr. Fairfax extends his regrets," the innkeeper said. "He left before sunrise."

"On foot?" Erin asked, clearly relishing the image of her attacker trudging away in defeat.

"Bought one of my horses. Paid handsomely for it, I might add."

"Dangerous, if you ask me," the coachman said, brandishing a pistol. "There's bandits on the road from here to New York."

"We're ready for them," Betsy said, patting her travel bag. Each of her sisters nodded in agreement. This journey clearly wasn't their first rodeo.

"And you, Mr. Johnson?" the coachman asked. "You'll be the only man in our party now."

"I'm armed as well."

The five passengers boarded the coach with faces set in grim determination, the driver's warning weighing on their thoughts. The King's Highway was sloppy, slowing their pace but easier on Gary's stomach.

"We didn't care for Mr. Fairfax much anyway," Clara said, breaking the silence.

"His eyes..." Betsy added, pursing her lips. "Quite unnatural if you ask me."

"Like a feral cat ready to pounce," Hannah concluded the pillory. Erin nodded, squeezing Gary's hand.

"You're much better off with Mr. Johnson," Clara said, toasting the couple with a swig from her jug.

"What brings you to New York?" Gary asked, changing the subject before the sisters could explore his relationship with Erin any further.

"We're only going as far as Princeton," Betsy replied, taking her turn with the jug.

"Our lands are nearby," Hannah added.

"You own property?" Erin asked. "I didn't think women

could..."

"Married women cannot own land in their own name, of course," Clara replied. She belched loudly as the coach bounced over a rough spot in the road.

"But there is no such restriction on unattached women," Hannah said, winking at her sisters. "We have no brothers, so Father, bless his soul, left our ancestral estate to us."

"It's only three hundred acres, but the rents allow us to live quite comfortably," Betsy said. "Without the encumbrances, shall we say, of a husband."

Erin smothered a grin as she looked at Gary. "You all must be quite popular among the bachelors and widowers in Philadelphia," he said.

"Our social calendar is quite full," Clara replied.

"Dr. Franklin calls regularly," Betsy chimed in.

"He's encouraging us to buy land in Pennsylvania," Clara said. "The Penn's are selling quite cheaply now."

"Before they lose it all," Hannah said, earning a tsk, tsk from her sisters but plowing forward regardless. "Dr. Franklin says the Executive Council - of which he is president - will confiscate the Proprietor's lands as soon as the new state constitution passes this autumn."

"That's the penalty for supporting the King," Betsy said. "The Penn family will never rule this colony again."

"As soon as the new constitution passes..." Gary said, the words tumbling out in his excitement. His hand instinctively went to the clasp of his pack, containing both his copy of the Declaration and the deed to the Penn estate. Perhaps Fairfax's broadsheet didn't get its facts right. "I recently purchased a modest parcel from the Penn's."

"You are a shrewd man, Mr. Johnson," Hannah said before shifting her gaze to Erin. "Even if your morals are suspect."

Erin refused to wilt, taking Gary's hand into her lap. "Mr. Johnson's morals sit perfectly well with me."

"Hannah, you are not the one to lecture on morals," Clara

piped in as she stiffened her posture. "Mr. Johnson, you must ensure that your purchase is well-documented and the land properly surveyed. Dr. Franklin is a fine man, but he is a buzzard when it comes to business. The Council will undoubtedly scrutinize every Penn transaction most carefully."

The stage slowed, then ground to a halt. The five passengers snapped to attention, reaching into satchels and pockets for pistols. Gary flashed a glance out the window. Nothing but greenery in sight.

"Just a herd of cows," the coachman called down. "We'll be on our way shortly."

Oxygen returned to the coach. "I'll drink to that," Betsy said, taking the jug from Clara.

"Surveyed?" Gary asked.

"You will need clear proof of title," Clara said, retrieving her jug. "The Lenape believe they were swindled out of their land by the Penn's in the Walking Purchase of '37 and will try to reclaim it."

"Walking Purchase?"

"The Penn's made a deal with the tribe to buy all the land that a man could walk in a day."

"Only the Penn's hired the fastest runner in Philadelphia and cleared a path through the woods for him," Hannah added with a titter sneaking into her voice. "He traveled twice as far as anyone imagined."

"We've been involved in several land disputes in New Jersey. They can get quite nasty," Clara said.

"It appears that some men don't believe that women can hold their own in court. We've already retained an experienced lawyer in Philadelphia to look after our interests," Betsy chimed in.

"Mr. Johnson may need to return to Philadelphia then," Erin said, a full-toothed smile lighting her face. "To see to his business interests."

The stage arrived at The King's Arms in Trenton in time for supper. The setting sun lit the treetops behind them in an amber glow. Gary clambered out first to help the ladies down. Erin bolted ahead of the three sisters, immediately heading inside to secure their accommodations.

"We have the Franklin suite," she told Gary. "I paid an extra two shillings to be sure we're alone."

CHAPTER 41

Every joint in Jennifer Tryon's body ached as her rolling prison bounced slowly westward along the King's Highway. Other than two rest stops, a musket-pointing Continental beside her while she squatted in the woods, Jenn had been hog-tied since dawn. She was relieved to watch the sun finally sink below the horizon, its rays frying her face since noon.

Propped up next to her, Robert Rogers seemed to handle the journey with more aplomb. "This ain't nothing compared to the weeks I spent in chains in the hold of a fur trader's schooner in '69," he said. "Stinking with beaver pelts."

Jenn didn't respond, but Rogers continued anyway. "I still limp a bit from that adventure."

"Hush," Sergeant Ferguson, the senior of the three guards sharing the wagon bed, commanded as he awoke from a lengthy nap, his graying beard flecked with spittle.

Jenn waited until he dozed off again. "Why were you arrested?" she asked Rogers.

"Treason against the Crown. General Thomas Gage had it

in for me ever since my Rangers jumped ahead of his dragoons at the siege of Ticonderoga in '59." He tilted closer to Jenn. "That aristocratic fop married a Jersey girl, you know. Turns out she spied for the American side in Boston."

"But you were acquitted, obviously."

"Yes, but my career in the British Army was finished. Left me dead broke and deep in debt."

And dead drunk too, most likely, Jenn thought.

"We'll be stopping outside of Trenton in less than an hour, I reckon." Captain Hawthorne called. Caleb, the junior guard, clean-shaven, sandy-haired, poked his head up, his musket wobbling as he surveyed the countryside.

"I thought you said General Washington had you arrested for treason too," Jenn asked, rolling to her side to look Rogers in the eye.

"That he did."

"Not many men can claim to be charged with treason by the commanders-in-chief of both the British and American armies."

"Guess they were both afraid I'd outshine them," Rogers replied, his gaze drifting off as he remembered his days as a celebrated war hero. "Would have too. If I was given the opportunity."

Not likely, Jenn thought. "Which side are you on now?"

"My side," Rogers replied, spitting into the road.

The wagon lurched off the King's Highway, coming to a stop in a vale anchored by a thirty foot high boulder formation resembling a haphazard pile of children's blocks. The three scouts must have found a shortcut through the woods as they had already set camp. Caleb and Ferguson tugged Jenn and Rogers off and shoved them towards the simmering fire. "We'll sup here and spend the night," Hawthorne said.

"There's a fine public house in Trenton," Rogers said.

"The King's Arms," Hawthorne replied. "That's why we're staying here."

"Don't want you reuniting with your fellow lobsterbacks,"

Caleb said as he jabbed his bayonet at Rogers' back.

"Don't care much for Tories myself," Ferguson added, evil-eyeing Jenn. "Even if they sport a fine pair of tits."

"We'll have none of that," Hawthorne said, stepping down. "Now, boys, go rustle us up some food."

The three scouts surveilled Jenn and Rogers as their captain untied them. With her ankles beet red, Jenn could barely hobble forward. Rogers stumbled to one knee, only righting himself with Hawthorne's assistance.

Caleb and Ferguson proved savvy hunters, returning before dark with four carcasses draped over their muskets. Hawthorne handled the cooking, roasting the rabbits on a spit and divvying the feast equally among his men and prized prisoners.

"You're Governor Tryon's daughter, eh?" he asked between bites.

"Yes."

"And he sent you to spy in Philadelphia?"

"He didn't send me to Philadelphia," Jenn declared, wiping grease from her lips with the back of her hand. "And I wasn't spying."

"Then why were you there?"

"To hear the Declaration of Independence with my own ears." Although she hadn't planned to travel to 1776, she needed to make the most of it. If - when - she returned to the twenty-first century, there would be many ways for Tryon Travel to capitalize.

Six heads snapped up, six sets of eyes lasering on her. "Why would you care about that, lassie?" Ferguson asked.

"Because I care about life, liberty and the pursuit of happiness. For men and women, black and white."

One of the scouts, bald, his bare scalp and face creased from years outdoors, picked a bone from his teeth. "You sound like a preacher's daughter, not a governor's daughter."

"What a crock of horse shite, if you ask me," another scout said. "Let's string her up right here."

"Is there any way to stop this war before good men like you

get killed?" Jenn couldn't stop the words torrenting from her lips.

"It's too late," Ferguson said, pointing a drumstick at Jenn. "The British have already arrived with the largest armada in the history of the world. They ain't going to just turn around and sail home."

"I don't want to die," Caleb said, fighting back tears.

"Stop sniveling like a swaddling bairn," Ferguson retorted.

"Would you be willing to back up your lofty words with action, Mistress Tryon?" Hawthorne asked as he tended the fire, stoking the dying embers with his bayonet. "Sign an oath of allegiance to the Continental Congress?"

"I might," Jenn replied.

"It might save your life," Rogers added, reaching cautiously for the coffee pot before it turned cold.

The party bed down under a boulevard of twinkling stars and a three-quarter moon. Hawthorne apologized as he chained Jenn and Rogers together at their ankles. One of the soldiers climbed the rocks to post a look-out, another stood sentry at the edge of camp, while a third stole away towards Trenton. Caleb and Ferguson slept, awaiting their turn at picket duty.

Despite the evening cool, the air was still thick with humidity. Jenn fell asleep dreaming of a dive into the icy ocean, waves crashing around her.

She awoke in total darkness to Ferguson's strident call. "The redcoats are here. Dragoons. They've stopped for the night at the King's Arms."

CHAPTER 42

Gary and Erin were asleep, naked and sweat-soaked, in the king-sized feather bed when the British soldiers knocked. "Who ..." he called out, too late.

The door crashed open: black-helmets, red coats, gold buttons, white sashes, polished boots. Too many colors to absorb in his drowsy state.

"Look what we have 'ere," Lieutenant Banastre Tarleton, only twenty-two, declared with a lusty leer. Although born into a merchant family prospering in the West Indies slave trade, he boasted the ramrod posture, regal cheekbones, and cream complexion of nobility.

Gary pulled the coverlet up; Erin ducked underneath it. "What do you want?" he asked, struggling to maintain an even tone as his pulse rate soared.

The dragoons positioned themselves at the foot of the bed, knocking over a wash basin, in no rush to answer. "I have an arrest warrant for Henry Fairfax for illegally supplying the rebels with arms and gunpowder," the lieutenant replied at last, pointing a long, slender finger in Gary's direction. "I understand that you might be his associate."

"I am not associated with Mr. Fairfax in any way. We met for the first time on the eastbound stage yesterday morning."

"But he dined at your table." Tarleton chose his next words carefully. "And shared your room."

The lieutenant must have had an informer in the Horny Goat last night, Gary realized. "Mr. Fairfax was assigned by the innkeeper to our room, but he left before we set out from Bensalem this morning."

"He's not here then?" Tarleton signaled for his men to poke around. One of the dragoons lit a candle.

"No. Fairfax purchased a horse from the stable at the Horny Goat and went off on his own," Gary said.

"Where did he go?"

"I don't know."

"Perhaps we should ask the tart hiding under the covers," a redcoat, sporting a bushy, handlebar mustache, said, prodding Erin's butt with the butt of his musket. "She was quite close to Mr. Fairfax last night, weren't she?"

"We'd ask her quite politely," another dragoon, youthful and apple-cheeked, added, reaching for the coverlet. "Wouldn't we boys?"

Gary slapped his hand away. Still hidden, Erin shuddered, wrapping her arms around his waist.

"Lieutenant Tarleton, the men haven't had a woman in months," Sergeant Thatcher, graying hair peeking from under his helmet, said, stepping forward. "The spoils of war, sir. It's their due."

Banastre Tarleton? Professor Pilgrim had warned him about the brutality of his Queen's Rangers. In 1780, they would massacre 120 rebels in South Carolina who were trying to surrender. "Tarleton's quarter" became a war cry for the Continental Army for the rest of the Revolution. Gary's heartbeat ratcheted up another notch setting off warnings of cardiac arrest in his seventy-year old brain.

Tarleton removed his helmet, polishing the brass insignia with his sleeve, apparently pondering the request, letting the fire build. The mustachioed dragoon started to unfasten his belt.

"She's my wife," Gary blurted as his twenty-five-year old brain took command, slowing his thoughts, enabling him to think - and lie as required. Erin squeezed harder, her clammy hands trembling.

"We'll return her. Don't you fret," apple-cheeks said, leaning his weapon against the bed. The other soldiers, standing behind the captain, cackled in anticipation like starving men waiting their turn at the buffet line.

"Out!" Tarleton ordered. "I'll not turn the entire countryside against the Crown by rousting an innocent man's wife from his bed."

He pointed his dragoons towards the door. Their disappointment was palpable, a wet blanket snuffing out a now roaring flame.

"Sorry to disturb you," he said, grandiosely tipping his helmet towards Gary. "Mister?"

"Johnson. Gary Johnson."

"We'll talk again in the morning, Mr. Johnson."

"Thank you," Gary replied, relieved, but well aware that Tarleton had only offered them a temporary reprieve.

"Perhaps we should examine Mr. Johnson's belongings before we leave for the evening," the sergeant said, peering inside the double wide, cherry wood wardrobe. "Seeing as he's wearing such a fine timepiece around his neck."

He tossed Gary's blue jacket to the floor, then reached for Gary's pack, dumping the contents on the bed for all to see. Gary swallowed hard. Lucie's gold bracelet still appeared securely wrapped but his precious documents lay exposed in their clear, waterproof holder.

Sergeant Thatcher picked it up, held it to the candlelight, turned it upside down. Erin poked her head up, but Gary shoved her back into hiding.

"*The Gazette*." Gary volunteered, realizing the sergeant couldn't read. But Tarleton likely could, so he needed to get ahead of the situation. "It's a copy of the Declaration of Independence. I'm bringing it back to Connecticut."

Tarleton snatched the document holder, fumbling with the zipper which would not actually be invented for another eighty years. He removed the broadside, the deed to the Penn property, and the Button Gwinnett signature, scanning them in the dim light.

"I traveled from Connecticut to Philadelphia to purchase land there," Gary volunteered. "I thought to bring the latest newspaper back home as well."

Tarleton held the tabloid above the flame, slowly inspecting it for signs of code or invisible ink. His troop grew restless waiting.

One dragoon, short, his face grotesquely scarred, reached for the sock holding Lucie's bracelet. His eyes opened as round as pancakes when the jewelry tumbled to the floor. The soldiers broke ranks, diving, fighting to secure it.

Tarleton had no chance, or inclination, to stop them. "What's that?" he asked Gary.

"A bracelet. It's been in my family for generations."

Sergeant Thatcher emerged from the scrum with the treasure, beaming despite a purple welt blooming under his eye.

"You'll sell the bauble and distribute the proceeds equally," Tarleton directed, nodding to his Sergeant. He pointed to the door. "Out!"

The men left silently, their unrest quelled by the realization that they would each have a share of the plunder. Tarleton turned back to Gary, smiling slyly. "The spoils of war. I'm sure you understand."

Gary was in no position to object, although his financial security had just taken a huge hit. The bracelet had been his insurance policy to cover any unforeseen difficulties on the trip to recover his Watch in New York...or fund the rest of his life in 1776.

He slipped his hand under the coverlet to stroke Erin's hand, thankful the dragoons had shifted their attention away from her, at least for now.

Tarleton waited until all his men had left. "Till the morning then," he said, placing Gary's pack at the foot of the bed.

"Thank you, husband," Erin murmured, kicking back the coverlet after the door slammed shut.

Gary donned his boxers, Erin her nightshift, before they curled together again, drifting into a troubled sleep.

CHAPTER 43

Gary stirred at first light, but Erin was already about, frowning as she peered through the threadbare curtains. "There's at least fifty redcoats camped outside, maybe more," she said, wrapping her arms around her chest.

"I'll protect you with my life," he said, joining her at the window, holding her close until her shakes subsided.

She sighed as color gradually returned to her cheeks. "Ye will. I know it." Neither wanted to face the reality that Gary's life might not be enough.

"Our stage will be ready shortly." A shirtless black youth led the horses one by one from the stable, snorting and stomping as they were harnessed into position.

"We can leave while the soldiers are still counting their gold."

Lucie's gold, Gary thought. Although Erin nestled into his arms, Lucie was still his love - and his wife. Gary realized he was now two personas, watching each other, taking stock, preparing for battle. That conflict, however, would only require resolution if he could return to the twenty-first century.

"That bracelet - and your Watch. I know they mean the world to ye," Erin said, reading his mind as she wriggled free. "But all is not lost."

To Gary's surprise, she leaned over and dipped her hand into the chamber pot, fumbling around until her face lit up with a black-toothed smile. She pulled her purse from the mess and jingled the coins. "I thought they might be safe here."

Gary shook his head, chuckling in admiration. "Let's wash up and go downstairs. Hopefully Tarleton will be occupied elsewhere."

Gary smoothed the sleeves on his blue jacket, polished the buckles on his shoes, and tucked the Quare into his shirt, while Erin knotted a bandanna around her neck, positioning it to shield her cleavage. Before they left the room, she straightened Gary's tricorn hat. "Now ye look like a proper sharp."

The lieutenant was standing in front of the bar, engaged in conversation with the three sisters and the coachman when they entered. The room immediately fell silent.

Ignoring the hush, Gary led Erin to the breakfast table, slicing bread for both of them. She reached for the jam, but Tarleton interrupted. "I understand, Mistress, that you are related to Mr. Johnson, but not by marriage," he said, his words like a stiletto jabbing between her ribs.

"The good Lord frowns upon fornication outside of wedlock," Clara said.

"Incest is even more sinful," Betsy added, pointing a crooked finger at Erin. Hannah ducked her head, but remained silent.

"We're not cousins," Gary said, stepping in front of Erin. "That was just a ruse..."

"Then who are you, Mr. Johnson?" Tarleton asked. Nodding towards the coachman, he added, "I understand you were seeking a Letter of Marque from the Congress in Philadelphia. To prey on British shipping?"

Tarleton didn't wait for answers, his hand signal summoned

six dragoons, all unfamiliar faces. They surrounded Gary and Erin. "Lock them in the root cellar until I return from patrol," he said. Gary stuffed the bread in his jacket pocket as the redcoats led them away.

The cellar was dark, but pleasantly chill, smelling of turnips and onions. Before their eyes could adjust, the door opened, the morning light spilling in. Clara entered, flanked by two soldiers. "The stage will be leaving shortly," she said.

No surprise, Gary thought, but she didn't come down here to tell us that. He waited silently. Clara's two guards looked to the door, anxious to leave.

"I understand Lieutenant Tarleton's men relieved you of your jewelry last night. They appeared quite excited this morning about the return it might bring," she said at last.

"They stole it," Erin said.

"A small price to pay for what remains of your honor."

"Let's leave the pleasantries aside," Gary interjected. "Why are *you* here?"

"We'd like to buy your land outside Philadelphia."

"It's not for sale," he replied instinctively.

"You might want to reconsider," she said, swiveling her gaze around the cellar. "Silver might secure better accommodations and, shall we say, treatment, for both of you."

"What price would you offer?" Gary asked. He hated to swallow his pride, but Clara was right. The deed might prove worthless anyway.

"We could offer half of what you paid for it. Quite fair, considering your circumstances."

"My husband said our property is not for sale," Erin reiterated through clenched teeth.

Clara ignored her, focusing her attention solely on Gary. "If you change your mind, Mr. Johnson, you can find us at our home, Sisterly, six miles northeast of Princeton."

She pivoted with surprising sobriety and left, her guards following. The slam of the cellar door echoed in the darkness.

"Why?" Gary asked Erin. "The sale might help save you...from them." He tilted towards the encampment outside.

"The British are pigs. They'd take the money and have me as well."

"Tarleton protected you."

"For now," Erin replied, shaking her head. "His kind have abused the Irish for centuries. Me great-great-grandfather had his fingernails plucked out for playing the harp; me widowed grandmother was tossed off her farm for teaching Gaelic. She starved to death within a year. Why do ye think I came to America?"

"I didn't know."

"Ye say ye are from the future, Gary. Will me boys have a fighting chance at a better life here?

"Yes. America is the one country in the world where any man, or woman, regardless of background, will be able to pull themselves up, provided they work hard."

"That won't be a problem with John and Timmy. I'll see to that. What about Ireland? Will me homeland ever be free of British rule?"

"Yes as well, but it's complicated, Gary replied, pacing about the cellar. "Blood - British and Irish, Protestant and Catholic - will be spilled for another 200 years."

"I feared that. Old grudges die hard."

"Enough of the future," Gary said. "Let's see if we can find a way out of this dungeon."

"This might help," Erin said, holding up Gary's spoon, aiming the flashlight into the abyss. "Most old houses have a hidey-hole."

An hour later, their fine clothes plastered with dirt and debris, they found a trap door in the back. It was barred, but Gary managed to carve out a peephole in the rotting wood.

The courtyard was deserted and silent. No dragoons in sight. The stable hand sat on a fencepost, whittling idly.

"The dragoons are gone," Gary said.

"Up to no good, I wager."

CHAPTER 44

"The dragoons are coming this way," Ferguson whispered to Captain Hawthorne shortly after first light. Jenn could hear the fear in every word, a far cry from the sergeant's bravado the night before. "Fifty men, maybe more. Riding up the King's Road."

"We can't outrun them," Hawthorne replied, smothering the fire and scattering the ashes. "We'll have to hide until nightfall."

"Nightfall?" Caleb squeaked like a mouse.

"The Stark farmhouse is three miles north of here," the bald scout said, sipping his coffee as if he was enjoying the free Wi-Fi at the neighborhood Starbucks. "Isiah Stark's a rebel. He'll look after us."

"Only Indian paths in that direction, if that. The wagon won't be much use," Ferguson said as he slowly sharpened his knife on his whetstone. Looking directly at Jenn and Rogers, still chained together, he trimmed his unruly beard with the blade.

He thinks we'll be a liability, too. Jenn's gut clenched. She turned towards Hawthorne, their best hope. Squatting, he returned her glare, his expression grim as he evaluated his options.

"Burn the wagon. Shoot the horse," he said, standing. "We'll travel on foot."

"All of us?" Ferguson asked, opening his weathered cartridge box, checking his ammunition supply.

"All of us," Hawthorne replied. "If these two are who they say they are, they'll hold some value." He unlocked the cuff on Jenn, then Rogers. "But, if they so much as fart..."

Jenn popped up, but stumbled to one knee, rubbing her ankle until the circulation improved. Caleb wheeled his musket towards her with an unsteady hand. Rogers rose more slowly.

"Let's move out," Hawthorne ordered, taking the point himself. Jenn and Rogers followed, trailed by Caleb and Ferguson. The three scouts slipped away into the woods. A musket rang out. "Poor Star," Caleb muttered. "She deserved better."

"Hush," Ferguson ordered.

For the first two hours, the going was easy: the trail discernable, the ground soft underfoot, the tree canopy providing ample shade. By nine, however, the sun peeked above the tree line, baking them. The path appeared to peter out, but the captain seemed to know his way, wielding his musket to slash through the underbrush.

When they came upon a pencil-thin creek, Hawthorne signaled a stop. His once crisp blue jacket was ripped and soggy with sweat. The bald scout reappeared like a ghost, pulling the captain aside for a private conversation. His two compatriots emerged from the bush as well.

"The redcoats have fanned out. They may be hunting us."

"They've got eyes and ears everywhere," Ferguson said, spitting into the stream.

"Can we beat them to Stark's?" Caleb asked.

Hawthorne shook his head. Jenn realized they had no phone or radio to call for help. No helicopter that could swoop down to rescue them.

Rogers stepped up, scratching his beard. "Let me go to them," he volunteered, his mettlesome self once again. "See if I can negotiate terms."

"Terms of surrender? To the dragoons?" Caleb visibly wet his breeches.

"Anyone have any better ideas?" Ferguson asked.

"You've treated us fairly. You have a hostage," Rogers said, looking towards Jenn. He swung his gaze around to the five Continentals. "It's your best shot to survive."

Hawthorne looked away, as if the gurgling brook might provide a better solution. Jenn didn't relish the prospect of being left behind, but Rogers was well-known to the British, she wasn't. He would have a much better chance to negotiate, if that's what he really intended to do.

"All right," Hawthorne said, pointing his musket at Rogers. "You take the lead, Major. We'll be close behind." His words dripped out as slow as molasses. "Any tricks, you'll be the first to die."

Rogers slung his pack over his shoulder and waded into the knee-deep water. He slipped once but righted himself quickly. Hawthorne waited until Rogers had ascended the far bank before following. Jenn was next, Ferguson close behind, musket at the ready, then Caleb. The three scouts spread out, bringing up the rear.

Jenn cupped her hands in the stream, splashing the icy water on her face and scalp. Ferguson frowned, but she ignored him, shaking her head vigorously in his direction, the spray almost reaching his boots. Caleb stared off into the woods, his eyes vacant, a dead man walking.

Rogers slipped in and out of sight as they threaded through the brush. Jenn kept the pace comfortably, as did the others. The major was clearly not trying to outrun them, which, based on past experience, he must have known he couldn't do anyway. Or was she the anchor that had slowed him down, enabling their capture? She didn't want to think so.

They marched in silence for two hours through the brooding forest, a vast cathedral, the pines soaring like pillars to the blue sky overhead. Jenn counted squirrels, savored the blaring yellows and muted purples of the wildflowers, and listened to the buzz of cicadas, but she couldn't evade Ferguson's glare boring through her back.

How did she get here? To 1776? To TimeR? To Harvard? Each question careened into the next as she re-traced the arc of her life.

Computer science in the oughts was the perfect haven for a mathematically-gifted gay girl. The department at Harvard was mostly male, tech nerds who considered themselves fortunate to simply hang out with a hot-looking woman, leaving Jenn free to pursue romantic liaisons elsewhere. Which she did with gusto, recalling her first real girlfriend, Eleanor, a strapping brunette from Milwaukee who rowed stroke on the heavyweight crew team.

With the innocence of youth, they talked about getting married, leading Jenn to get involved in crusades supporting same-sex marriage and LGBTQ+ rights. While Jenn's passion for activism steadily grew, Eleanor retreated to her oars and her boatmates. Unsurprisingly, Jenn dumped Eleanor and fencing in the same week. When the Supreme Court approved same sex marriage in 2015, her senior year, Jenn looked for new mountains to climb.

"Pick up the pace, lassie," Ferguson growled.

Jenn refused to turn around, but quickened her step nevertheless. She stared at a puffy white cloud, shaped like an ocean liner, wishing she could climb on board and sail away. Within fifteen minutes, her mind had drifted back to her past again. Or was it forward to her past?

Sun Li suggested that Jenn further the Uyghur cause in the land of her birth. Labeled "terrorists," over 1 million Uyghurs were detained for "reeducation" in camps by the Chinese government. While the cause was just, Jenn rightfully feared that she might end up spending the prime years of her life in a Chinese prison. Her mother's activism alone would place Jenn under suspicion the moment that she entered the country.

Accordingly, after graduation, she joined the Peace Corps, spending two years teaching English in Rwanda where she experienced the crippling legacy of Britain's colonial past firsthand. Her time in the jungle convinced her that she could do more with her tech skills than her teaching skills. She answered a LinkedIn ad for an opening at Microsoft and headed off to Seattle.

She first met Gary when he presented at Microsoft soon after selling his third company, WorldR, which created virtual worlds for time travel and gaming. While his vision was intriguing, Gary's ability to execute was questionable at best. She sought him out afterwards to explore the details and left the conversation unimpressed. She wasn't surprised when Microsoft cut him loose a year later.

Jenn spent the next five years in Seattle, coding away. Under her girlfriend Naomi's tutelage, she sharpened her martial arts skills, competing in amateur octagon tournaments around the northwest.

"Shall I tell the redcoats that you are now in support of our rebel cause?" Ferguson called out as Jenn nimbly scaled a fallen tree blocking the path. "The governor's daughter might not be so welcome then, would she?"

She stopped on the far side, watching Ferguson struggle, his cartridge box tumbling off his shoulder. As both Tryon's daughter and a prisoner of the rebels, she expected to be welcomed by the British, but she couldn't be sure. She had no papers to prove her provenance. "Tell them what you please. Major Rogers will vouch for me." Fuck Ferguson.

The sergeant righted himself and retrieved his box. He scrunched his lips as if digesting a foul tonic. "Perhaps you'll put in a good word for me," he said, the plea searing his tongue. "And Caleb, too. The boy needs his mother."

"Perhaps, I will," she replied, before stalking off in pursuit of Captain Hawthorne.

Jenn met Molly Brant, who had just joined TimeR as its head of research, when she tagged along as Naomi's date at a national conference of Native American leadership. Molly convinced Jenn to come to Connecticut.

Ding Yu started recruiting her three years later. She rebuffed him at first, but Gary's doddering management finally convinced her to make a move. Ding was youthful, brash, rich, and, most important, committed to time travel for good. He could help make her dream come true.

Jenn completed the circle of her life just as Hawthorne signaled a halt at a crest in the landscape, not quite a hill but high enough to see the roofs of Trenton in the distance. Down below, on the King's Highway, a single lane dirt road, Rogers had stopped as well, raising his hands high over his shoulders as he was surrounded by a gaggle of redcoats, weapons drawn, pointed at his ample belly.

Rogers parlayed with his captors for several minutes before he was allowed to lower his hands. All eyes turned towards the ridge. A black-helmeted dragoon rode a pale gray horse towards them, stopping halfway up. "I will accept your surrender," he bellowed. "Leave your weapons and come down, if you please."

Hawthorne nodded to his men. He knotted a white kerchief around his saber and raised it so the British could see. The scouts hung their heads, disarming with obvious disdain. Ferguson shoved Jenn forward, positioning her as his shield. Caleb knelt in prayer before following the others down.

"Lieutenant Banastre Tarleton, the King's First Dragoons," the horseman, now backed by a dozen of his squadron, introduced himself as the Americans approached.

"Captain Jeremiah Hawthorne, First New..."

"You are a rebel, Mr. Hawthorne," Tarleton cut him off. "The Crown does not recognize your rank."

He signaled to his dragoons who surged forward, engulfing the rebels in horseflesh. Sergeant Thatcher dismounted first, conducting a rough search of Hawthorne. A half dozen redcoats also jumped to the ground, prodding and poking for concealed weapons. Once they were satisfied, the mounted dragoons bullied the Continentals forward.

Thatcher saved Jenn for himself. He spun her around, kneeling so that he could run his hands up her skirt, checking her ankles, calves and thighs, inside and out. Jenn endured stoically, looking off into the horizon rather than into the faces of the snickering redcoats.

Before the sergeant could explore any further, his lieutenant's voice rang out, "We'll have none of that, Thatcher. Bring Mistress Tryon to me. Immediately."

Thatcher cursed, groping Jenn as he rose, to the amusement of his men. She wheeled and slapped Thatcher's face, the smack resonating on the deserted hillside. "My father will hear of your impudence."

"Just doing my duty, ma'am," he replied, leering for all his men to see.

Tarleton jumped down from his mount, bowing elegantly to Jenn. "Apologies for my sergeant's rudeness, but we must take every precaution out here in the countryside."

"My father will not be pleased."

"I will apologize to His Excellency myself when I have returned his daughter safely to his care."

Jenn held her head erect as she stomped by Tarleton towards Major Rogers. "Thank you," she said.

"The least I could do - since I got you into this predicament," he replied.

Tarleton handed the reins of his horse to his aide. "The Major speaks quite highly of you," he said to Jenn. "I hope you will share my table at supper this evening.

Before she could reply, Thatcher hustled to Tarleton's side. "The prisoners, sir?" he asked. "Where should I quarter them?"

"We give no quarter to rebels, sergeant."

"Understood, sir. I'll see to it."

"Now to supper," Tarleton said, signaling for his mount.

He offered his elbow to escort Jenn, but she sidestepped, looking for Captain Hawthorne, lost in a blur of redcoats. The glint of sunlight reflected off their bayonets.

"No," she shouted as the murderous meaning of Tarleton's command sunk in.

"Mama!" Caleb's scream pierced the air.

CHAPTER 45

Jenn bull-rushed past Tarleton, but she was too late. The dragoons pumped their bayonets over and over into the six unarmed Continentals, their bodies writhing as they crumpled to their final resting place on the rock-strewn hillside. She jumped on Ferguson's back but he tossed her off like a sack of corn meal, stabbing Captain Hawthorne's lifeless form one more time for good measure before stalking off to rejoin his commander.

Caleb gurgled, scarlet leaking from the gash across his throat. Jenn knelt at his side, holding his hand as he died. The other Continentals didn't even twitch. She wanted to cry, to scream, to rant at the heavens, but no sound escaped her throat. Caleb's hand slipped from her grasp as she sat back on her haunches, surveying the butchery.

Jenn had no idea how long she stayed in place, catatonic, before Rogers appeared at her side, helping her to her feet. "Nothing you could have done to save them," he said, leading her back to the dragoons, mounting up to return to the King's Arms.

Lieutenant Tarleton, astride his stallion, offered his hand to pull Jen up into the saddle. "You'll ride with me."

"I prefer to walk," she replied, her brain numbed by grief and anger.

"It's too far. You won't make it by nightfall."

"I don't care."

"I'm sorry, mistress, but the rebels are everywhere," Tarleton said, extending his arm again. "You're in my charge now. I can't allow harm to come to you."

Rogers formed a stirrup with his hands, boosting Jenn. She looped her arm around Tarleton's waist and swung her leg over his horse's back. Settling into the saddle, she swallowed hard, her survival instincts kicking in. Rogers nodded his approval as he climbed up behind Sergeant Thatcher.

"You've ridden before?" Tarleton asked. When Jenn nodded, he kicked the flanks of his mount, eager to escape the scene of the massacre as quickly as possible. The dragoons followed, galloping down the King's Highway in tight formation.

They arrived at the King's Arms after three hours of hard riding and no conversation. Although arcing down towards the treetops, the sun still baked the courtyard. The aroma of roasting meat was a welcome respite from the stench of sweat, both human and equine.

Dismounting, Jenn's butt felt mashed like a potato, while the insides of her bare knees were scraped strawberry red from clinging to the saddle. Regardless, she stood upright, refusing to give Tarleton any glimpse of weakness.

He strode into the inn, returning quickly. "The Governor Franklin suite," he announced, handing her a key. "We'll sup at seven."

Jenn thought to check the time on her wrist watch, but then remembered its demise. "I'll need fresh clothes," she said. Torn and tattered after a week of constant wear, her frock barely provided cover. She didn't want to even consider the state of her undergarments.

"I've already spoken to the innkeeper's wife. She'll find

presentable attire for you among the household staff.”

"And draw a hot bath?” Jenn asked. Why not, she was the governor's daughter.

"A bath as well then,” Tarleton replied, ordering Thatcher to see to it. He turned from Jenn to his men, cursing and groaning as they unsaddled their mounts and led them towards the field where they would spend the night. The campfires were already burning as the cooks and camp followers prepared the evening meal.

"The Benjamin, I mean William, Franklin suite...,” the dog-eared innkeeper announced with a sloppy smile as they climbed the stairs, "... reserved for our most honored guests. Our Negro, Angel, will see to your bath.”

Rebels and Tories stayed here, Jenn realized, appreciating the nimbleness required to run a tavern in border territory. Plopping down on the king-sized feather bed, she briefly wondered who had slept there the night before. Images of Caleb and Captain Hawthorne tossed her mind, keeping her exhausted body from sleep. A rattle on the door interrupted her torment.

"Your bath is ready, ma'am,” Angel, her frizzy hair tightly capped, said. "It's in the keeping room.”

Jenn sat up, nodding slowly, although her eyes saw nothing but punctured corpses.

"Are you all right, ma'am,” the girl, roughly Jenn's height but likely a dozen years younger, asked.

Jenn nodded again, still lost in her private hell. She rose to her feet, finally shaking off the nightmares.

"I'll show you the way.” An indigo blue bodice, embroidered with the King's Arms' seal, displayed Angel's coffee-toned bosom.

They walked through the kitchen, vibrant with the bustle, sounds and aromas of supper preparation. Heads turned to glimpse the governor's daughter. The keeping room, a cozy nook behind the main fireplace, featured two benches and a table, which had been upended to make room for a cast iron tub filled with steaming water.

"Do you need assistance with your bath?” Angel asked.

Jenn shook her head, happy to be left alone to soak. A midnight blue gown, maroon sash and matching bonnet hung on a peg next to the tub. A stout corset, linen drawers and flouncy petticoats lay on the bench.

"I'll wait in the kitchen then," Angel said.

"I may need your assistance later," Jenn called after her.

"Of course, ma'am."

Jenn eased into the tub, stretching her legs as far as possible in its tight confines. The filth seemed to melt off her skin as she washed. Leaning on Rogers' admonition that she could not have tempered Tarleton's barbarism, she tried to cleanse her conscience as well. Scarily, the lieutenant now appeared committed to taking her towards New York and her "father."

As her head cleared, her libido stirred. Good sex would calm her nerves; it always did. But where could she find a willing woman in the eighteenth century?

"Ready to dress, mistress?" Angel called as she opened the door.

"In a minute," Jenn said as she stood, dripping wet, and turned, studying Angel's face for any signs of interest.

The serving girl held up a towel but didn't make eye contact. Too bad, Jenn thought as she dried off and began to dress. Angel tied the stays behind Jenn's back, pinning her breasts tight to her chest with just a peek of cleavage visible on top. The gown was snug in the waist, but Jenn sucked in her stomach and soldiered on.

"Master said to bring you straight to supper," Angel said, kneeling as she buckled Jenn's shoes, high-heeled with an intricate floral pattern.

"Master?" Jenn sputtered, almost tripping in her new shoes. "Are you a...?"

"Slave?" Angel replied. "Yes, ma'am. Born right here in the tavern. My mama works in the laundry."

While Jenn had seen enslaved people during her stay in Philadelphia, she had not had the opportunity to converse with one. Now, she didn't know what to say.

Angel stood, handing Jenn her cap. "Would you like me to do your face, Mistress Tryon?"

"My face?"

"A bit of color might be helpful, ma'am," Angel said, reaching into her basket for a looking-glass, holding it up so Jenn could examine herself.

Jenn thought her face, tanned from a week outdoors, looked healthy, but Angel was already dipping a brush into a crock of white paste.

"What's that?" Jenn asked.

"Why it's powder, ma'am," Angel said, looking confused. "To whiten your skin. I melted the lead myself this morning."

"Lead?" Jenn croaked, shaking her head.

"Your lips then," the slave girl said, displaying another crock containing a ruby red concoction. "Beet juice fresh from our garden. Mixed with cinnabar."

Cinnabar? A mineral laced with mercury? Jenn shuddered. No wonder few colonials lived past fifty, "No thank you," she said. "I think my face looks just fine."

"My master will thrash me if I don't dress you proper."

"I have an earring." Jenn fastened the gold hoop to her right ear, but Angel still looked disappointed.

"What else do you have in there?" Jenn asked, pointing at the basket.

"Patches," Angel replied, brightening. She took out a star shape, brushed on an adherent, and stuck it on the right side of Jenn's forehead. "To show your allegiance to our King."

When Jenn nodded her approval, Angel displayed another patch, a purple circle. "Are you married, ma'am?"

"No."

Angel did not seem surprised, fastening the adornment just left of Jenn's upper lip.

"And if I was married?"

"It would go on your right side," Angel said, stepping back to examine her handiwork, shaking her head. "That will have to do,

I reckon."

Robert Rogers burst in before Angel had time to make up Jenn any further. "Everyone's waiting for the guest of honor," he said, offering his elbow.

CHAPTER 46

"Mistress Jennifer Tryon.   Daughter of the esteemed Governor of our New York colony," the butler, a stately black attired in the tavern's livery, announced. Eight guests surrounded the dinner table, a battered pine fancied up with tablecloth, fine china and two candelabras, each glowing with four candles. Lieutenant Tarleton, jacketed in dress scarlet, gleaming black boots and powdered wig, stood at the head, fidgeting with the hilt of the saber scabbarded on his hip. The innkeeper, sweating nervously in his Sunday meeting suit, hovered at the kitchen door.

"Here, here," two older men, fashionably attired in shades of brown, tapped their spoons on crystal goblets as Rogers, underdressed in his weathered Ranger jacket, guided Jennifer to the vacant seat at Tarleton's right hand before strutting to his own place at the lieutenant's left. The five women, gowned, coiffed, and hatted, were more muted in their approval.

The sight of Tarleton again soured Jennifer's stomach as she sat down, a task made even more difficult by the strictures of her corset. She nodded politely towards the other guests as the butler poured claret and the innkeeper deposited a tray heaping with cornmeal fried oysters in the middle of the table.

"Let me introduce Lord Rutherford and his wife, Lady Anne," Tarleton said, smiling pompously as he gestured towards the couple who bowed their heads in response. "And Minister Greene and his wife, Charlotte," he added, tilting towards the other side of the table. The minister, his bald pate crowned by a ring of gray curls, raised his glass in a toast.

The three as yet unannounced women, dressed in turquoise, lavender and almond, respectively, fidgeted in their seats waiting their turn. "Staunch patriots, the Wishingwell sisters, Clara, Hannah and Betsy," Tarleton declared. "I've persuaded them to delay their return home to Princeton to join us this evening."

"A pleasure to meet you all," Jenn said, breathing deeply to calm her nerves. The three sisters, all in their thirties, she thought, were obviously unattached, but still sought-after guests. There must be more to their story.

"The lieutenant was just telling us about your rescue from the rebels," the minister said, puffing on his corn cob pipe.

"Quite exhilarating," his wife added, adjusting the red roses pinned to her hat.

"My rescue?" Jenn asked. "The Continentals were..."

"Heavily armed, I understand, and intent on pillaging the countryside," the minister said.

"Were you scared amidst all that skirmishing and bloodshed?" Charlotte Greene asked.

"Quite a brave woman, if you ask me," Lady Anne said, raising her glass in a toast.

Jenn stared daggers at Tarleton but remained silent.

"Mistress Tryon thinks me a barbarian," Tarleton said sheepishly. "But that is the nature of warfare."

The lieutenant was a murderer, a war criminal actually, but she needed him on her side. She speared three oysters and plopped them onto her plate, embossed with the GR monogram of King George.

"Did they harm you?" Clara asked before taking a long swill of red wine.

"The Continentals? Not at all," Jenn said. "They treated me with respect."

"Most admirable," Lord Rutherford replied, signaling for a refill of his goblet. "Especially since I understand you were practically naked when the dragoons appeared."

"We are at supper, dear," Lady Anne scolded, patting her lip with a napkin. "Please save that coarse talk for the drawing room afterwards."

"Practically naked?" Hannah interjected, her languid blue eyes leaping to life. A purple circle was pasted just left of her upper lip, Jenn noted as she slurped an oyster and adjusted her bodice. Hannah's gaze closely followed her movements.

"To the King!" Tarleton raised his glass in a toast.

"To the King!" Everyone, including Jenn, echoed.

Taking his cue, the innkeeper proudly appeared with a tray bearing a suckling pig, complete with an apple stuffed into its mouth, surrounded by golden potatoes and root vegetables. The butler circled the table ladling gravy as each of the guests filled their plates.

Tarleton and Rogers engaged in a comparison of warfare in the North American wilderness compared to the plains of western Europe. Jenn made small talk with each of the three sisters, careful to say as little as possible about her own background, while the two older couples largely gossiped among themselves.

"Are you still holding the Johnson's in the cellar?" Clara asked Tarleton as the butler cleared the supper plates.

"I do believe so," the lieutenant replied. "Frankly, I'd forgotten about them amidst all the excitement this afternoon."

"What will you do with them?" Clara followed up.

"That depends on the information I receive from Connecticut."

At the mention of Connecticut, Jenn shifted her attention from Hannah to Tarleton. Did he say Johnson's?

"They seemed like such an enterprising young couple," Betsy said. "Hard to believe they could be spies or pirates."

"Not pirates, sister," Clara corrected. "Privateers."

"I don't see the difference. They both prey on British shipping and drive up the price of all sorts of goods here in the colonies."

"Privateering is quite legal during wartime, Mistress Wishingwell, on both sides of the Atlantic," Tarleton said. "Provided the captain has received a letter of marque from his government."

"So as yet Mr. Johnson has committed no crime?" Clara asked, pointing a chubby finger towards the lieutenant.

"No, not yet."

"Then I would suggest treating him with a bit more respect."

"And how would you suggest I do that, my dear?" Tarleton asked.

"Perhaps, we could ask the innkeeper to deliver the remains of our meal to them. They must be famished."

"Clara Wishingwell, I sense an ulterior motive," Tarleton said.

"Whatever do you mean?"

"Tell the truth, sister," Betsy said.

"Well, I do have a small business proposal that I'd like Gary Johnson to consider."

"Gary Johnson? From Connecticut?" Jenn asked, her breath shortening with excitement. "I know a man by that name. A good man, in fact."

"Let's invite Mr. and Mrs. Johnson to join us then," Tarleton said, standing to call for Sergeant Ferguson.

Jenn's thoughts raced. Mr. and Mrs. Johnson? Was Lucie here too?

While the sergeant hastened to the cellar, the lieutenant turned to Jenn, taking her hand. "I hope you will recognize that I am a reasonable, law-abiding man, Mistress Tryon. Not a barbarian."

"I will be certain to inform my father accordingly," she replied, steepling her fingers in her lap to prevent slapping the Lieutenant across the face.

Hannah Wishingwell slipped away from her sisters and sidled next to Jenn. "I believe we might share a common passion, Mistress," she said, tapping the purple circle pasted above her own lip.

Jenn's head spun as she inhaled Hannah's musky jasmine scent. She had to stay focused on Gary - if it really was him. But her body willed her closer to Hannah, their forearms brushing, a charge shooting through her loins.

"A discreet passion," Hannah whispered, making no move to disengage.

"Most discreet," Jenn replied, her breath quick, the words barely escaping. Angel, the little devil, had played matchmaker.

Clara and Betsy wandered towards their sister. Hannah pressed a key into Jenn's hand. "Perhaps we could rendezvous later this evening," she whispered.

CHAPTER 47

"Someone's coming," Gary called to Erin, who dozed with her head resting on a sack of dried peas. He gripped the handle of a shovel that he'd found lying underneath a pile of debris in the cellar.

"Who?"

"Can't tell. It's too dark." He kept his eye pinned to the peephole, tracking the swinging lantern. Erin sat up, shivering. "It's only one man," Gary added, reaching for her hand. "We'll be fine."

"Does he have supper?"

It was Sergeant Thatcher, Gary realized, the redcoat he'd least like to see. He stood off to one side, ready to swing the shovel, as the door opened.

Thatcher entered with his pistol drawn. "Figured you might have prepared a warm welcome for me," he said, pointing his weapon at Gary. "Now, put that down."

When Gary complied, he announced, "Lieutenant Tarleton invites you both to join his guests for supper in the dining room."

"Supper?" Erin asked in wonder, as if the sergeant had

invited them on a trip to paradise. She wasted no time nudging Gary towards the open door.

"Guests?" Gary asked warily. He smelled a trap.

"You'll find out soon enough," Thatcher replied, ostentatiously ogling Erin's backside while his pistol aimed squarely at Gary's chest. "If it was up to me, we'd come back down here for dessert."

The threesome crossed the tavern's empty courtyard, moon rays providing the only illumination. When Erin stumbled over a wagon rut, Thatcher offered his hand, but she slapped it away.

The butler opened the front door and escorted them inside. The air was ripe with the scent of pipe smoke and roasted pig. Gary noted the red ensign flag of the British navy tacked above the bar in the spot where the stars and stripes had rested last night. The innkeeper backed away as they approached.

"Mr. and Mrs. Gary Johnson from Connecticut," the butler proclaimed. Gary swiveled his gaze around the room, taking in an array of familiar faces: Tarleton, Clara, Hannah, Betsy, Jennifer.

Jennifer? Jennifer Tryon? His mind thundered like a runaway train. He had finally connected with a fellow time traveler. Was she friend or foe? Would she even recognize him now?

He squeezed Erin's hand, flashing a smile to calm her while hopefully concealing his excitement. At first, she barely noticed the guests, her attention captured by the fleshy feast resting in the center of the table. Gary's goofy expression, however, hinted at a more nuanced puzzle.

"Sit, sit," Tarleton commanded with a broad gesture. "Fill their plates, man," he ordered the butler.

"So nice to see you both again," Clara said. Her sisters bobbed their heads in agreement.

Gary nodded, rapidly trying to take the temperature of the room. His life - and Erin's - might depend on it. Erin was clearly torn between her growling stomach and her mistrust of all people English. She held a drumstick, dripping with gravy, in one hand, but waited for Gary's signal before gnashing it.

He stared at Jenn, noting that she occupied a position of honor at the table. His "wife," however, had no clue to her identity.

"Enjoy your meal, Mr. Johnson," Jenn said, breaking the tension. "I understand you've had a difficult day."

Gary's shoulders sagged in relief. He was over the first hurdle but still far from the finish line. While he knew that the Committee of Safety had destroyed Jenn's Watch, he doubted that she knew that he was Watch-less as well. He tapped the Quare hanging underneath his shirt. It might be more useful than he thought.

Erin's brow wrinkled as she picked up on the interplay between her "husband" and Jenn, but she was not perturbed enough to delay her meal any longer. Gary also succumbed to the aroma of freshly cooked meat. Upon a gesture from Tarleton, the butler opened another bottle of claret, a '69 St. Emilion, and refilled everyone's glasses. Gary politely declined.

After clearing the supper plates, the innkeeper brought dessert, an apple pie topped with fresh cinnamon and a bowl of clotted cream. Hannah dug in with gusto. The cream smearing her lower lip appeared to draw Jenn's attention.

Sergeant Thatcher and two dragoons slipped into the dining room, but a hand signal from Tarleton kept them at bay. The lieutenant had fattened up the goose, Gary understood; now it was time for trial by fire.

"Mistress Tryon, do you know this man and his wife?" Tarleton asked. Clara leaned forward, savoring her front row seat. Hannah wiped her lip with her napkin.

"Yes, Lieutenant. I am well acquainted with Mr. Johnson, but must admit this is my first meeting with his lovely young wife," Jenn replied.

"And how are you acquainted with him?"

Gary cringed as he reached for Erin's hand.

"Our families conducted business quite regularly. In New York and Connecticut."

Jenn had covered both bases, Gary thought, but he still

wasn't sure where she was headed.

"What type of business?"

"Trading. My father, Governor Tryon, needed foodstuffs in New York and later in exile aboard the Duchess. Mr. Johnson supplied them."

"Do you remember the name of his ship?"

"*The Lucie*, I believe. Quite a seaworthy vessel."

Gary smiled at the reference. Yes, Lucie could weather any storm.

"Are you aware that Mr. Johnson has applied for a letter of marque from Congress to prey on British shipping?"

"No, but that is hardly a surprise. A good businessman must trade with both sides," Jenn replied. The innkeeper dropped a dessert bowl, pie splattering the rug.

"You do not believe Mr. Johnson is a rebel spy?" Tarleton continued, ignoring the mess.

"Lieutenant, do you have any evidence whatsoever to accuse Mr. Johnson of such a heinous crime?" Hannah asked. "I manage our family's China trade. I am quite sure our captains are quite, shall we say, nimble in their dealings."

"Crime?" Lord Rutherford snorted as he snapped awake. "What crime?"

"Never mind, dear," his wife said, patting her husband's hand.

"I have no such evidence," Tarleton admitted.

"Then I insist that you remove all restraints on the Johnsons," Clara said, nodding towards her sisters. "The Wishingwells, staunch friends of the Crown, will vouch for them."

"I will let my father know of your patriotism," Jenn added.

"Here, here," Hannah toasted, her eyes twinkling at the governor's daughter.

Erin's gaze spun from Tarleton to Gary to Clara to Jenn to Hannah. She took a large draught of wine. "Are we done then?"

"For the moment, yes," Tarleton replied, standing. "I do believe the King's Arms is fully occupied, but, seeing as you are old friends, you may share the Franklin suite with Mistress Tryon this evening."

"Thank you," Gary whispered to Jenn as the party broke up.

"It's truly good to see you. You look so...youthful. And in love."

"As do you." Gary tilted his head towards Hannah.

CHAPTER 48

Waking well before sunrise, Gary found himself alone in the dining room, surprisingly clean after last night's festivities. With the threat from Sergeant Thatcher and his men receding, Erin slept so soundly that a cannon blast wouldn't have roused her. He helped himself to what he thought was a cup of coffee from the crane hanging over the smoldering fire, but found out quickly enough that it was tea.

Jennifer Tryon - tech guru, hard-working, idealistic, gay. He tried to recall all he knew about her from the twenty-first century, realizing it was not much. As founder and CEO of TimeR, he had been much more concerned with his company's mission than its people. While Jenn had deserted him in 2026, she appeared to be on his side in 1776. Would she stay in his corner once she learned that his Watch was gone?

At least his Watch was recoverable, not smashed to smithereens like Jenn's. That was his ace in the hole - and he would have to play the card carefully. But, to play it right, he needed to better understand Jenn's situation. Why had Jenn traveled back to

1776? Was she sight-seeing, following him, or on the run herself?

A tear welled in Gary's eye as he thought of the twenty-first century. He hadn't been in touch since his Watch was taken by the Committee of Safety almost a week ago. How was Lucie holding up? Was she searching the sands of time for him? How long until she gave up, presuming him lost or dead? In fact, he had blocked out all thoughts of 2026 in order to focus on survival here in the eighteenth century.

At least that's what Gary told himself every morning. It assuaged his guilt and sugared over the cold, hard truth that he savored being twenty-five years old again. How many seventy-year old men, or women, would have felt otherwise? He had already plunged into the deep end with Erin. There was no going back. What would he tell Lucie? He'd cross that bridge when, and if, he got there.

Gary's introspection was cut short by the sensation of another presence in the dining room. He looked up. A candle flickered in the window, but it was still too dark to see much. A spectral shape, masculine, short but lithe, swathed in black robes, glided towards the door. Had he been hiding here the whole time? The man turned, his face oval-shaped, like a Chinaman, Gary thought. Then he was gone.

The innkeeper stepped through the kitchen door, rekindling the fire. "Bread and jam, sir?" he asked.

Gary nodded, as he forced his brain back to the problems at hand. A Chinese intruder? He must have been dreaming.

Clara waddled down the stairs, jug in hand. She sliced a wedge of bread, lathered it with strawberry jam, and ladled a steaming helping of porridge into a bowl. "May I join you?" she asked, plopping her broad butt down next to Gary.

"Of course," he replied, as if he had a choice. The elder Wishingwell had come to his defense last night, but he still only trusted her as far as he could throw her.

Clara ate heartily, while the innkeeper ambled over to fill her mug with tea. When he walked away, she tilted towards Gary.

"Tarleton is a devious man. I would keep my guard up, if I were you."

Gary nodded. No surprise here. He focused on his breakfast, the less said the better.

He fidgeted on the bench as the dining room steadily filled: the lieutenant, Betsy, Lady Rutherford, the Greene's. But no sign of Jenn yet. Or Erin. "I have to attend to my wife," he said, pushing away his plate.

"I would like a word with you - in private - at some time today," Clara replied.

"Have you seen Jenn...I mean Mistress Tryon?" he asked.

"She was engaged with my sister last night but I have yet to see her this morning."

"Must have been quite the engagement," Lady Rutherford said, smothering her leer with her napkin. "For them both to be tardy for breakfast."

"Yes, well, Hannah is quite the engaged woman," Clara said.

"As is Mistress Tryon, I gather," Minister Greene replied with a knowing smile.

Tarleton looked a bit lost as the innuendo swirled around the table. "We leave for Princeton in thirty minutes," he announced, standing.

So much for time alone with Jenn or Clara, Gary thought as he climbed the stairs. Erin was already dressed, insistent that she not miss breakfast. They packed and returned to the dining room, half empty now. Through the window, he watched an elegant two horse coach, likely carrying the Rutherford's and Greene's, clatter away. Four horses, harnessed to a more road-worthy vehicle, stamped restlessly in their wake.

Gary helped Erin, Clara and Betsy climb aboard. Electing to ride with the troops, Rogers mounted a coal-gray mare and tucked into formation behind Sergeant Thatcher. Still no sign of the lovers.

Tarleton circled his stallion several times, clearly hesitant to leave. Jennifer Tryon, the woman he thought to be the Royal Governor's daughter, was his prize, Gary realized. What would happen when Tarleton found out the truth?

Hannah Wishingwell emerged from the King's Arms first. While her dress, the same almond one as last night, and matching cap were neatly in place, she couldn't camouflage her bloodshot eyes. "Mistress Tryon will join us shortly," she said, looking almost like a circus clown, her cheeks smudged cherry red with make-up.

Jennifer, however, looked regal. She had wiped off all colonial cosmetics and left her short blond hair uncapped. A gold hoop glittered on her right ear. Angel, the slave girl, lifted the train of her gown off the dirt as she approached the stage.

The thought of sitting in the cabin, alone with five women, was more than Gary could bear. Fortunately, Major Rogers came to his rescue. "You might want to ride up top," he said, sidling his mount close enough to nod his respects to Jenn.

"Well then," Clara harrumphed as Jenn settled into her seat.

As Gary scrambled up the side of the coach, his watch popped out of his shirt, swinging freely. Jenn peered at it through the open window, a broad smile creasing her face. He returned the grin with a knowing nod. The Quare was his only leverage in this relationship right now.

"Tally ho!" Tarleton shouted, waving his saber as he led his men off at the trot, the coach following. A squad of six dragoons brought up the dust-choked rear.

CHAPTER 49

The formation stayed on the King's Highway for six hours before turning off to a country lane taking them to the Wishingwell estate. Riding unencumbered in the coach was certainly more comfortable than riding trussed up in the back of the Continental Army wagon, but the thinly padded seats did little to cushion Jenn's ass from the bumps in the dirt road. Whoever invented shock absorbers would make a fortune.

She and Erin sat on one side, facing forward, while the three sisters squeezed next to each other on the bench facing rearward. The glimpse of Gary's watch sent her heart soaring, while the sight of Hannah, sitting opposite, kept her blood pressure up. Jenn's mind machine-gunned between thoughts of returning home to the twenty-first century and visions of her lover's parting thighs.

As the coach swerved to avoid a mud patch, Hannah's boot curled forward, nudging Jenn's ankle. "You'll love Sisterly," she said. "Particularly the library."

"What are your favorites?" Jenn asked, allowing her leg to remain in proximity to Hannah's.

"We have several first editions - Swift, Voltaire, Defoe," Betsy chimed in.

"Our newest is *Tristram Shandy*. It was only recently published in London," Clara said proudly.

"I prefer adventure," Hannah said. "I've read *Robinson Crusoe* several times."

"I read that at Harvard," Jenn said, immediately realizing her gaffe. Harvard did not admit its first female student until 1936.

"Harvard?" Clara asked, eyebrows arched in disbelief.

"I was visiting the school - with my father, of course." Jenn held her breath waiting to see if her backtracking had placated her audience.

"I'm sure your father had access to the best books from England," Hannah said.

"Sister, I thought you preferred adventures of another sort," Clara said. "Defoe's *Moll Flanders...*"

"She was a whore, wasn't she?" Erin asked, while looking out the window at the rolling hills. Jenn exhaled as the conversation was clearly moving on.

"And a thief," Hannah said. "A most successful one at that."

"More power to her then," Erin replied, her hands fidgeting in her lap.

"But she repents, of course. And travels to the colonies to start a new life," Betsy said.

"A worthy end," Erin replied.

"Do you have *Fanny Hill*?" Jenn asked. The sisters tittered.

"Another story of a whore," Betsy said. "No reputable lady reads that rubbish."

"But the illustrations..." Hannah raised her eyebrows seductively. "I caught a peek on my visit to London last summer."

Pure pornography, Jenn remembered, but nevertheless impressed at Hannah's Atlantic crossing.

"Why do novels portray any woman who enjoys relations as a whore?" Erin asked.

"Because that's what men want. A whore in the bedroom,

but a princess in the drawing room," Clara said.

"Perhaps women should write their own books," Erin said. The three sisters gasped, but Jenn 's respect for Erin catapulted.

Tarleton appeared in the window, leaning over his mount to announce that they had arrived. Sisterly's graveled entrance stretched a half mile through pasture and farmland. Jenn noticed three low-slung thatched homes along the way. Men tilled the fields while women and children were out in the yards. Blacks and whites, separate but at least appearing equal.

The drive culminated in a red brick, three story, Georgian manor house. A Black in powder blue livery waited at the foot of the front steps, while the household staff, all similarly uniformed Blacks, lined up on either side.

Clara was first out. "Benjamin...," she commanded the butler, "...see to our guests."

"Of course, Miss Clara," he replied, taking her valise. "What time would you like supper this evening?"

Hannah was last out, trailing close to Jenn. "I'll have Sally show you to your room," she whispered. "It's next to mine."

"Your slave?" Jenn asked.

"We have no slaves here, Mistress Tryon," Hannah said, stepping back. "We granted all our Blacks manumission upon our father's death. They labor here now on their own free will."

Jenn beamed as she touched Hannah's hand. "Well done, Mistress Wishingwell."

Prior to supper, they bathed together in Hannah's suite in an enormous oval tub fronting the bay window overlooking the garden. Fortuitously, the suite connected to the guest room via a discreet door set into a bookcase.

Afterwards, Sally helped Jenn dress in the same blue gown she had worn the night before. She had no choice, although they did change the look somewhat with a lacy white apron and summer scarf. Like Angel, Sally professed disappointment at Jenn's disinterest in cosmetics, although they did apply the purple patch above her lip once again.

Befitting the governor's daughter, Jenn was the last to arrive in the drawing room prior to supper. With her lust quenched, she turned her attention to Gary, sharply dressed in blue jacket, white linen shirt and cravat. The wrinkles in his face had melted away. His shoulders were square, not slouched; his step had a spring, not a shuffle. A far cry from the man she knew at TimeR.

She chuckled thinking of Gary's first look in the mirror after his journey backwards in time. How would it feel to regain forty-plus years of life? Would he even want to return to 2026 and become an old man once again?

Jenn sipped a glass of claret, watching Gary and Erin chat with Clara, Betsy and Major Rogers. Her former boss seemed in no rush to leave, although the Watch dangling around his neck gave him the means to do so any time. She rested her goblet on a side table, marveling at its detailed workmanship particularly the intricate fretwork, gracefully curved legs and claw feet. A creation of Thomas Tufft, prominent eighteenth century cabinetmaker, she guessed, likely worth millions in the twenty-first century.

When could she safely go home? In Jenn's struggle to simply survive the past few days, she had lost sight of the reason she had traveled here in the first place. To escape the Chinese. They were relentless and would squeeze Ding Yu for all the information he had. Then they would come after her – if they could find her. Sun Li's activism in the Uyghur cause had already put them both on the MSS black list. Tryon Time would have to wait until she got the all clear.

Gary had a Watch. Would he send a message ahead on her behalf? Arrange for her to receive a new Watch of her own – even though she had stolen TimeR's technology?

No need to rush him. Hannah had promised to talk to Tarleton about extending their stay at Sisterly.

Supper was served mercifully fast. Nothing like a long stage coach ride to exhaust a traveler. In modern times, the trip from downtown Philly to Princeton might have taken little more than an hour, not the entire day. Tarleton announced they would leave for

Staten Island at dawn before excusing himself early to check on his troops, camped in the high meadow.

Jenn was just about to head upstairs to bed when she noticed Clara and Gary closeted in a corner of the great room, underneath the twenty point antlers of a massive deer killed long ago. Erin was not in sight. She edged close enough to overhear the conversation.

"I'm still interested in acquiring your land in Pennsylvania," Clara said.

"It's still not for sale," Gary replied.

"I thought you might reconsider."

"Why would I do that?"

"The Watch you're wearing around your neck? It's a Quare, is it not?"

Gary nodded, reaching under his shirt to cradle his timepiece.

"Daniel Quare crafted it for my great-grandfather, William Wishingwell, in 1701."

"Your great grandfather?" Gary asked, although not as surprised as Jenn would have expected.

"If you look closely by the stem, you will see the initials 'WW.'"

Gary examined the watch in the dim candlelight. "There are no initials."

"Look closely," Clara said, leaning over. "I imagine the thieves tried to grind them out but I saw a trace this morning in the sunshine when you climbed up the stagecoach."

"Thieves?"

"There...," Clara pointed. "You can see the grooves. A bit of polish will bring them out more clearly."

"This is your watch?"

"Our father's," Clara replied, pointing to her sisters. "It was stolen from him in Philadelphia several years ago. Right before he passed."

"Why should I believe you?"

"I have the provenance upstairs. Would you like to review it?"

"I..."

"No mind. I'll allow you to keep the timepiece. And your life as well," Clara said, her eyes as cold as stones. "In exchange for the deed to your land."

"I'll have to discuss it with my wife," Gary replied.

"We hang thieves here in New Jersey, Mr. Johnson. And their wives do not receive much pity."

"I'm no thief."

"Tell that to Lieutenant Tarleton."

Jenn had heard enough. She bustled up the stairs, her head spinning.

CHAPTER 50

"Give her the deed," Erin said, sitting up in bed, her bare breasts damp in the night heat. "We have ye treasure. More than enough for the five of us to get by."

Gary had forgotten about Erin's two boys and Mamo. "Can we trust Clara any more than we trust Tarleton and his troops?"

"Do we have any choice?"

Gary parted the brocaded drapes and stared out the window, savoring the wisp of a breeze. The crescent moon cast eerie shadows in the garden. "I guess not."

Erin found a pink silk robe in the wardrobe, cinched it around her waist and joined Gary in the moonglow. She reached around his chest, unfastened the top of his shirt, and reached for the Quare. "Make sure Mistress Clara gives ye a proper bill of sale and the papers detailing the history of her watch."

"Yes, a good idea," Gary said, distracted as Erin's hand wandered.

"I can go back to work at the City Tavern," she said soothingly. "Ye can find a ..."

"Job? What could I do here? In colonial America?" Gary pulled away.

"What did ye do in ye time?"

"I was an entrepreneur, an inventor."

"So invent something here. I have faith in ye."

"Well..."

"Ye should have an edge, aye? If ye are really from the future."

"You do have a point."

"Go now. Give Clara what she wants..." She said, snuggling close again, her robe parting, "...and come back to me."

A thump on the door interrupted their embrace. "It's me, Jenn..., Mistress Tryon."

Gary let her in, careful to secure the latch behind her. "What do you want?"

"Your Watch? Where is your Watch?" she asked, still in evening dress, desperation wearing on her features. "The one we built at TimeR."

"I suppose I could ask you the same question," Gary replied, feigning ignorance as he stalled for time. Erin re-cinched her robe and wandered towards the nightstand, rinsing her face in the bowl of warm water.

"The Committee of Safety destroyed it when they interrogated me," Jenn said.

"The Committee got mine too," Gary said, proceeding to spill out the story of his arrest and duel with William Sands.

"So you think your Watch is in New York? Intact?" Jenn asked.

"That's our only hope," Gary said, wincing as he saw Erin's scowl.

"So ye are from the future as well?" Erin asked Jenn. "Ye look just as lost here as him."

Jenn's expression betrayed her shock, but she answered calmly. "Yes. I worked for Mr. Johnson's company. Helped him to build the Watch."

"A woman? Working with her mind, not her body," Erin commented softly. "Tell me more about the future."

"I don't know where to start," Jenn said, shuffling her feet as Gary shrugged his approval. "In the twenty-first century, women can vote, own property, even write books."

"And rut with other women?" Erin asked, looking Jenn eye to eye.

"Yes," Jenn blushed. "How could you tell?"

"Will you help us find my Watch?" Gary asked Jenn, anxious to change the subject.

"Yes."

"Who's to say ye won't try to steal it from us?" Erin asked Jenn. "If we can find it."

"It won't do me much good without Gary," Jenn replied. "We could all end up with our necks in a noose if we don't work together."

"As Dr. Franklin said last week: we must hang together, or we will surely hang separately," Erin said, smiling again.

"Touché," Gary replied.

"It's getting late. We leave for New York at dawn," Jenn said. "I don't expect Lieutenant Tarleton to tolerate our tardiness again."

Your tardiness, Gary thought. "Say our farewells to Mistress Hannah," Erin said.

Jenn smiled softly and left.

"We can trust her," Erin said, crawling under the sheets.

"How do you know?"

"A *tribade* knows how to keep a secret."

"What's a *tribade*?"

"Come to bed, dear."

CHAPTER 51

Connecticut 2026

Lucie prided herself on her ability to keep her emotions in check, but Gary had been out of touch for six days now. He had texted the office on Saturday saying he was coming home, but then followed up with a message that indicated trouble. Trouble that had blocked his return. Where was he? Was he still alive? She drove the last question from her thoughts. He would come home soon - or she would go find him.

The FBI man, Gibson, had been incensed, threatening to arrest her, when Gary disappeared into the sands of time. Fortunately, Rob Mangano showed up within the hour. He convinced Gibson that there was now little risk in letting the time travel mission play out. The FBI monitored all communications, but appeared to be rooting for Gary's safe return.

The Johnson house was a mess, but largely a pleasant mess. Mirabel and Remy had moved in. The grandkids scampered about. Lucie tripped over a fire engine and tossed batting practice to

Derek. But, mostly she toiled in her garden, often with a glass of Chardonnay within reach.

Lucie's mobile buzzed. "I've got something to show you," Molly Brant said. "Can I come over?"

Since Gary left for 1776, Molly had reached out multiple times per day, but never with this urgency. Within an hour, the engine blast from a submarine gray Ferrari reverberated up the Johnson driveway. TimeR's head of development clambered out of the driver's seat but her step lacked its usual zest. Lucie ushered her into the library.

"Looks like I should sit down," she said, dread numbing her limbs as she eased onto the plush sofa. Molly sat next to her, pulling a blue folder from her satchel.

"You know we've been tracing and retracing Gary's route through time. Ley lines, wormholes, every possible place he could have detoured enroute from Philadelphia 1776 to Connecticut 2026."

"Detoured? Gary never mentioned any detours."

"Not by choice. I thought there might be a bug in the software that sent him off-line."

"Gary said you'd tested the software thoroughly. He swore you'd never let him go if it wasn't safe."

"He was right, but...," Molly replied, looking away. "...it looks like he never left Philadelphia."

"Never left? What happened?" Lucie asked, bewildered. "Did he change his mind?"

"He got arrested," Molly said, pulling a copy of a three column clipping out of the file. "We dug through a database of old newspapers. Look at this."

Pennsylvania Packet
Wednesday July 10, 1776
Vile Murder

Constable Huckleberry has detained Mr. Gary Johnson of Connecticut on suspicion of murder in the death of Mr. Owen

Sullivan last Saturday. Mr. Johnson claimed he acted in self-defense when Mr. Sullivan assaulted him in an alley off Market Street. Mr. Sullivan was in service in the household of Mr. William Sands, a well-respected agent of Cary and Company in Philadelphia.

If anyone witnessed this vile deed, please come forward immediately. Constable Huckleberry would also welcome information on the moral character of Mr. Johnson who claims to have no relations in Philadelphia.

"Saturday - that was the day Gary was coming home," Lucie said. "So this assault must have happened right after he texted you."

"This Sullivan guy could have seen the Watch and mugged Gary," Molly added, tapping the article with her finger.

"So what happened to Gary after his detention?" Lucie asked.

"We haven't been able to find that out yet either, but at least he's alive."

"As far as we know, *Dieu merci*," Lucie said, standing, rising from the sofa and staring out the window at the front yard. A Verizon truck was parked across the street; a blue Tesla cruised by. The twenty-first century...but her husband was likely locked in a dungeon in the eighteenth century. "What can we do?" she asked, shuddering.

"We'll continue to scour the newspaper files...there were so many tabloids back then," Molly replied, putting her arm around Lucie's shoulder. "My team has already started building another Watch, but we need to know the identity of the time traveler before we can go much further."

"I'll go," Lucie volunteered, head high, shoulders straight, just like the French resistance fighters she had seen in old World War II movies.

"That's a noble gesture," Molly said.

Remy burst in, laptop in hand. "Dad's alive!" he shouted.

"We know," Lucie and Molly answered in unison. "But he's

in jail...for murder."

"No, he's not. He escaped!" Remy plopped his computer on Gary's desk, knocking over the photo of Pee Wee Reese. Lucie and Molly crowded around.

Pennsylvania Gazette
Tuesday July 16, 1776
WANTED: DEAD OR ALIVE
The Pennsylvania Committee of Safety has placed a bounty of $50 for information leading to the arrest of Mr. Gary Johnson of Connecticut and his accomplice, Mistress Erin Duffy of Southwark. They escaped from custody and are believed to be traveling to New York City together. Mr. Johnson is now believed to be a spy for our mortal enemy, the British Crown, as well as the murderer of Mr. Owen Sullivan.

"Won't everyone in the colonies be hunting for Dad now?" Remy asked.

"*J'en doute,*" Lucie said. "There was no internet in 1776. It might take a month or longer for this tabloid to circulate."

"I'll Google Erin Duffy," Molly said, pulling out her phone.

"I haven't been able to find her name in any historical database," Remy replied.

CHAPTER 52

Princeton 1776

Hannah playfully nibbled on Jenn's earlobe, awaking her lover before dawn. "Take me again," she whispered. When Jenn finally stirred, Hannah lay back atop the sheets, legs askew.

Jenn peeked out the diaphanous curtains enclosing the king-sized feather bed; the room blushing with the first sprouts of light. She shook her head. "We don't have time, my love. I can't be late again."

"Tarleton will wait," she said, tugging Jenn to mount her. "We pay him well. And feed his men."

Jenn shook her head, parting the curtains as she rose. She gazed at Hannah, possibly for the last time. So much hair, she thought. Legs, pits, pubes. Did colonial women ever shave? What a difference from her own bare skin, broken only by a rainbow crescent tattoo cradling her navel. Perhaps that was the attraction - for both of them. Something different, exotic, exciting. A little spice in the life of two successful, single ...middle-aged...women.

She washed at the basin while Hannah pouted. Admitting defeat at last, Hannah, still naked, stalked past Jenn to her dressing table, toying with the pipe left over from last night. "One more?" she asked. "It will make your ride a bit more manageable."

Jenn had enjoyed recreational drugs, weed, gummies, an occasional line of coke, in the twenty-first century, but she had never smoked opium before last night. Fortunately, they had just one hit before tumbling into bed. "No," Jenn replied, tying her cap and straightening her bodice. She would need to be a proper British aristocrat today.

She kissed Hannah, savoring the sweet narcotic residue on her lips, but broke off before their embrace could progress any further. "I'll write from New York," she promised.

"Wait," Hannah said, offering a packet of what looked like brown gum. "*Hul Gil*, the joy plant. A farewell gift." Jenn tucked the opium into her skirt pocket as she left.

Clara and Gary were already seated at the breakfast table when she started down the stairs. She slowed, watching as they exchanged envelopes, broke the seals and read the contents.

"The Penn property is yours," Gary said.

"A fair trade for my grandfather's watch...," Clara replied in a hushed tone. "...and your life."

Erin emerged from the kitchen holding two mugs of steaming tea. The cook, a rotund black woman sporting a bronze hoop piercing her nose, followed with a tray of pastries, serving Clara first. The lady of the house declined, however. "I'm going to return to bed," she said, standing.

"Perhaps my sister will see you off," Clara added, brushing by Jenn.

"Perhaps she will."

Clara reached the top before turning. "I'd almost forgotten," she said, holding an envelope. "Benjamin said a man, a Chinaman he noted, delivered it this morning."

"A Chinaman?" Jenn asked as she scurried up the steps. She took the missive, sealed with a scarlet wax imprinted with the head of a dragon. "Is he still here?"

"I haven't the foggiest idea," Clara replied, pivoting and marching towards her room.

"We ride in fifteen minutes," Lieutenant Tarleton announced, removing his helmet as he strode into the dining room.

Jenn ducked into the "water closet," Sisterly was too civilized to require its guests to retreat to an outhouse, and broke the seal of the envelope. A shriveled, severed pinky finger tumbled out. It bore a gold ring engraved with Ding Yu's personal emblem. The note, written in block letters, was unsigned. It said: MEET ME OUTSIDE THE BLAZING STAR TONIGHT AT MIDNIGHT. TELL NO ONE.

They were scheduled to spend the coming night at the Blazing Star tavern on Staten Island. How did the Chinaman know? Who was he? What did he want? Jenn trembled as she realized that none of the answers would be to her liking.

Before boarding the stage, Jenn looked up towards her lover's room. Hannah, robed now, stood at the window and waved. Contrary to her better angels, Jenn waved back.

"A lusty woman, eh?" Erin said, waiting to board as well.

"That she is," Jenn replied.

"Would ye like to see her again?"

"I really don't know," Jenn said, stealing one more glance at Hannah.

"She'll not let ye go easily, I wager."

"All aboard," the coachman shouted, cracking his whip in the air, as Gary emerged from the mansion. Tarleton circled his horse, reviewing the route with the coachman, before trotting off to lead his men. Rogers trotted his mount up next to the lieutenant, further establishing his martial bonafides.

Gary clambered up next to Erin, holding her hand, while Jenn sat opposite. Without the Wishingwell sisters, there was plenty of room. The coach jolted forward, bouncing its passengers off their seats. It was going to be a long day.

Once the pace settled into a rhythmic pounding, Jenn closed

her eyes but sleep wouldn't come despite her exhaustion from the previous two nights of lovemaking. "What's your plan?" she asked Gary who stared out the window while Erin dozed.

"Plan?"

"To get your Watch back."

"We'll need to get into New York first."

"The city ferry docks right outside the Star," Erin said, obviously more alert than she looked.

"Will Tarleton let you go?" Jenn asked.

"We'll need to think of a good reason," Gary replied.

"We can tell him we're going to visit my cousin, Hercules Mulligan," Erin added "His tailor shop is on Wall Street. He suits many of the fine gentlemen of the city."

"Your cousin?" Gary asked. "I thought Hercules was Black."

"Black? Are ye daft?" Erin corkscrewed her face in disbelief.

"That's only in *Hamilton*, the play," Jenn laughed.

"My cousin was Black in a play?"

"Never mind," Gary said. "Can Hercules get us into Washington's headquarters?"

"You're going too fast," Jenn said. "Why would Tarleton let you out of his sight? He still doesn't trust you."

"We'll promise to bring the good lieutenant news from the city," Erin said. "News that he might bring to General Howe."

The next three hours bumped along uneventfully. The King's Highway grew wider, although not much smoother, as they left the New Jersey wilderness. They stopped briefly in New Brunswick, a bustling port on the Raritan River. Several copies of the Declaration of Independence, which had been read on the village green on July 9, were still tacked to the wall of the Indian Queen tavern. Gary took one down and stuffed it in his pack. "A souvenir," he said.

Jenn was more interested in the postings concerning Blacks. A notice of an upcoming sermon from an abolitionist Quaker minister was displayed next to bounties for the capture of runaway slaves. How could Americans fight for liberty *and* own slaves?

After a short ferry across the river, the stage set out for Perth Amboy. The travelers kept the windows open but still baked in the summer sun. Robert Rogers slowed his mount to drift back to the stage, making sure to tip his cap to Jenn before galloping off again. Tarleton remained on the point, keeping on the lookout for a rebel ambush.

"A bit different than your time?" Erin asked Jenn.

"Not as much as you think," she replied, smiling. "Traffic on the Jersey Turnpike is still backed up on the weekends even in the twenty-first century."

"Tell me more about women - in the twenty-first century," Erin pressed. "How do they dress?"

"Any way they want to," Jenn said, taking off her lace cap.

"Can they go uncapped in public?" Erin asked.

Gary chuckled as Jenn replied. "Women can choose to wear a hat - and many do - but no one is required to wear one."

"And skirts can be shorter, a lot shorter," Gary said.

"Women can show their ankles?" Erin asked, her mouth gaping wide.

"Their ankles?" Gary laughed heartily. "Skirts come all the way up to here," he added, pointing to the top of his thigh. Tapping his navel, he added, "And tops can be slit open down to here."

"No!" Erin was even more gobsmacked. "Have they no shame."

The trio remained quiet as the stage rolled on to another ferry to cross the Arthur Kill to reach Staten Island. "Three hours till we reach the Blazing Star," the driver announced as he snapped the reins to get the horses going.

Just past the village of Tottenville, the road grew more crowded with sweaty pedestrians, galloping horsemen and lumbering farm wagons. No surprise since the vast might of the British armada slowly came into view. Row upon row of white tents lined the fields. Red-coated soldiers drilled in formation. Sure-footed mules lugged cannons towards the coast. Finally, as the stage approached its destination, the masts of hundreds of ships sprouted skyward from the Lower Bay of the port of New York.

"Looks like all of London sailed here," Erin said, eyes glued to the British war machine. "How will we ever win?" she added, shifting her gaze to her husband.

"George Washington," Gary answered. "He single-handedly kept the Continental Army together and the Continental Congress in line. Without him, we'd still be singing *God Save the King*."

"I don't know," Erin said, shaking her head. "I think I'd rather skip the war and live in ye time."

"I'm sure you would," Gary replied, his expression showing more concern than his words. "But no one can go forward in time - only backwards."

"That doesn't seem fair," Erin said.

"It's the science," Jenn explained. "The calculations can re-trace your gene tree but can't project it. There are simply too many variables to compute - even for the largest server farms."

"Gene trees? Server farms?" Erin asked. "Who will tend them? Slaves?"

"No slaves," Jenn answered before realizing she had lost her audience.

"So I could go back to me great-grandma's time and save her from the British?" Erin asked, moving on, perhaps not as lost as Jenn thought.

"Well, that's complicated," Gary stepped in. "A time traveler can basically observe events, but not change them."

"It's the Novikov self-consistency principle," Jenn said, hoping to help Gary by dissuading Erin from pursuing the subject any further.

"That sounds about as foolish as freezing my cunny wearing a short skirt on a cold day," Erin replied with a sly grin.

"The grandfather paradox might be easier to explain," Gary said. "If you traveled back in time and killed one of your grandparents, then you couldn't be born."

"Therefore it could never happen," Jenn concluded, folding her hands in her lap.

The stage slowed as the Blazing Star, a two story clapboard structure fronted by a broad veranda, came into view. Candles burned in every window although the sun had not dipped completely out of sight. The rapid-fire twang of a fiddle bade them welcome. Jenn was last out of the stage, swiveling her gaze to search for the mysterious Chinaman.

CHAPTER 53

Jenn lingered over her tea and cherry pie as Gary and Erin excused themselves early from supper. Like newlyweds on their honeymoon, she thought. Gary appeared to have adjusted to life as a youthful colonial gentleman quite well. Would he even want to return to the twenty-first century? She wouldn't be the one to push him - or tattle if they both managed to return. What happens in 1776 stays in 1776.

What about Erin? Did she know that she was married to a seventy-year old grandfather? Just as well she couldn't travel forward in time.

Jenn realized she was ahead of herself. They both needed a Watch to return to the twenty-first century. Currently, they didn't have one and didn't even know if Gary's still existed. On the other hand, the mysterious Chinaman had to have a Watch to travel here carrying Ding's finger.

How did he get it? The Watch not the finger. She didn't think the Chinese were even close to completing their time travel software. Ding couldn't really help much - even if they cut off all his fingers.

"You look lonely, Mistress Tryon," Robert Rogers said as he slid next to her.

"Just thinking."

"I'm sure you're looking forward to seeing your father again. How long has it been?"

"Years."

"Lieutenant Tarleton sent a fast rider up ahead to tell him of your pending arrival." Rogers pushed a little closer, the smell of horse wafting over Jenn.

"He did? That was thoughtful of him." Jenn wanted to dive into her pie and disappear.

"He was surprised you didn't write yourself."

"I wanted to surprise my father," she said, shifting a few feet away from the major.

"Of course. Well, I'm sure he will be quite pleased to see you."

"As I am him."

"Does he know of your gay-ness, may I ask?" Rogers said, leaning towards her.

"My what?"

"That you prefer women to men for...companionship."

"He knows I have shown little interest in acquiring a husband."

"Not quite the same though, particularly at your age."

"You are being quite forward, Major Rogers," Jenn replied, more displeased with the reference to her age than her sexual preference.

"I was just thinking...if you were in need of practice...with a man, I mean ...I might volunteer."

"I'll keep that in mind."

"With proper opportunity..." he added, reaching for her thigh with a devilish gleam in his eye "...I might even be able to persuade you ..."

"Not a chance, Major." She slapped his hand away before it

got close.

"Well then, I'll take my leave." Rogers stood and doffed his hat.

"I'll see you in the morning."

"Probably not, Mistress. I'll be leaving before dawn to seek Major General Howe and reclaim my commission in his Army."

When would Tarleton receive a return message from Governor Tryon? Jenn didn't want to be around to find out. Alone now in the tap room, Jenn nervously sipped her tea until the hands on the tall case clock showed eleven-thirty.

She slipped outside and wandered down to the ferry landing, lit only by the tavern torchlights and the moon. Across the Narrows, the Brooklyn shore was pitch black. It was little more than a Dutch farming community in this time. She looked for the Statue of Liberty and the Verrazano Bridge, but of course they weren't built yet.

"Mistress Tryon," a reedy voice called from behind her. "So glad you could come."

Jenn turned slowly to face a figure swathed in black from hooded head to slippered toes. She squeezed her knees together to stop from pissing herself as he pranced towards her. "Shall we walk?" he asked, taking the lead.

He stopped under the canopy of a spreading oak, its leaves blocking the moonlight. His eyes, a sapphire blue, projected menace, like Star Wars laser swords. "You almost eluded me," he said. "I salute you."

"Who are you? Jenn asked.

The Chinaman bowed. "Forgive my impoliteness. I am Colonel Lai Ming of the Ministry of State Security of the People's Republic of China."

"How did you find me?"

"Your arrest, or rather your vicious assault of the Committee of Safety man, was reported in the tabloids of the day, the *Gazette* I believe. What other woman than Jennifer Tryon could kick like that?"

"I didn't realize I was so famous."

"Your escape, along with Major Rogers, was also reported."

Jenn's eyes drifted to the bulky, rubberized Watch on Lai's left wrist. "How did you get here?"

He held up the Watch. "I have one for you as well...providing you cooperate."

Jenn said nothing, biting her lip, forcing herself to maintain a stoic facade even though she was boiling underneath.

"What do you want me to do?" she asked at last.

"Ensure that Mr. Johnson never returns to the twenty-first century."

"Destroy his Watch?"

"If it is still operational - yes."

"And if it's not?"

"Then he will be free to live out his days in colonial America."

"Why do you care if Gary returns to 2026?" she asked.

"We do not want any witnesses to surface."

"Witness to what?"

"You will see. Suffice it to say, my actions here will reverberate through the centuries. China, the country of your ancestors, will assume its rightful position as the dominant world power by 2026. America, if it exists at all, will be in no position to challenge our superiority." Spittle leaked from Lai's thin lips as his patriotic fervor bubbled over.

"But a time traveler can't change history - only observe it," Jenn said.

"I beg to differ."

A lantern flickered at the tavern door. It appeared to be growing closer. "Who's out there?" the night watchman called out.

"Don't disappoint me," Lai said, gripping Jenn's wrist in a crocodile grip. "The consequences will be dire."

"How can I find you?" Jenn asked, her eyes flicking between Lai and the approaching light. Her boil had metastasized into a full body cancer.

She now faced a life or death mission – not just for herself but for the free world. Lai or Gary? The choice was easy. She knew how totalitarian the Chinese were. If they became the dominant power in the twenty-first century, human rights around the globe would suffer, the complete opposite of all she hoped to accomplish with Tryon Time. She would have to stop Lai. And count on Gary – bumbling, love-sotted Gary - to get her home someday.

"I'll find you," Lai whispered before disappearing into the darkness like a puff of smoke.

"Mistress Tryon, what in damnation are you doing out at this hour?" the Watchman asked, illuminating Jenn's face with his torch.

"Taking the night air."

"Now why would you be doing that?" The Watchman asked. "The night airs ain't nothing but trouble." He swept his torch towards the tavern and beckoned her to follow him.

CHAPTER 54

Gary woke at dawn to the sounds of commotion in the tap room shortly followed by the pounding of boots climbing the tavern steps. Since it was Sunday, he was not expecting any early morning military activities. Erin rolled over, her sinewy shoulder peeking above the coverlet. He stroked her hair as her body tensed in fear.

He held a finger to his lips to shush her. The boots reached their door - but kept on going - the snap of leather on the wood floor receding. Erin relaxed, pulling the pillow over her head to block the light.

Gary rose, stepping into his breeches. Cautiously, he parted the shade, expecting to see a mounted troop of redcoats in the courtyard, but it was deserted, save for two sentries and Tarleton's mount, tethered to the rail. A cloud of dust from a vanishing horseman rose from the road. He opened the door and peered down the hall.

The lieutenant, waving a parchment in one hand like the Holy Grail, rapped on Jenn's door with the other. "Mistress...Tryon," he boomed. Silence. Tarleton rapped again, then kicked the door open. "Your charade is..." he shouted, but could not complete the sentence.

A sneakered foot lashed out from inside the room catching him flush in the stomach. He doubled over, breath whooshing from his lungs like a deflating balloon. Jenn, fully dressed, stepped from the shadow, chopping down on Tarleton's neck. He sank to his knees, then toppled face forward. Jenn looked down the hall, eyeing Gary with relief. "Help me," she mouthed, tugging the body into her room.

"He's dead," Gary said, rushing to her side, still not fully comprehending what had happened.

"No. But he'll be out cold for a good while." Jenn grabbed Tarleton by the boots, motioning for Gary to man the other side. Together, they dragged the body into the room and closed the door.

Jenn pulled the parchment from Tarleton's clenched fist and unrolled it, nodding her head as she read. "Tarleton wrote ahead to Governor Tryon who informed him that his daughter died in London in April."

"Didn't you know that?"

Jenn shrugged. "It wasn't exactly posted on X."

"Since you vouched for us..." Gary said, the wheels spinning in his brain.

"...we're all in trouble," Jenn finished his sentence. "We need to leave immediately."

Wearing only her night shift, Erin opened the door and peered inside. "What...?"

"Close the door before anyone sees you," Gary said, kneeling down, relieved to feel Tarleton's beating pulse. He peeled off the lieutenant's scarlet jacket. "Let's put him in bed," he said, looking up at the two women. "It may buy us some time if people think..."

"...he slept with me?" Jenn asked, crinkling her nose in disgust.

Erin nodded as she grabbed an ankle. They struggled, almost impaling Tarleton on his sword, before finally succeeded in laying him flat in bed. Erin unbuttoned the Lieutenant's shirt, then reached for his flies. "A rather wee pintle," she noted with a giggle as she pulled down his breeches, breaking the tension in the room. Gary quickly covered him with the sheet.

Jenn reached into her satchel, pulling out the envelope of opium that Hannah had given her, and smeared it on Tarleton's lip. "Let him explain that."

"We need to get to the ferry before he wakes up," Gary said.

They reconvened, fully packed, outside Gary's room in less than five minutes. He had never seen Erin dress so quickly.

Unfortunately, Sergeant Thatcher and the two sentries were waiting at the bottom of the stairs. "And where might you be going?" he asked.

"To the ferry. I believe it departs at seven," Gary replied, bluffing. The ferry might not even run at all on Sunday but he was not going to quibble over details right now.

Thatcher looked confused, his eyes darting up the steps and then back down to Jenn. "Your lieutenant is in my room," she said. "Asleep."

"In your room?" Thatcher asked, an expression of disbelief captivating his face.

"He came to me in the middle of the night," Jenn replied, holding her head up defiantly. "Drunk and who knows what else. My father will not be pleased."

"Bloody hell." Thatcher pushed past Jenn and stormed upstairs.

Gary led Erin and Jenn into the courtyard. "The lieutenant will settle our bill when he awakes," he said to the tavern master, watching the scene unfold in horror.

Gary walked purposely down the gentle slope towards the landing, forcing Jenn and Erin to slow as well. No one looked back.

Morning fog cloaked the Narrows in a gray shawl, while a ragged surf nipped at the shore. A skiff, a flat-bottom ferry and a single mast schooner lay at anchor. The ferryman's hut, a squat stone structure with a crudely fenced vegetable garden out front, was dark with the shades drawn. A shaggy goat chomped on the grass outside its perimeter, occasionally looking up to inspect the visitors.

Gary was about to ring the ferry bell, but Erin stopped him. "Let me try," she said, removing her cap as well as the scarf that covered her bodice. She mussed her hair as she approached the ferryman's gate which swung open at her touch. She knocked on the door and waited.

"Stop yer hammerin'," a raspy voice with a thick brogue hacked from inside. A shade parted displaying the brawny torso of the ferryman. "What ye want at this ungodly hour on the Sabbath?" he asked, his tone noticeably softer at the sight of Erin.

"We need ye help," she said.

The door opened and the ferryman stepped outside, pulling a louse from his curly head and tossing it into his garden. He looked over the three travelers, then scanned the sky and the treetops. "Ye won't be going far today," he said at last. "There's nary a hint of breeze."

"County Cork?" Erin asked.

"Aye."

"County Donegal," she said curtseying. "I promised me mum I'd visit her relations in York City."

"Can ye wait till the wind picks up?"

Erin shook her head, stealing a glance at the tavern, still asleep from all appearances.

"Yer not running away from trouble, are ye?"

She stared silently at the riverbank.

"The lobsterbacks?" he asked. She nodded.

"They're scum," he said, spitting into the dirt. "No respect for women or property."

"Can you take us to Brooklyn?" Gary asked, stepping to Erin's side.

The ferryman eyed the Narrows as if counting the waves that lapped the rocky beach. "Aye, but I'll need some help at the oars."

"They're coming now," Jenn said, pointing up the bank. Sergeant Thatcher, joined by a half dozen dragoons, had started towards them.

"We'd best be leaving smartly then," the ferryman said, leading the way towards the boats.

Gary and Jenn helped launch the skiff while Jenn stowed their belongings. Thatcher shook his fist from the bank as they drifted away from shore.

"Will they come after us?" Erin asked.

"Not likely, lass. Brooklyn is foreign territory. At least right now."

CHAPTER 55

The voyage across the Narrows took over two hours, taxing the endurance of Gary and Jenn who had alternated at one oar while the ferryman effortlessly handled the other. The tide was out so they clambered from the skiff into the mud thirty yards from shore. Gary offered a fistful of coins but the ferryman shook his head, tilting towards Erin. "Ye keep the *cailin* safe now."

"On my life," Gary vowed.

"And you?" Jenn asked the ferryman.

"My sons will notice I'm missing and come fetch me soon enough," he replied, glancing back across the Narrows. "Ye be off now."

The threesome climbed up the bank to the Shore Road, empty on a Sabbath morning, and trekked uphill towards the Gowanus Heights. From the ridgeline, visible in the distance, it would be only a few miles downhill to the flat boat ferry to cross the East River to Manhattan Island.

Gary reminisced as they walked. He had grown up nearby, played Little League in a park fronting the water, watched the "submarine races" with his eager high school girlfriend from the back seat of his rusty Chevy Malibu.

Was Brooklyn in his past...or his future? He looked at the heavens. The fog had lifted, not a cloud in sight. Erin held his hand as they walked. She was the epitome of contrasts: fiery red hair and pale complexion; street smart but little formal education; devoted mother and indefatigable lover. Where did she fit in his timeline? A weeklong fling or a lifelong romance?

He stepped smartly over a heaping pile of horse dung - no pain in his left knee. No doctor appointments on the calendar either. Back home in 2026, his buddies marked time by their visits to the orthopedist, cardiologist, ophthalmologist, dermatologist, endocrinologist, oncologist. The list was endless, the appointments both terrifying and mind-numbing.

"We should have killed Tarleton when we had the chance," Erin said, breaking his reverie. Gary had told her about Tarleton's butchery later in the war. "Think of how many of our boys' lives we could have saved," she added.

"We couldn't murder Tarleton in 1776," he replied, although the thought had crossed his mind. "Think how many lives, multiplied over generations, would have changed. Most for better, but some for worse no doubt. That's why time travel has rules."

"Ye sound like a schoolmaster," she replied, ducking her head, muttering to herself as she trudged forward. "Who would have stopped us anyway?"

Gary looked to Jenn for assistance, but she appeared lost in her own private space, frequently spinning her head as if she suspected they were being followed. By whom, he wondered, glancing back down the empty road.

"I've nay heard of a woman striking like ye did," Erin said, wiping the perspiration from her eyes when they stopped under a shade tree. "Gary said ye were as quick as a cat."

Jenn sipped from her water bottle, her taut biceps glistening with sweat. "Tarleton's got to admit to the opium or the fact that he was beaten up by a woman," she said, obviously savoring the lieutenant's conundrum.

The grunts of hard labor greeted them at the ridgeline. White and black men, most bare-chested, a handful in uniform, broiled in the July sun building the Continental Army's defenses against the expected British assault. Some chopped brush, assembling the debris into fascines and clearing lanes for musket fire. Others towed wagons of felled timber, lashing the harnesses across their shoulders, manpower replacing horses which were scarce and expensive to feed. Gary could see the outline of a diamond-shaped bulwark guarding the hilltop. A third regiment dug a latrine trench on the far side of its walls.

"A fine sight," Erin said. Gary wasn't sure if she meant the half-built fort or the half-dressed men.

"Who goes there?" a sentry in an orange jacket asked, pointing his bayonet at the threesome.

"Gary Johnson from Connecticut. Returning home with my wife and... cousin," he said, surprised by the challenge.

"Connecticut eh? Quite a long way from here. What's your business in Brooklyn?"

"None, sir. We are simply passing through on our way home from Philadelphia."

"Passing through?" the sentry asked, circling them suspiciously. "Why are you on this side of the Narrows then? You should be traveling in the Jerseys and crossing the Hudson further north."

"We're going to visit my cousin, Hercules Mulligan. He has a tailor shop just off Broadway," Erin said, reaching into her pack, withdrawing a card printed in a vivid swirling script on stout paper stock. "His particulars."

Gary exchanged a surreptitious glance with Jenn, encouraging her to stay silent, while the sentry inspected the card. "I'll be in need of a new suit after this journey," he added, taking off his jacket in an effort to distract the sentry.

"Why would you be venturing abroad to visit your cousin in the middle of a war?" the sentry pressed.

"I went to Philadelphia to obtain a Letter of Marque," Gary said.

"And where is that letter?"

"The congress had more important business to attend to, so my letter has been delayed," Gary said, backtracking. "However, Congressman Sherman assured me it will be forthcoming shortly."

"And you, mistress," the sentry looked towards Jenn. "Why are you traveling unaccompanied?"

"Unaccompanied by a husband, you mean?" Jenn asked.

By now, three more orange-coated privates had arrived, training their muskets on Gary. The air crackled with tension.

"The Declaration of Independence?" Gary asked. "Have you men read it?"

"General Washington read it to the troops on the common last week," the first sentry said. "A fine document."

"I've got a copy in my pack. I'm to bring it back to Connecticut to share with my friends," Gary said.

"So you're not a Tory then?" a second sentry asked.

"Why would you believe him, turd brain?" a third sentry asked.

"I'm sorry, sir, but we're going to have to detain you until we can verify your particulars," the first sentry said, shepherding Gary, Erin and Jenn close together. "The British are swarming these heights with spies."

CHAPTER 56

The orange coats frog-marched Gary, Erin and Jenn into Fort Box, the stronghold already named for a major in the Massachusetts line although not yet completed. To Gary's consternation, Jenn checked for pursuit one last time before they entered. Her shoulders appeared to slump with relief as the gate closed behind them.

Fort Box's palisades, barely waist height at this point, provided little relief from the baking sunlight. A nest of boulders, too big to move, lodged near the center of the enclosure. A half dozen Continentals appeared to be digging a well behind it. Drenched with sweat, Gary hoped they would finish soon and be generous with its output.

The threesome sat on the rocks watching the soldiers scurry like ants around the perimeter, racing to complete the fortifications before the mighty British Army could attack. No one seemed to pay them much attention.

From their high perch, Gary looked down on the Narrows, the Upper Bay and the lower tip of Manhattan. The Hudson and

East Rivers snaked around the island. Gary imagined the daunting task George Washington faced trying to defend the city without a navy of his own.

"What will happen here in the War?" Erin asked, fluttering a fan in front of her face in a barely successful effort to create a breeze.

"The Battle of Brooklyn, August 1776," Jenn replied, a bit fuzzy on the details. "A major defeat for our side."

"Washington was badly out-flanked by the British, but he managed to evacuate his entire army in the dead of night," Gary added. "If not, the war would have ended right then."

"George Washington saved the day. As he would again and again over the next twenty years," Jenn said, staring wistfully out to sea. "Commander-in-chief of the Continental Army and then President of the United States of America."

"President? If Washington commanded the army, why didn't he become King?" Erin asked. "Who could've stopped him?"

"Good questions," Gary said. "Washington stopped himself. He retired to Mount Vernon. Twice actually – after the Revolution and then after his second term as President."

"Washington believed in democracy, the will of the people," Jenn said. "In our time, he's still revered as the Father of our Country,"

"Foolish man, if you ask me," Erin said. Suddenly, smiling as if the future was too much to contemplate, she jumped down from the rock and kicked her right foot into the air. "Teach me how you do it?" she asked Jenn.

Jenn rose slowly, stretching her arms over head, looking to Gary for approval. When he nodded, she extended her right arm until it was shoulder height parallel to the ground, then kicked her foot up to touch her hand. Five reps. Slow and steady. She took a deep breath and repeated the exercise with her other foot.

"That's all there's to it?" Erin asked.

"Go ahead. Give it a try," Jenn said, barely concealing a smile.

Erin hitched up her skirt and tried to kick, but her leg faltered just past knee high. She sprawled backwards, landing smack on her bum. She scrambled up, her lips set in determination. Jenn demonstrated her kick again, faster this time, more violent. Erin kicked, her toes only reaching her waist, but she managed to stay upright. Gary clapped, trying to be supportive, but his action only drew an angry glance.

Jenn positioned herself behind Erin, leaning her shoulder into her. "More knee flex this time."

Three sweat-drenched, bare-chested soldiers wandered over to watch the women. "I love a good catfight," a baby-faced private leered, swiping his raven-black locks from his eyes.

Jenn and Erin continued to practice, ignoring the men. "Shake your arse for us, lassie," the fattest one of the bunch, his hairy belly sloshing over his belt, guffawed. "I'll wager on the wench with the bigger titties," the third private, a jagged scar slicing across his stubbled, unshaven cheek, said. He waved a handful of bills in Erin's direction.

"Why don't you men go back to work?" Gary asked, stepping in front of the women.

"We're just having fun," Scarface said, shoving Gary away. His two compatriots surrounded Gary. Baby Face pulled a knife from his belt.

"Slow down, gentlemen," Jenn said, positioning herself at Gary's side. "If you want some fun, I'll give you all the fun you can handle."

"Lift your skirt lassie," Fat Man replied, bucking his hips at Jenn.

"Not that kind of fun," Jenn said, flexing her fingers. "I'll fight all three of you hand-to-hand, man-to-man."

"Fight? The three of us? You're a feeee-male," Scarface drew out the word to the delight of his pals. "Why would we fight you? Unless of course you let us take turns after we thrash you."

"Even better than that," Jenn said, unfastening her gold earring. "If you thrash me, this is yours."

"For the sake of the devil," Scarface whistled, admiring the jewelry.

One against three? Gary calculated the odds were heavily in Jenn's favor. "If she wins, you walk us out of here," he announced, hoping Jenn got the message that she shouldn't kill, or even maim, her opponents.

"You're spies," Baby Face said.

"We are not spies," Gary said. "We're just trying to go home to Connecticut. Do you think we'd be left alone like this if we were spies?"

"Connecticut? We're in the 19th Connecticut," Fat Man declared. "From New Haven."

"Yale College. Connecticut Hall. I've been there," Gary said, quite truthfully. The soldiers' frosty scowls began to melt.

"We're not college men," Scarface said, grinning at his friends. "But our captain is a Yale man, I believe."

"Nathaniel Hale," Baby Face added. "A most righteous man, if I do say so myself."

"Can you take us to him?" Gary asked.

The three soldiers shuffled in place for a long second, discreetly ogling Jenn and Erin, then glancing at each other, sharing their disappointment that there would be no orgy today at Fort Box.

"Hale's over by the well," Fat Man said.

CHAPTER 57

Although Jenn was not attracted to men, she had to admire Captain Nathaniel Hale. Standing a full head taller than most, tawny hair braided into a ponytail that bisected his broad shoulders, aristocratic cheekbones and pox-free complexion, he cut a handsome figure, particularly shirtless with an ax in hand. His statue outside CIA headquarters in Langley, Virginia barely did him justice, she thought, remembering a job interview there during her senior year at Harvard.

"A pleasure to meet you, sir," she said, curtseying after Fat Man's brief introduction.

"And you, Mistress..." he replied, toweling the sweaty sheen from his chest before donning a white linen shirt.

"...Coldstream," she said. It was her grandmother's maiden name, an alias she had used in the twenty-first century for incognito registration on porn websites. Gary nodded, almost too vigorously, clearly relieved that she had ditched the Tryon moniker.

Hale barely heard her, his attention instead diverted to Erin. "Captain Nathan Hale, at your service," he said, bowing low in her direction.

"Erin Duffy," she replied instinctively, blushing scarlet before correcting herself. "Mrs. Gary Johnson."

"I'm Mr. Johnson," Gary said. "From Connecticut."

"So, I've heard," Hale replied. "You're leading these women home, I gather. After a visit to a cousin in New York?"

"Yes, sir."

"There appears to be some question as to the veracity of your story."

"I've been to your schoolhouse in New London, close to the harbor," Gary said. "And I have visited your family farm in Coventry."

"You know my father?" Hale put on his weathered jacket, a dull brown, and tricorn, marked with a simple yellow feather signifying his rank.

"Deacon Hale, a good man, although we're not well-acquainted," Gary replied. "I am aware, however, of the classes you offered for young ladies at the Union School. The first of their kind in our colony."

Jenn marveled at Gary's bullshit. How did he know anything about the Union School in New London, Connecticut in the eighteenth century?

"Yes, well, the classes were in honor of my mother..."

"Elizabeth," Gary interrupted.

Enough already, Jenn thought, although her respect for Gary continued to grow.

"All right, Mr. Johnson," Hale said. "I accept your bonafides as a Connecticut man."

Gary beamed at Erin, although Jenn swore his "wife's" gaze leaned more towards Captain Hale than her "husband."

"Why have you not enlisted in our Glorious Cause?" Hale asked, snapping Gary back down to earth. "You certainly appear to be an able-bodied young man."

Erin doused a smile as she waited for Gary's answer. "Dear, you should tell the Captain of your business dealings in

Philadelphia."

"There is no business more important than driving the British back into the sea," Hale said, fixing his saber securely around his waist.

"Here, here," Jennifer added. She furtively glanced around the fort, relieved to see no sign of Lai.

Hale checked the timepiece in his jacket pocket. "We could use another hand digging this well, Mr. Johnson. If you would be inclined to help, I could arrange for you, your wife and Mistress Coldstream to ferry back to Manhattan under my guard at the end of the day."

"Of course," Gary sputtered.

Hale summoned his orderly. "Put Mr. Johnson to work with Sergeant Hempstead's team. And arrange a canopy so the ladies can have some shade. I'll look in on them as soon as I can."

"I guess we'll have to go sit in the shade," Jenn said, sharing a furtive smile with Erin.

True to his word, Captain Hale supervised his men for an hour before meandering over to their oasis, a sail strung out over four fence posts. "Your husband appears to be struggling with his shovel," he said to Erin.

"He's a merchant, not a laborer," she replied. "But his heart is in the right place."

"And you? The calluses on your hands suggest you have not shied away from labor - unusual for the wife of a prosperous merchant."

Erin clasped her hands in her lap. "I do what is needed," she said, squirming in her seat atop a hogshead.

"Tell us about yourself, Captain Hale," Jenn asked, coming to the rescue. "How did you come to be in command of such a fine group of men?"

Hale laughed. "Fine men? Surely you jest. They are a dog's stew of wastrels and scoundrels. I had to pay each one to enlist."

"Me first husband died on Bunker Hill," Erin said, looking squarely at the captain. "He was neither a wastrel nor a scoundrel."

Hale's head snapped, as if he had been slapped. "My sincere apologies, Mrs. Johnson. The first men to join the fight were indeed fine men and true patriots. Three of my brothers enlisted in April '75, the day after the battles at Lexington and Concord. But, it has been much more difficult attracting recruits as the war progresses."

"Will we win?" Erin asked, apparently skeptical of the answer provided by Jenn and Gary just an hour earlier. "We have seen the might of the British Empire on our travels through Jersey. Will ye fort, ye army, be enough to stop the redcoats?"

"Upon my honor," Hale replied, straightening to stand at attention. "We will do all that is necessary to achieve victory, or die most valiantly in the struggle."

"And ye wives and children and parents will suffer the consequences," Erin said, standing now, her voice just audible.

"It's too glorious a day to dwell on such morbid thoughts," Hale said. "Our cause is righteous. Our liberty is precious. God in heaven will look favorably upon our endeavors."

"Amen," Jenn added. Hale was right in the long term. Would he survive the battle? The war? She couldn't remember.

"Mrs. Johnson, perhaps you would like to tour the redoubt with me?" the captain asked, gesturing towards the ramparts rising to face the Shore Road. "You will see for yourself the commanding position we hold. The redcoats would be foolhardy to attack here."

"Yes, I would," Erin replied. "Can Mistress Coldstream join us as well?"

"No thank you." Jenn felt safer in the center of the fort, protected from Colonel Lai.

"As you wish," Hale said without any trace of disappointment.

Jenn watched them walk away, an appropriate distance apart, but chatting amiably nevertheless. Gary put down his shovel, his gaze following them as well. He had to realize his relationship with Erin was doomed, didn't he?

Was Gary doomed too? Colonel Lai had a plan and Gary Johnson was evidently in its way. What heinous act would Lai commit to change history?

Assassinate George Washington. The answer had lodged in the back of Jenn's brain since their meeting last night. Washington's elimination would virtually insure that the American republic would be stillborn.

Could Lai change history? Time travel theory said no, but they were the first travelers, so who really knew. And weren't scientific theories made to be tested anyway?

CHAPTER 58

Salty sweat stinged Gary's eyes, a blister in his right palm popped cherry red, and Erin had just walked off with the dashing Captain Hale. Fortunately, the day had the distinct possibility of improving from here.

If he finished his shift at the well, Hale would take them to New York. If Gary could get into the city, he might be able to get to Washington's headquarters, where the Philadelphia Committee of Safety had supposedly shipped his Watch. If his Watch was there, if it still worked, and if he could negotiate its return, he could travel back to the twenty-first century immediately. Lots of ifs and nagging questions.

A slate gray cloud slid across the sky, bringing modest relief from the fulgent sun. But, it also fostered turbulent thoughts. What if his Watch had been destroyed? Would he be stranded in the eighteenth century for the rest of his life? Would that be so bad?

He missed Lucie - and his family - but he certainly didn't miss being seventy years old. Whenever he returned home, he'd be lucky to live ten more years, fifteen on the outside, hobbled by arthritis and who knew what other ailments. If he stayed here in 1776, he could capitalize on his knowledge of the future to make a fortune. Buy land, government bonds, fine jewelry. He knew for certain that prices would rise as soon as the Revolutionary War ended.

He would become wealthy. Wealthy young man. Had a nice ring to it. And he could be with Erin.

Gary realized he was way ahead of himself. He would never be stranded in colonial America. Molly and the TimeR team were probably building another Watch right now. Someone would come and fetch him.

Instinctively, he checked the latch on his backpack. The documents he would bring back to the twenty-first century - the Declaration of Independence, Button Gwinnett's signature, maybe a personal note from Nathan Hale or even George Washington - would secure his family's financial future. But, his nights with Erin would have to end.

"Struggling a bit, Mr. Johnson?" asked Sergeant Hempstead, a cowbell of a man topped by a thatch of curly hair.

"I'll be OK," Gary replied.

"OK? Can't say I've heard that expression before."

"Never mind. I just needed a breath. I'll be fine now."

"Back to work then."

Gary put his head down and dug for another hour, the effort numbing his mind to the decisions ahead. Erin's laugh snapped him from his crucible. She was back under the canopy, chatting with Captain Hale.

Erin also had to be pondering her future, he realized, with or without him. If he left, Nathan Hale would certainly appear to be an appealing pinch-hitter, maybe much more.

Unfortunately, Hale was destined to die in September 1776. The idealistic young captain would volunteer to become America's first spy; however his mission on Long Island would last less than a week before he was captured and hanged by the British from an oak tree on the east side of Manhattan. His last words, "I regret that I have but one life to lose for my country," would resonate for centuries, but would provide little comfort to Erin.

Stripping off his shirt, Hale joined his men for the final hour of hard labor before ordering the company's drummer boy to beat a retreat, signaling an end to the day's labor. "Huzzah, Mr. Johnson," he said, slapping Gary's back, nearly knocking him over. "You've earned your passage to Manhattan."

The surrounding treetops diffused the sun's fading rays like a prism as the 19th Connecticut, plus its three visitors, tramped out of Fort Box. The march to the ferry was largely downhill, much to Gary's relief, on a well-worn Indian path, passing through forest, field and meadow.

"What did you and Captain Hale talk about?" he asked Erin. The soldiers formed a loose cordon, but didn't appear to be paying them much attention.

"He was curious about Philadelphia and the Congress," she said, slowing down her gait so Gary could keep pace. "He wondered if I knew Franklin, Adams or Jefferson."

"And?"

"I told him the truth," she said, head defiantly upright. "I knew Doctor Franklin quite well, the others only in passing."

Gary thought about pressing her relationship with the esteemed, if elderly, Doctor, but decided otherwise. "Did Hale have any news from Connecticut?"

Erin shook her head. "He left home almost a year ago to join the army and only returned for a brief Christmas visit. His family are true patriots."

"I'm sure his parents are proud of their sons," Gary answered, wondering how he and Lucie would feel if Remy, or Maribel for that matter, went off to war. Proud of their service, but afraid for their safety, he decided.

"And how did ye fare with the shovel?" she asked. "Ye looked quite swell at it."

"I'm exhausted."

"Not too worn out, I trust," she whispered, her ruby lips slyly curling.

Gary winced as Erin's verbal needle struck home. "Don't you worry," he laughed. "I have plenty of gas left in the tank." He was a young man for at least one more night. Erin looked thoroughly confused, but he marched along with a bit more zest in his step.

The column halted at the edge of the tree line, a flat, grassy field separating them from the hamlet of Brooklyn, comprising a dozen clapboard houses gathered around an intersection of two trails. Several men peeled off into the trees while others rested on a fallen tree limb, slurping rum, ale or cider from their canteens. No one dared drink water after a vicious bout of diarrhea had swept through camp last month.

Scarface pulled a gray ball from his pack. "A quick game of rounders?" he asked Captain Hale.

"It's called baseball here in America," Fat Man said, holding a flat bat, like Gary had seen at a cricket match in England. Scarface tossed his ball to Baby Face who caught it cleanly with one hand. Five soldiers, then ten, then twenty, gathered round, clamoring for a throw. No one had a glove.

Captain Hale checked the sky, blue morphing to gray, but no sign of rain. "Excellent idea," he said, reaching for the bat. "Anyone who needs to return to New York immediately can go with Sergeant Hempstead."

Gary leaned towards the Sergeant, but stopped when he saw Erin's frown. "I'll play," he said, handing his precious backpack to a now beaming Erin for safekeeping. Jenn said nothing, her tightly pressed lips conveying her displeasure, as she again wheeled 360 degrees to scan for pursuers.

Hale split the men into two teams of ten with Gary on the opposition. Scarface and Fat Man laid out the four bases, shirts weighted with stones. Erin and Jenn sat cross-legged in the grass near first base. A soldier, sporting a handlebar mustache, shared his flask of whiskey.

"Have you played before?" Scarface asked Gary. When he

nodded, although failing to mention it had been over two hundred years in the future, Scarface pointed him to the open position at third base. Since it was his ball, Scarface was the first pitcher. He tossed it casually around the infield and the game was on.

Neither the day's hard labor nor the day's hard drinking had taken a toll on the men, who bobbed up and down in the field, maintaining a steady stream of chatter. Gary earned a huzzah by fielding a grounder cleanly then throwing across the diamond to beat the batter to first base. The recognition rose a notch when he backpedaled into the outfield to catch a pop up. Gary performed admirably at the plate as well, singling sharply to left field in his first at bat and hitting a deep fly in the second that was caught by the centerfielder.

When Scarface's arm gave out in the third, he motioned to Gary to relieve him. Limbering up, Gary remembered the last time he had pitched - in the driveway with Derek. He gripped the seams of the homespun ball, a tightly wound mass of stockings, as Fat Man stepped to the plate, swinging his bat menacingly.

Gary's first two pitches bounced well in front of the plate, earning catcalls from the bench. His third one started right down the middle, enticing Fat Man to swing, before the ball broke down and away. Strike one. Gary threw another darting curve with the same result: a mighty swoosh as Fat Man's bat hit nothing but air.

For his fifth pitch, Gary decided to change speeds, tossing a fastball, but Fat Man, wary of the curve, decided not to swing. Too bad the game had no called balls or strikes, Gary thought. Another curve, another Fat Man flail, the effort landing him flat on his butt to the derision of his teammates.

Hale, up next, nodded appreciatively, although Gary wasn't sure whether the captain was acknowledging his pitching or his wife, who had stood to watch. He was tempted to try a beanball to garner Hale's full attention, but decided against it. Erin was his, at least for tonight; he had nothing to gain by trying to embarrass the good captain.

If anything, the opposite was true. Gary ditched his curve

and threw a fastball, knee high, instead. Hale's biceps rippled as he swung, but he could only nick the ball. It dribbled weakly in front of home plate; he started to run towards first base.

"Foul ball," Gary called, waving Hale back into the batter's box. If Hale was the athlete the history books said he was, he would have his timing down for the next pitch. Gary set his hands and took a deep breath before launching another fastball down the middle.

Hale's eyes bulged with anticipation. The smack of his bat smashing the ball resonated as loudly as a musket blast. The ball arched over the left fielder's head, rolling through the meadow. Hale trotted around the bases, head down with humility, as the outfielders vainly searched the woods.

After ten minutes, Hale directed everyone into the trees. The ball was too valuable to lose. Baby Face's scream brought the men racing together. The ball was lying at his feet, but his face was fright white. "A witch threw it to me," he mumbled, stepping back as if the ball was radioactive.

"A witch?" Hale asked, trying to conceal a smirk as he nonchalantly picked up the ball. "On a broomstick?"

"No broomstick," Baby Face replied, still shaking. "But all wrapped in black robes."

Gary's brow furrowed. Dressed in black... like the Chinaman he thought he saw in the King's Arms?

Fat Man handed Baby Face his canteen when they returned to the ball field. Baby Face took a long slug, a ruddy color slowly returning to his cheeks.

"Ready to go, boys?" Jenn asked, her impatience obvious.

The Chinaman, that's who Jenn's been looking for, Gary realized. She was either collaborating with him, or running away from him. Either way, trouble loomed.

Captain Hale led his motley crew towards the ferry as the sun set over the still waters of the Upper Bay. A cooling breeze rippled the treetops. The soldiers shared their supper, hardtack and dried peas, with their three guests. Gary soaked up their camaraderie, holding Erin's hand as the street lamps of New York City finally came into sight.

CHAPTER 59

Erin shivered as the ferry approached Murray's Wharf on the east side of Manhattan Island. The sky was cloudless but drained of light except for the twinkle of distant stars. Gary put his jacket over her bare shoulders and wrapped his arms around her waist.

"Ye enjoyed the game, didn't ye?" she asked, leaning back into his embrace as the boat swayed with the current.

"I did."

"Ye appeared quite good at it."

"Thank you." He nuzzled her neck.

"It did appear that Captain Hale got the best of ye though."

"He did, but..."

"But ye allowed him to, didn't ye?" Erin wriggled around in his arms to face him.

"How did you know?"

"Ye face gave it away," she said softly before kissing him.

"We need Hale, so I thought..."

"Shush." She kissed him again, her lips lingering. They

broke off as Captain Hale approached.

"Well played today, Mr. Johnson," Hale said. "You've had some experience at baseball in Connecticut, I gather."

"A bit, yes."

"With what side, may I ask?"

"The Yankees, the Connecticut Yankees."

"Can't say I've heard of them. Do you have a captain?"

"Mr. Judge. Aaron Judge. One of the best … in the colonies, I believe," Gary couldn't resist having some fun. Erin turned her head towards the Bay.

"We won't have much more time for baseball, I'm afraid," Hale said, missing Erin's tell as he looked out towards the Narrows where the British Navy was anchored.

"No, we won't." Gary replied, smothering any trace of humor from his tone.

"I hope you'll consider enlisting in my regiment. We need good men like you for the fight ahead."

"I will look to return as soon as my business in Connecticut is complete. My family is depending on me." A morsel of truth at least.

"I'll see to it," Erin added.

"I'll draw up the papers then. We can date your enlistment as of October 1."

Gary saluted. "I look forward to serving my country."

"Huzzah!" Hale returned the salute before stepping away to help the dockhands tie up the ferry. His men shuffled on to the pier, illuminated by three flaming torches. Gary, Erin and Jenn were the last off.

"The captain is flush with revolutionary spirit," Erin said, smoothing her skirts. Too flush for his own good, Gary thought. "But, he must learn to look behind men's words," she added, squeezing his hand to make her point.

"Behind women's words as well." Gary didn't want to shoulder all the blame for the lie.

"Ye plan to be gone well before October, don't ye?" Erin

challenged him with her tone as well as her jutting chin.

"Yes." Gary had hoped to avoid this conversation tonight, but had resolved to tell the truth.

"And if ye Watch is broken beyond repair?" Erin asked, a sparkle glinting in her eyes.

"I'll stay…" Gary sighed, deciding whether to continue, but again honesty got the better of him. "…until someone from the future comes back to get me."

"Ye will leave me either way then." Erin's expression drooped into a moue of defeat as she digested Gary's intentions.

"I don't have a choice," Gary replied, his stomach knotting as he realized how lame his words sounded. The night, quite possibly their last night together, had soured without any drumroll, like a black thundercloud spontaneously massing in a clear blue sky.

"Perhaps I should seek to provide… counsel… to the good captain." She did not attempt to mackle the truth either.

"I wouldn't…" He wanted to warn her not to get too close to Nathan Hale, but decided it would just make him look like a jealous ex-lover - which is what he would, in fact, likely be soon enough.

She cupped his chin in her hands, her eyes reading his, like a poker player reading the table. "Tonight will be our last," she said, breaking away, pushing all her chips into the pot.

Hale returned before Gary could reply. "Where will you and Mrs. Johnson be staying this evening?" he asked.

"We'll find a boarding house," Gary muttered half-heartedly, his mind still spinning from Erin's gambit. Would she really leave him even if his Watch was broken? The thought had not previously crossed his mind.

"Not likely," Hale replied. "New York's a military camp now. The good citizens evacuated once the British warships appeared. The respectable taverns have shuttered."

"Me cousin, Mr. Mulligan, can accommodate us," Erin said. "His last letter indicated that he planned to stay the course in the city."

"Perhaps, but it's past curfew. Too late to go calling," the captain said. "You can stay at my camp on the Bowery. Mistress Coldstream as well. I'll accompany you in the morning to visit Mr. Mulligan."

Hale led a ragtag procession across Wall Street towards Broadway, the intersection marked by the tallest building on the island, Trinity Church, dark now like a hulking sentry. Gary reached for Erin's hand but it held little warmth as they walked silently past the shuttered warehouses, counting houses, and market stalls of the city's commercial district.

The cries and clinks of revelry filtered from behind the church, as if it was the sidewalk bouncer outside a hip nightclub in modern-day New York. Fat Man poked Baby Face with his musket, gesturing towards the noise. Sensing the restive stirrings behind him, Hale stopped and turned, "Not tonight boys. We have an early start tomorrow."

"That's the Holy Ground," Erin said. "As wicked a collection of brothels and public houses as you'll find anywhere in the colonies."

"The Holy Ground?" Jenn asked.

"Aye," Erin replied. "The land is owned by the Church."

"That's rich," Jenn said, her sarcasm obvious.

Did Erin know the Holy Ground from firsthand experience? The question surfaced from the depths of Gary's mind but he forced it to submerge. Her face betrayed no guile or guilt. She had never hidden her vocation, albeit not her only vocation, from him. Single women drew the short straw in colonial times. They did what they must to survive and feed their families. Erin was young, beautiful and full of life. He was in love with her, even though he hoped to soon leave her.

Hale turned right at the church, leading the troop north on Broadway towards their encampment. Erin stopped, looking left for a brief second, trying to discern her cousin's establishment, but the flickering street lamps provided little more than an ethereal radiance to the deserted boulevard. She caught up to Gary before the night watchman opened the city gate.

Less than a mile from the wall, they reached a pasture off Bowery Lane that served several Continental Army regiments. Hale led them through a haphazard maze of tents, shanties, campfires, trash pits and barely dressed men sleeping on open ground. The corner of the field that the Nineteenth Connecticut had claimed stood out for its orderliness even in the darkness.

Hale opened the flap of his marquee, twice the size of his men's accommodations, and ushered Gary, Erin and Jenn inside. The air stifled from the summer heat, but the room was well-appointed with a rope bed, chest, trestle desk, and field chair. "Breakfast is at six," he said before leaving.

Jenn rummaged through her pack, smiling victoriously as she withdrew a bottle of rum. "A parting gift from Major Rogers. He said to save it for a special occasion." She handed the bottle to Erin. "I trust you can put it to good use."

"Where are you...?" Gary started to ask as Jenn slipped out of the tent, but Erin shushed him again with a wet kiss. She broke off to take a long draught, whiskey dripping down her dimpled chin. She almost passed the fiery liquid to Gary, but decided to take another swill instead. "Lie down," she commanded, pushing him back towards the bed.

After Gary obeyed, she stood over him, shrugging off her bodice, her formidable breasts tumbling loose. She raised the bottle to her lips a third time as her frock slithered to the floor. "I'll drink ye out of me memory – if I must."

CHAPTER 60

Jenn latched the flap as she exited Hale's tent into the warm, inky blackness. Farewell fucks could get quite spirited, she knew from experience, still sore from her last night with Hannah. Wouldn't want the lovers to wake up the troops who appeared to have taken their captain's admonition seriously: campfires smoldering, tents dark, voices silenced.

Surrounded by hundreds of soldiers, Jenn almost felt safe from Colonel Lai, although not safe enough to sleep. Accordingly, she sat cross-legged on a flat, grassy stretch and checked her iPhone which had remained off since she had last used it at Widow Hauser's. To her relief, the battery icon still showed 75% remaining. Her home screen displayed no calls, texts or emails, as expected but still disheartening. She chuckled, better than crying, at the knowledge that high speed messages in her current world traveled via horseback.

But, the cold hard truth was that, without her own Watch, Jenn was stranded in Revolutionary America, perhaps forever. Regardless, she had to stop Lai – even though he terrified her. He would reach out again soon enough. And she had to be ready.

After that? She allowed herself to hope. Gary would retrieve his Watch, return home and send someone back for her. Or someone from TimeR would come back for him. Either way, Gary was her only ticket home. How ironic, since she had left TimeR to escape him.

Facing an extended stay in 1776, Jenn needed to bone up on "current" events. She tapped the Kindle icon on her phone and dove back into her history books. Nathan Hale's imminent demise stung like a hard slap across the face, driving her to stand and shake a fist at the cruel God in the heavens. She couldn't imagine that winsome young man hanging from a tree with a rope looped around his neck, but had no doubt that it would in fact happen on September 22nd.

Sitting down again, Jenn read more about Washington's strategic blunders leading to the rout in Brooklyn as well as the Continental Army's defeats at White Plains, Fort Washington and Fort Lee. The mighty British army would chase Washington and his dwindling force across New Jersey into Pennsylvania.

But the British didn't finish Washington off when they had the chance. Why not? It turned out that General William Howe, the British commander-in-chief, was in no rush to end the war and return to his matronly wife in England. He had a beautiful, young, American mistress, Betsy Loring, ensconced right here in New York City, her arms sarcastically referred to as the most powerful weapons of the Continental Army. Pussy ruled, apparently, even in pious Puritan times.

Given a reprieve, Washington miraculously rallied his troops, crossing the Delaware River on Christmas Eve 1776 to seize Trenton and then Princeton, two weeks later. How would Hannah and her sisters fare? Just fine, Jenn thought. They were chameleons, adopting the colors of whichever side was winning. If Jenn was stranded here, a return visit to Sisterly would be her consolation prize.

Colonel Lai? Jenn snapped from her book to scan the perimeter. Her heart pounded loud enough to wake the entire camp. Satisfied she was alone, Jenn put away her reading, set her pack as a pillow and lay back. A sliver of moon adorned the starstrewn sky. She started to count the distant specks of light but was out cold before she reached fifty.

Footfalls in the grass snapped Jenn awake. She jumped to her feet, fists up, ready to defend herself. "Who's there?"

"It's me," Erin replied, her white night shift clinging to her damp body. She walked unsteadily towards a waist high shrub. "I've got to piss."

Watching Erin, the tension sweat from Jenn's body like a breaking fever. She dropped her fists, resting them on her hips, while Erin completed her business.

Two nights ago, at Sisterly, Hannah's opium had sent her head spinning, so Jenn stepped onto the balcony for fresh air. In the wan moonbeams, she had seen a ghostly figure slip out the window of Gary's room. At the time, she thought it might be Gary himself, venturing to meet with Lieutenant Tarleton. When Hannah called her back to bed, Jenn had dismissed the episode as a narcotic-induced nightmare.

Thinking about the episode again last night, she feared it might have been Colonel Lai, striking a deal with Gary that would leave her out in the cold - or worse. The figure had walked with a spectral gait, disappearing around the side of the mansion. Now, she realized the figure had been Erin.

Listening to Erin tidy up, Jenn realized the "why" likely didn't matter much. There were no other eligible men at Sisterly except Tarleton and his soldiers. Erin would piss on the British before she'd sleep with them. So Erin had her own reason for sneaking out at night. Maybe she just needed fresh air.

On the return, Erin slipped and slid. "Who were ye expecting?" she slurred, still sodden with rum.

"No one. Just a bit jittery," Jenn replied. "How's your evening going?"

"Bonny well - for a last night."

"I might not be so quick to leave Mr. Johnson," Jenn said,

sitting down, motioning for Erin to join her.

"And why not?" Erin asked, still standing, albeit a bit wobbly. "He plans to leave me."

"Captain Hale is not the answer."

"I'm not looking for answers, just a good man. For me and me bairns."

Jenn clambered back to her feet, eye to eye with Erin now. "The good captain is going to soon volunteer to be a spy for General Washington," she said with the gravity of a physician delivering a diagnosis of terminal cancer.

"A spy? That's lower than a whore..." Erin replied before belching. "... and I should know."

"Captain Hale is a brave but naive young man."

"Aye, that he is."

"And naive men do not make good spies," Jenn said, adopting a more strident tone. "You know what happens when a spy is caught, don't you?"

Erin crooked her neck and stuck out her tongue, giggling like a drunken schoolgirl. "I won't let him run off spying then."

"You won't be able to stop him."

Erin pursed her lips and flicked her glance up towards the stars. "Ye time travel rules don't apply to me."

"Perhaps, but they apply to Captain Hale. He would willingly sacrifice his life for his country."

Erin appeared to ponder Jenn's words, then turned towards Hale's marquee. "Gary's likely to want one more go before dawn."

"Don't keep him waiting on my account."

CHAPTER 61

Gary stirred as the first gilded arrows of daylight pierced Captain Hale's tent. He rolled over, the sheets moist and musky, reaching for Erin, but she was gone. Alarm bells rang in his brain.

Fortunately, the scuffling of bare feet alleviated his concern. "What are you doing?" he asked, sitting up, the Quare bouncing on his chest.

"Thinking," she replied. Dressed in her night shift, translucent in the gauzy pre-dawn, she paced back and forth in the cramped space.

"Think here. Next to me."

"Something's not right," she said, sitting on the edge of the bed, resting a hand on Gary's shoulder.

"What?"

"I may have been wrong about Jenn."

"Wrong?"

"I'm not sure we can trust her."

"We don't have much choice," Gary said, alert now, trepidation about the monumental day ahead seeping into his thoughts.

"She told me about the fate of Captain Hale last night - when ye were asleep. For no good reason."

"I'm sorry about Hale."

"So am I." Erin replied, standing again. "But the good captain is not me worry today. Ye are."

Gary poked his feet out from under the sheets, dropping them to the floor, sitting up slowly. "I am?"

"Ye need me to make the introduction to my cousin Hercules. He can help ye reach General Washington and get ye watch back."

"And you're OK with that?"

"OK?"

"Good with that. You'll help me get my Watch back?"

Erin nodded. "What's me choice?"

"Thank you." Gary replied. Erin was right. He would do whatever necessary to get his Watch back. "What will you tell Hercules? That I'm not a spy, just a time traveler from the twenty-first century?"

"Leave it to me."

"And after that?" A stupid question, he realized too late.

Fortunately, Erin just shrugged. Her attention appeared to switch seamlessly from Gary to her wardrobe. Although she didn't really have many clothes, she appeared to be pondering her attire with more care this morning.

He washed his face and slipped on his shirt, but stopped with it only half-fastened to admire the curve in Erin's hip as she bent over her satchel. *No!* He forced his gaze away.

She peeled off her night shift, further testing his resolve. "No more tomfoolery," she snapped, as she joined him at the wash basin. "Ye made ye choice."

"Yes, ma'am," he replied, shifting his attention to the errant buttons on his shirt. He donned his boxers and breeches before sitting on the bed to buff his shoe buckles vigorously. The activity kept his head down as Erin finished dressing.

Erin smoothed her petticoats and flounced her skirt. She started to tie her bodice but stopped midway. Reaching into her valise, she withdrew a pink coral necklace and held it out to Gary. "Ye help here please?" she asked, turning to expose the back of her neck to him.

He hesitated. The necklace was new, at least he had never seen Erin wear it before. "A pretty piece," he said, standing behind her, rubbing the coral in his fingertips. "How did you come by it?"

"I have me ways," she replied, bending her head so he could secure the necklace.

"Your ways?" He slowly realized the necklace looked familiar. "Clara Wishingwell wore one just like it to supper at Sisterly, didn't she?"

"Aye." Erin's smirk foreshadowed his next question.

"You stole it?"

"That's rather harsh," she replied, but showed no remorse.

"How would you phrase it then?"

"A transfer of property? Quite justified, in me opinion. Mistress Wishingwell forced ye to transfer ye land deed to her, didn't she?"

Gary paused, mulling his response.

"An eye for an eye," Erin rolled on.

Gary shook his head, eyeing her in a new light. "What else do you have in there?" he asked, not sure if he wanted to know.

She dumped the valise on the bed. After sorting through worn undergarments, a kerchief and a cap, she snatched up a diamond stickpin, her green eyes brimming with triumph. "I believe this once belonged to Mr. Fairfax."

"You stole that too?"

"That beard-splitter deserved worse. Don't ye think?"

"I'm not sure what to think."

"Ye thought I was going to throw myself at Captain Hale, didn't ye?"

Gary slowly nodded as he put on his business-blue jacket.

"I can support me self and me bairns without a man."

"What if you get caught? Who will look after your bairns then?"

"I'm hurting no one. Worst I'll get is a night in the stocks and a whipping."

"Seems like you've thought it through."

"Aye," Erin replied, fixing the stickpin to Gary's lapel. "These fingers do more than fondle ye cock, ye know."

"I can see that," he said, removing the ornament and handing it back to Erin. "You'll need this more than I will."

Erin palmed the diamond and put it in her skirt pocket. Gary's mind twirled like a ceiling fan as he tried to come to grips with Erin's pickpocket skills.

Was she any different from him? He looked at his pack, containing the Declaration of Independence and Button Gwinnett's autograph. Wasn't he trying to support his family too?

"Huzzah," Captain Hale called through the tent flap.

CHAPTER 62

After breakfast, Hale led the return trip down Bowery Lane. The baked, dusty thoroughfare yearned for rain, preferably an all-day soaker. Gary and Erin flanked the captain, while Jenn trailed closely behind. Baby Face and five other brown-jacketed soldiers marched in the rear, reminding Gary that they were not yet clear of suspicion, if not actually prisoners.

The city gate was clogged with the traffic of an army preparing to withstand a massive British invasion. A squadron of two dozen men attired in bright blue bisected by white sashes wheeled a cannon northward while a wagon stacked with tree trunks lumbered south. Drums rolled, fifes tooted, officers shouted orders to cherry-cheeked privates, most still teenagers, who stared vacantly into the distance.

Hale, exuding the enthusiasm of the undefeated and unbowed, signaled a halt under the branches of a towering oak. He feigned frustration at the delay, but not-so-subtly shifted his attention to Erin. She wore a demure white cap which did little to restrain her scarlet locks from curling insouciantly to her shoulders.

They complemented the pink coral necklace which lay flat across her bodice, buttoned up as befitting the wife of a prosperous merchant.

"When did you see your cousin, Hercules, last?" Hale asked.

Erin dwelled on the question, swiping a bead of sweat from the tip of her nose. "Two years ago, maybe three. Before little Timmy was born."

"Little Timmy? You have a child?"

"Two. With my first husband. Rest his soul."

"You'll look after these youngsters, won't you?" Hale asked Gary. "Their father was a true patriot."

"Most certainly," Gary replied.

The conversation halted as another troop, clad in maroon, marched by, followed by a third, dressed in well-worn homespun. One soldier even sported a coonskin hat despite the stifling heat. How Washington molded this riffraff into an army was a mystery Gary hoped he would not be around to find out.

"Captain Hamilton," Hale called, spinning away to greet a friend, apparently the commander of the white sashed artillerymen.

"Hale Captain Hale," Alexander Hamilton replied, tipping his tall, yellow-feathered hussar's hat in their direction. Although a head shorter than Nathan, Hamilton twitched with the nervous energy of a young man on the move. "Always a pleasure to encounter a fellow college man."

"And you as well."

"Who are these beautiful women?" Hamilton asked, obviously ignoring Gary. "Surely not under your command."

"Mrs. Erin Johnson and her cousin, Mistress Jennifer Coldstream. And Mr. Johnson," Hale replied. "They are under my supervision. Temporarily."

Erin curtsied. Jenn followed suit. Gary nodded, hoping he disguised his offense at Hamilton's slight.

"Ah, well. Welcome to New York." Hamilton gestured grandly towards the crowded city gate. "What brings you to our beleaguered city?"

"Business," Gary replied, stepping to his wife's side. "We're returning from Philadelphia. I've applied for a letter of marque from the Congress."

"For a privateering vessel?" Hamilton mused. "I believe General Washington has profited quite handsomely from his naval investments."

"I hope to do so as well," Gary said. "I might be looking for capital to fund my first voyage. To help the war effort, of course."

"Of course," Hamilton said. "I may have some contacts..."

Seemingly uninterested in the conversation, Hale looked at the city gate which had cleared, then at Erin and Jenn. "Huzzah," he proclaimed. "We must be off."

"I trust we will meet again, Captain Hale," Hamilton said. "If not..."

"To a good death, Captain Hamilton," Hale replied, tipping his tricorn. Once Hamilton was out of earshot, Hale added, "My friend is a fervent supporter of our Glorious Cause, but he is too commercial at times for my tastes."

"A bit of a socialite as well," Gary said.

"Truly?" Erin asked.

"He is known to dally with the Schuyler sisters," Jenn piped in. "Elizabeth Schuyler in particular."

"Quite the catch, I believe," Gary said, looking sternly at Erin.

Broadway might have been a grand boulevard before the Continental Army arrived, but now it was a skeleton of its former self. Mansions had been ransacked for firewood, metal and bricks. Campfires burned in the street, cluttered with household debris, roving dogs, and feces of all shapes, sizes and smells. Soldiers, some smartly uniformed and battle-ready, others barely dressed and tottering, clustered behind barricades. Their heads poked up as Hale and his entourage proceeded downtown.

The Holy Ground was unsurprisingly quiet at this early hour. Slowing to walk beside Jenn, Gary noticed she appeared at peace, more focused on what lay directly ahead, than constantly swiveling to see who trailed behind. The Chinaman? Gary searched the shadows, but saw no sign of him.

Erin drifted between Jenn and Gary, taking his hand as they passed Trinity Church. Jenn flashed a nod of approval before swerving to avoid the rotting remains of a goat. When Jenn gagged, Erin dabbed perfume on a kerchief and handed it to her, then fixed another nosegay for herself. If Erin mistrusted Jenn, she disguised it well.

"There's Mr. Mulligan's shop," Hale said as they reached Wall Street. A neatly painted sign hung in the downstairs window of a three story, red brick home which bordered the Bowling Green. They stopped in front. Hale rang the brass knocker. Feet shuffled to the door, freshly painted navy blue. It opened slowly.

"Can I be of service?" a well-fed, bespectacled man, sporting a garishly striped jacket of scarlet, pumpkin, and daffodil, asked.

"Cousin Hercules," Erin called, moving to Hale's side, raising her fan to shield her eyes from the morning sun. It had just risen behind Mulligan's shop, illuminating her like a spotlight.

Hercules squinted, wiped his glasses on his sleeve, and looked again. Hale shuffled his feet, his right hand dropping to the hilt of his saber. Gary held his breath. Erin dropped her fan.

"Cousin Erin," Hercules said, opening his arms to greet her. "You're a sight for sore eyes."

After a brief exchange of pleasantries, Hale bowed gallantly. "I'll leave you then," he said. "Mr. Johnson, I look forward to seeing you upon your return from Connecticut."

"On October the first," Gary replied, nodding his approval.

Erin offered her hand. "Captain Hale, thank ye for escorting us here. I hope we will meet again." Jenn did the same.

Hercules ushered them inside. His studio was cluttered with swaths of cloth, bolts of moleskin, and balls of yarn. A mannequin outfitted in a purple suede jacket dominated the center of the room while a spinning wheel sat in the other. A mahogany roll top desk, probably worth millions today, looked over a bay window.

"Now who is this winsome young man and what brings you both to travel abroad in this perilous time?" he asked with a mischievous smile.

"This is Gary Johnson," Erin replied, ushering him forward. "We were recently married."

"Excellent news. It's not healthy for a woman to remain unattached for too long."

"My sentiments, exactly," Gary said, putting his arm around Erin's waist. "And this is my cousin, Jennifer Coldstream," he added. Also unattached, by her own design however, he chuckled silently.

"How can I be of assistance?" Mulligan asked. "I am quite sure you didn't appear at my shop to purchase a wedding suit."

"I'm in need of an introduction to General Washington's household. My Watch, an irreplaceable family heirloom, was stolen from me in Philadelphia," Gary said, unfastening the top of his shirt to display his current watch. "I thought I had retrieved it - with my wife's assistance - but learned to my dismay that this watch might have been made by Mr. Quare, but it is most definitely not my Quare."

Mulligan fussed with the lapels on the mannequin's jacket. "Mr. Hancock favors a purple suit, you know," he said before turning to face Gary, Erin and Jenn. "Why do you believe that your watch now resides with General Washington?"

"The Committee of Safety in Philadelphia posted it here," Gary replied.

"The Committee of Safety? Your tale grows even more intriguing. How would the good Committee have come upon your watch? And why would they post it here?"

Gary looked at Erin, but she remained silent, hands in her skirt pockets. "William Sands..." Gary continued, "...a well-known businessman, who occasionally trades in stolen goods, proffered it to the Committee in exchange for immunity for his previous transgressions."

"Ah, I see. Sands is an agent of Cary and Company in

London, I believe," Hercules said. "And also a British spy, I'm quite certain."

"I have little doubt," Gary said.

"So, how did Mr. Sands come about your watch?"

"I stole it," Erin declared, her head down, staring at the floorboards. "Or at least I helped Sands steal it." Jenn loosed a low whistle.

"You what?" Gary said, his eyes gaping wide as he stepped away from Erin. "You stole it?"

"Me bairns were hungry. Mr. Sands pays well. Ye were a foreigner," Erin replied, slowly raising her head.

"The hold-up? In the alley? It was all a setup?" Gary struggled to control the anger, and the hurt, in his voice.

"Aye. I partnered with Sands after me husband fell on Bunker Hill."

"My cousin - your wife - deserves a modicum of credit for her honesty," Hercules said, stepping between Gary and Erin, as if he feared Gary would strike her. "She's a good woman at heart. And a good mother."

"Thank ye."

When Gary made no violent move, Hercules turned away, pacing to the window. "I must tell you, Mr. Johnson, that your watch has aroused quite a stir here in New York."

"It has?" Gary asked, his heart skipping a beat. "It's here then? Intact?"

"I believe so," Mulligan replied, circling slowly behind his desk. "I fit two of the General's officers for suits - brown, not purple, by the way - just yesterday. They commented about it directly. Believed it was an instrument for espionage. Are you a British spy, Mr. Johnson?"

"Absolutely not. I'm a Connecticut man staunchly devoted to the patriot cause."

"I wouldn't have married him otherwise, cousin," Erin said.

Hercules withdrew a page of parchment from a drawer and dipped his quill in the inkwell. He wrote for several seconds without looking up. "Here is a letter of introduction to Captain Benjamin Tallmadge in General Washington's service. He is most interested in gathering intelligence. I believe he will know the whereabouts of your watch."

CHAPTER 63

Retreating to an alcove at the back of Hercules' workroom, Jenn reassessed her situation. Erin was not just a pretty face. She was an accomplished thief whose skills might prove useful in their quest to reclaim Gary's Watch. In fact, now that she thought about it, the coral necklace adorning Erin's throat looked uncannily similar to the one Clara Wishingwell had worn.

Jenn followed Gary and Erin out of Hercules' shop back onto Broadway. Mid-morning traffic was light. A weary draught horse lugged a wagonload of watermelons downtown while a lone horseman, dressed in a tattered white hunting shirt, galloped towards the city gate. They crossed Bowling Green, stepping over the rubble of the gilded statue of King George. It had been ripped down by a rebel mob last week after the first public reading of the Declaration of Independence. All that remained was a barren marble pedestal.

What remained of her dreams to launch Tryon Travel, promote time travel for good, and expand democracy around the world? These worthwhile ends, she once thought, justified her theft of TimeR's technology. Colonel Lai's appearance at the Blazing Star, however, crushed her noble ideals. She had unwittingly helped the Chinese government, as autocratic as any in the twenty-first century.

The trio stopped on the unpaved street outside the Kennedy mansion, George Washington's city residence and de facto command post on the lower tip of Manhattan. The facade was all yellow brick, imported from Holland, punctuated by a lusciously carved door. A three-section Palladian window rested above the entranceway, set there to light the great hall and grand staircase lying within.

Archibald Kennedy had made his fortune by captaining a British privateer in the French and Indian War and augmented it further by marrying into the British aristocracy. He was arrested in New Jersey for his Loyalist activities later in 1776, but paroled unharmed, eventually returning to England. His opulent residence, however, became a spoil of war.

Before Gary could bang the door-knocker, the front door burst open. A blond-queued officer, crisply attired in blue jacket, yellow sash and matching cockade in his hat, bustled out. Washington had browbeaten Congress to grant him six aides in residence, personally selected from the best and brightest young men in the colonies. This "family" primarily drafted and hand-copied the commander-in-chief's military correspondence, including the General Orders distributed each day to outposts throughout the city. No laser printers in the eighteenth century.

"Don't just stand there and gawk, man," Edmund Randolph scolded Gary. At the time, a twenty-three-year old lawyer, Randolph would go on to be governor of Virginia, America's first attorney general and second secretary of state. "We're in the midst of a war."

"We're here to see Captain Tallmadge, Benjamin Tallmadge." Gary could barely stammer the sentence.

"We're...?" Randolph asked, the lightbulb flashing as he first noticed Erin and Jenn. He quickly doffed his tricorn. "A pleasure to make your acquaintance, ladies, however His Excellency does not encourage social visits until supper time."

"Our visit is of military importance," Gary said, regaining his composure. "We have a letter of introduction from Mr. Mulligan."

"Tallmadge you said?" Randolph looked back up at the front door. "From Mulligan? Hercules Mulligan?"

"Mr. Mulligan is my wife's cousin." Gary replied, flourishing the letter.

"Hercules Mulligan is quite well-respected in this house," Randolph said, taking the letter, reading it slowly. "He's privy to a great deal of information."

"That's why he suggested that we meet with Captain Tallmadge. As soon as possible."

"Come with me then," Randolph said, pivoting back up the steps to the front door. Jenn crossed her fingers, praying the Watch was intact.

The inside of the Kennedy mansion was hot and steamy. Four of Washington's Life Guards, tall, fit men formally uniformed in blue and buff with a white plume adorning their helmets, stood at attention at the foot of a sweeping stairway, an indication that the Commander-in-chief was in residence.

Randolph led them through a sitting parlor into what was once a grand ballroom, large enough to host a wedding for a hundred guests, but now converted into office space for Washington's staff. They stopped in front of a jacket-less officer, head down buried in paperwork, scribbling rapidly with his quill. To his rear, palatial windows opened to a verdant garden which descended to the Hudson River, bringing in the trilling of birds and the shouts of sailors, but little cool air. A ceiling fan would have been welcome, Jenn thought, but she was a century too early.

"Captain Tallmadge?" Randolph asked. When he got no reply, he repeated the question.

"Yes," Tallmadge grunted, finally looking up.

"This gentleman is here to see you. He has a letter from Hercules Mulligan."

Tallmadge took the letter. His head bobbed between Gary and the two women as he read. When he finished, he nibbled at the tip of his quill for a second. "Let's talk outside," he said, standing.

Tallmadge led them to the veranda overlooking the garden, grown wild due to neglect during the military occupation. He peered over the railing confirming their privacy. "What do you have for me?"

Gary swept aside the lapels of his jacket, unfastened the top of his shirt and displayed his Quare. "I believe this Watch may be a tool of the enemy," he said, recounting his story of the duel with William Sands.

Tallmadge's countenance perked in recognition of Sands' name. "Mr. Sands is certainly a character of dubious loyalty, but I am not certain what harm his watch can do."

"I'm not skilled in matters of intelligence gathering," Gary said, rolling over his Quare in his hands. "But I believe it might harbor a mechanism for encoding messages."

"Or a secret compartment to hide a poison," Erin blurted, letting her eyes roll towards the second story windows.

"May I examine it?" Tallmadge asked, holding out his hand.

"Of course," Gary said, unfastening the chain around his neck. "I would propose to exchange it for my Quare, merely a family heirloom but a most cherished one, that I believe you have in your possession."

"My office has examined your watch in great detail," Tallmadge said.

"And it still works?" To Jenn's dismay, Gary couldn't camouflage the urgency in his voice. "May I see it?"

Before Tallmadge answered, a great bustling erupted in the mansion as His Excellency, George Washington, descended the grand stairway. At forty-four, Washington stood over six feet tall, regally attired in a royal blue jacket sporting gaudy epaulets on each shoulder. Underneath, he wore tailored gold breeches and matching waistcoat. A tricorn, adorned with a black cockade, rested atop meticulously coiffed reddish brown hair touched with powder and queued with a black ribbon. Silver spurs, gold sword hilt, and polished boots glittered in the morning light. He strode with a regal gait, every bit as imposing as the history books said he was.

As he approached, Jenn blinked in disbelief. She was actually in the presence of George Washington. Better than an audience with the Pope. Or a meet and greet with Mohamed Saleh, her favorite Premiership footballer. Cocktails with Taylor Swift might be a close call though, she chuckled silently. If Tryon Time could deliver this experience to the mass market, she could make the world a safer place for everyone.

Billy Lee, a stout Black whose permanent smile belied ever-watchful eyes, walked a step behind the General. Attired in red and white livery, Lee was Washington's most trusted personal servant and slave.

The Life Guards escorted Washington and Lee towards the stables at the rear of the house. While this cordon looked formidable, it would not protect the General from Lai, armed with twenty-first century weapons and skills. Tallmadge stood at attention as Washington approached. He gave Jenn and Erin a thorough review before nodding to Tallmadge, "Carry on, captain."

Jenn's mind playfully wandered forward in time. What if she could film a clip with her iPhone. Post it on Tik Tok? Sell it to CNN? Millions of views, maybe billions. She would use the profits to help impoverished Black women in Africa and the Caribbean.

Washington mounted Nelson, a spirited chestnut gelding. He waited impatiently as the rest of his entourage climbed into the saddle. All appeared to be expert horsemen. On the commander's signal, the troop trotted onto Broadway, heading north. Soldiers, as well as most of the ordinary citizens left in the city, appeared on the street to watch the pageantry of their leader's departure.

"My Watch?" Gary asked, slowly recapturing Tallmadge's attention.

"Ah, well," Tallmadge replied. "It rides with our Commander-in-Chief."

Gary and Jenn raced to the street, but they were too late. All they could see was the hind ends and wagging tails of six horses.

"Where's he going?" Gary asked Tallmadge who trailed them out.

"That's not for public dissemination," he replied, somewhat annoyed. "You may return tomorrow to inquire about your watch."

"Then I will hold this watch until tomorrow as well," Gary said, linking the Quare back around his neck.

"But..."

"No buts. I demand the return of my property."

Tallmadge looked for assistance, but he was the only uniformed man remaining on the street. "As you wish," he said. "I'll see you promptly at eight tomorrow."

The captain returned to the mansion, leaving Gary, Jenn and Erin to their own devices.

"What now, Mr. Johnson?" Jenn asked.

Gary shrugged in frustration, but Erin stepped forward, a mischievous smile on her face as she withdrew a parchment from her skirt pocket. "General Orders for Monday July 15, 1776," she read the scribbled cursive aloud, albeit with some hesitation: "Fortifications along the coast in Harlem and Greenwich Village will be reviewed...War Council will meet at Mortier House at 3pm." The two villages, as well as Mortier, Washington's country residence, were north of the city.

Erin must have swiped the document from Tallmadge, or some other officer's desk. Jenn shook her head in disbelief at the security lapse. While Tallmadge had refused to disclose Washington's whereabouts to Gary, the General's paperwork was easily found. British spies, who were undoubtedly plentiful in New York, would have had a field day garnering information. No wonder Nathan Hale had been captured so quickly.

How could they get uptown? Uber?

"I believe there's a stable on Wall Street," Erin said, as if reading Jenn's mind. "We can rent horses for the day."

Jenn had a more immediate worry than her mode of transportation. Colonel Lai, black robed, had just appeared on

Broadway. Astride a stone gray stallion, he stopped briefly across the street. He nodded to her before pulling up his hood and riding north.

CHAPTER 64

Growing up in Brooklyn, Gary had occasionally bet on horses running at Aqueduct race track, but he had never ridden one. In fact, his immigrant parents would have laughed at the thought. Horses were for farmers, cops or wealthy aristocrats. Flush with cash from the sale of his first company, however, he would not deny his children the equine experience. Accordingly, they vacationed at a dude ranch in Colorado for several years when Mirabel and Remy were young.

At the stable, Gary swung his right leg up into the saddle like the wranglers in Colorado had taught. He prayed that his mount, Spur, a mammoth, cream-coated creature would be as obedient as the horses at the ranch. The women had changed into borrowed breeches, tucking their skirts into their saddlebags. Jenn appeared surprisingly comfortable atop a fidgety turkey brown mare; Erin, however, sat as if she had a dozen needles poking her ass. She swore in Gaelic although her ride, a stout sorrel, barely shuffled in place.

Fortunately, the trip to Greenwich Village, a rural expanse of country estates, was only three miles, easy trotting along a dirt track wide enough for two wagons to pass. They arrived at noon, learning from a roadside vegetable vendor that Washington's entourage had passed through but not tarried.

Gary pushed forward, hoping to catch up with the commander-in-chief when he stopped to inspect fortifications. The trail tracked the Hudson River, its ripples visible whenever they crested a ridgeline. Scattered farmhouses and meandering meadows dotted the landscape. A mansion sporting four chimneys rose in the distance.

Gary recalled bicycling with Lucie along what might have been this same path in the early oughts. Of course, in the twenty-first century, it was fronted by a solid wall of skyscrapers while automobiles whizzed by on the adjacent West Side Highway. He never thought he'd miss New York City traffic, but he did now.

Gary lurched forward as Spur bucked to avoid a red fox. He wrapped his arms around its neck, dashing all thoughts of the twenty-first century. Jenn snickered as she cantered up, grasped the bridle, and soothed the agitated animal. Sitting upright, Gary patted the saddlebags containing his precious artifacts, invaluable proof of his journey to the eighteenth century.

As he led the way northward again, Erin remained in the rear, silent, her repertoire of curses apparently exhausted. She gripped her reins so ferociously that Gary thought her fingers might remain permanently clenched.

An upturned farmer's wagon blocked the road just outside the hamlet of Bloomingdale. A short, roughly dressed man, gray-streaked beard tickling his chest, stepped forward, pointing a musket at Gary's chest. Five others, apple-cheeked but armed as well, swaggered behind him.

"Morning," the leader said, spitting tobacco juice in Gary's direction. "I'm Josiah Worthy."

"Good morning, Mr. Worthy."

"Where yer headed?"

"Connecticut."

"Long way off."

"It's home."

"Who are these lovely ladies?"

"My wife and her cousin."

"Nice looking. Real nice looking."

"May we pass? Our family's expecting us before dark."

"Soon enough." Worthy walked slowly around Spur, reaching up to pat the overstuffed saddlebags. "Eliphalet, this gentleman travels with a heavy load," he called out. "And he appears to be in a hurry."

"We'll have to lighten his load then, Father," Eliphalet, tall but skeletal thin, said. He grabbed Spur's bridle with one hand while keeping his pistol pointed with the other. The nubs on his chin marked him as no older than twenty. "Why don't you come down now mister."

The four other boys, all younger-looking, surged forward, surrounding Jenn and Erin's horses. "It might be a good idea if you all dismounted," Josiah said. "I'd prefer we parley a bit more privately." He pointed to a trail leading into the woods.

Gary hesitated, but he couldn't argue with Josiah's musket which prodded his ribs. He climbed down, his right hand lingering on the saddlebag. Jenn and Erin followed suit.

Josiah placed his hand over Gary's. "Don't you fret. We'll take good care of your belongings, won't we sons?"

The youngsters gawked as they helped the women down from their mounts. "Got anything to eat?" the smallest, his nose topped by a cherry red wart, asked. "We's hungry."

"Hush your mouth, Ezekiel," Josiah commanded as he led Spur off the road, while Eliphalet shoved Gary along on foot. Erin and Jenn walked close behind, trailed by the Worthy's and their horses.

After ten minutes, they stopped in a clearing bisected by a frothy brook. Two fresh horses were loosely reined to the low hanging branches of an oak. They nibbled on wildflowers, looking up expectantly as their masters returned. The air smelled pleasantly of jasmine and river moss.

Josiah opened one of Gary's saddlebags, dumping its contents in the grass. He kneeled, sorting through clothes, utensils and toiletries. Nothing of value. He kicked Gary's trencher into the stream.

"I'll make you an offer," Gary said before Josiah could toss through his other saddlebag.

"Don't reckon you're in much position to bargain," Eliphalet said, nudging his pistol into Gary's back. His brothers snickered in agreement.

Holding Spur's bridle, Josiah stepped around the horse's head to get to the other side. He was about to unlatch the bag when the rumble of mounted men seeped through the woods. "Go see who's coming," he said, pointing to Ezekiel.

The youngster sprinted back towards the road. Josiah and Eliphalet kept their weapons trained on Gary while they waited. The other three Worthy's stayed close to Jenn and Erin, but their attention wandered.

Ezekiel crashed through the underbrush, his face contorted with excitement. "It's General Washington..." he blustered, gulping air.

"You sure boy?"

"Got Continentals with him. All fancied up in uniform."

"His Life Guards," Eliphalet said. "They won't take too kindly to us."

"No they won't," Josiah said, rapidly surveying his situation. "Mount up boys. Take all the horses. "Eliphalet you ride this one." He handed over Spur's reins. "We'll meet at the King's Bridge."

The Worthy's needed no further encouragement. Each boy grabbed a horse and swung into the saddle. Eliphalet extended his arm to his youngest brother and pulled him up. Ezekiel clung to his back as they rode off.

"Hate to leave without a proper farewell," Josiah called as he followed his boys across the brook and into the trees.

"Wait!" Gary screamed to no avail. His precious documents were gone.

The thrashing of a horse pounding through the woods stunted any conversation with Erin and Jenn. A Life Guard mounted on a colossal black steed approached. "Are you harmed?"

"No," Gary replied, his face frozen in shock, the single word barely escaping his lips. He forced himself to take a deep breath. "Those thieves - they stole my horse and my possessions. Can we chase them down?"

"Could be British patrols in the vicinity."

The rest of Washington's procession arrived at the clearing. The General surveyed the scene but said nothing.

"Highwaymen," the Life Guard explained.

Washington nodded. "My army must prepare to repel the British. Sadly, we lack the resources to police the countryside."

"But my valuables...and our horses."

"You have your lives," Washington said.

"They were just boys," Jenn lamented.

"Hungry boys," Erin added.

"What do we do now?" Gary asked.

"My men can transport you back to Mortier House," Washington said, reaching into his pants pocket. He removed a silver watch, flicking it open to check the time. Nodding towards Gary, he turned his horse around. His Life Guards surrounded their charge, waiting patiently for his command to depart.

"Supper is served promptly at five," Billy Lee announced, ambling his mount behind his master.

CHAPTER 65

"That's my Watch," Gary said to Erin, barely keeping his voice level.

"Shush," she cautioned, squeezing his hand, steering him a few feet away from the cordon of Life Guards and their fidgeting stallions.

"I think we should take the good General up on his offer of hospitality," Jenn added.

The Life Guards looked to Washington. "Assist these people," he said, his lips barely moving.

The lead Guard trotted to Erin and offered his hand. She clasped his forearm, allowing him to swing her up into the saddle. Jenn and Gary mounted with two of the other Guards.

Washington surveyed his retinue, now almost double in size. "To Mortier," he said, nudging Nelson's flanks with his boots. The seasoned war-horse sprung to life, leading the way through the woods.

They took the Bloomingdale Road at a canter, arriving at Washington's country estate just before three. The house, originally built by Abraham Mortier, paymaster of the British Army, stood atop Richmond Hill. It was two stories high with Greek columns supporting a broad portico on the ground level and a porch on the upper one.

The sun beat down unmercifully, parching Gary's throat. Uniformed soldiers, black-aproned artisans, and cravat-necked merchants milled about the front steps, all hoping to snare a word with the general. The air was fouled by horse droppings and human grime. Dust swirled with every new arrival or departure.

Gary tried to worm his way through but couldn't penetrate the perimeter. He retreated, joining Erin and Jenn by the stables. Erin somehow had a pocketful of carrots which they shared to pass the time. Her eyes flitted to the shuttered windows as if she was casing the joint, but she made no move.

"Billy Lee said supper at five, didn't he?" she asked as the sun finally began its descent.

"Yes," Gary replied, checking the Quare nestled against his chest. "In thirty minutes."

"We should get dressed then," Erin said.

"Dressed? With what?" Jenn asked. "Those brigands rode off with our clothes - and everything else we owned."

Erin untied her white day cap and shook out her hair, fluffing it with her fingers. She removed her lacy summer scarf and opened the top two buttons on her bodice, airing out her sweaty bosom. Finally, she wrapped the scarf over her head and tied it under her chin, forming a fashionable evening bonnet. "There," she said. "Follow me."

Gary went a step further, hauling a bucket of brackish water up from the well and washing his face, neck and armpits. Jenn followed suit, exchanging a glance that needed no amplification. A shower would feel so good right now.

"Give me ye watch," Erin said before Gary could rebutton his shirt.

"Why?"

"Do ye want ye true watch back?"

"How...?"

"Trust me," Erin said, touching two fingertips to her tongue to wet them. "As ye well know, me fingers can be quite nimble."

Gary handed over the real Quare which Erin quickly deposited in her skirt pocket. Propelled by the hope that his time traveling might soon be at an end, he barged forward, pushing aside a spindly man, dressed in an orange suede jacket and powdered wig. Two Continental soldiers, armed with bayonet-tipped muskets, barred the way.

"General Washington is expecting us," he volunteered.

"Do you have a pass?"

"Let them up," Billy Lee called down from the veranda. "His Excellency will receive his guests shortly."

Erin slipped her arm into the crook of Gary's elbow as they climbed the steps, but Jenn hesitated, swiveling her head to search the courtyard. The mysterious Chinaman? Gary didn't see him, and didn't care. He could practically smell Lucie's beef bourguignon in the oven.

CHAPTER 66

After his brief fox hunting conversation with George Washington on the porch, Gary led Erin and Jenn inside Mortier House, far less pretentious than the Kennedy mansion in the city. Its entry foyer was single story with a well-worn plank floor. A narrow New England style staircase, shielded by two Life Guards, led to the General's private quarters. Bay windows framed a view of the Hudson, its calm waters glistening in the fading light of the early evening sun.

The parlor slowly filled with other guests, a dozen in all. A fiddler played while they took their assigned seats at the table, set with brass candelabras, sterling cutlery and crystal goblets. The Washington's entertained in style both in the city and the country. Jenn was paired with Captain Tallmadge, who must have ridden up from headquarters on short notice to squire the three travelers.

Four black waiters, wearing the same red and white as Billy Lee, served the wine, an excellent '66 Bordeaux, and the first course, root vegetables simmering in cherries. After everyone was served, Gary was about to dig in when he noticed that his compatriots had stood, eyes fixed on Washington.

The commander-in-chief rose solemnly, raised his glass, and intoned: "May God in heaven look kindly upon our United States and upon our army that seeks to defend it."

Glasses clinked; wine sipped; food left untouched. The fop in the orange suit stood next. "May America become an asylum to the persecuted of the Earth," he toasted. A twenty-first century sentiment, Gary thought.

"To the memory of those heroes who have already fallen for our freedom," the third toaster proclaimed.

"How many more to go?" Gary asked Ben Tallmadge.

"They usually do thirteen. But we save the last three until after supper."

"Good thing no one here knows America will have fifty states one day," Jenn whispered to Gary.

After the fifth toast, everyone sat and enjoyed their first course. Tallmadge signaled for a waiter to refill their empty glasses. "Would you prefer ginger beer to wine?" he asked, patting Jenn's hand, but she shook her head. Erin used the diversion to spill her wine into her vegetable dish.

The very pleasant aroma of a roasting turkey trailed from the kitchen. Once the plates were cleared, the toasts began again. By the ninth round, gulps replaced sips. After the tenth, Washington sat down, the indicator for supper to be served. "Your turn after we eat," Tallmadge said to Gary.

Anticipation of his toast spoiled Gary's appetite. He forced his brain back to his history lessons. At last, the staff replaced his barely touched plate of fowl with a bowl of apple crumble and clotted cream. Washington again stood, tipping his head in Gary's direction.

"Be at war with your vices, at peace with your neighbors, and let each new year find you a better man," Gary said, raising his glass.

"Here, here," the General said, bowing for the first time. "Quite original."

"Didn't Benjamin Franklin say that?" Jenn asked.

"Not for another ten years," Gary whispered.

Two fiddlers and a fifer began warming up in the drawing room before the final toast was fully digested. Washington led the way, his penchant for dancing well-known. As was his penchant for partnering with attractive young women.

"Mrs. Johnson, I hope you will accord me the honor of the first dance," the General said, reaching for Erin's hand.

"The honor is all mine," she replied with her deepest curtsy.

The guests formed a square in the center of the room. Washington led Erin into the middle as the band struck up "Yankee Doodle Dandy."

Martha Washington, only five feet tall, sidled next to Gary. "Music and good company help my husband bear the responsibility of his office," she said.

"It is a weighty responsibility," Gary replied, trying to keep his eyes on Erin as Washington whirled her around the floor. Another couple joined in, followed shortly by Jenn and Captain Tallmadge.

"Would you entertain a dance with me?" he asked Mrs. Washington.

"Dancing is not my strong suit, I'm afraid," she replied with a deprecating smile. Erin appeared to stumble, leaning into her partner for balance. "Nor is it George's, if I can be honest."

"He appears to be enjoying himself."

As the tune wound down, General Washington led Erin back to Gary. "Your wife is a most accomplished dancer," he said.

"George, you need your rest," Martha said, taking her husband's elbow. "We should leave the floor to the young people."

Erin took Gary's hand as the First Couple ascended the stairs. "We should leave too," she said. A tear welled in her eye.

CHAPTER 67

Gary and Erin left by the front door, the courtyard empty of the jostling throng that had assembled there all afternoon. The gibbous moon provided just enough illumination to lead them along the winding path through the woods down Richmond Hill. An owl high up a tree hooted a greeting.

At the river's edge, Erin broke away, staring out at the brooding waters coiled like a snake around Manhattan. Gary followed, wrapping his arms around her waist, trying to draw her close. She wriggled free, turning to face him.

"Here's ye Watch," she said, holding out his timepiece.

"You swapped...?"

"I didn't say that."

Gary wasn't listening. His mind raced like a Formula One car around a hairpin turn as he clasped his treasure in both hands. The Watch face showed 830. Looks right. He pressed the stem, holding it for three seconds. Lucie's photo appeared. His breath caught; his eyes lit; his palms grew clammy. It worked.

"Ye can go home now," Erin said, biting her lower lip.

Gary swallowed hard, barely noticing Erin. He tapped the Watch face three times. The clock dissolved, replaced by the menu screen. "Coming home," he whispered. A swish indicated his text was in route to Molly.

"What was that?"

"The sound of my message going through."

"No." Erin shook her head, pointing back up the hill "Over there."

Gary pulled out his pistol, cocked the hammer, and aimed it at the underbrush. Erin slipped behand him.

Jenn thrashed through, capless. A jagged scratch painted her right cheek.

"What happened to ye?" Erin asked.

"It's nothing. A branch," she huffed. "You can't leave now, Gary."

"And why not?" Erin pressed.

"Colonel Lai. A Chinese assassin. From the future. He's here to kill General Washington. And cripple America forever." Jenn slowly regained her wind. "We've got to stop him."

"Lai can't kill Washington." Gary forced his mind to slow down. The Chinaman was real. He had seen him with his own eyes. But his threat was false. "The laws of science won't allow it."

"How do you know for sure? No one's ever time traveled before."

"I'm sure. If the science was flawed, we wouldn't be here in 1776, would we?"

Jenn pursed her lips, mulling Gary's question. "How do you think Colonel Lai got here?"

"He has a Watch," Gary replied, enunciating each word to control his growing anger. "You helped him build it, didn't you?"

"I didn't know I was helping the Chinese government. I wanted to change the world for the better."

"Fine job ye did," Erin interjected.

"Do you understand?" Jenn asked, stamping her foot. "The Chinese government wants to kill George Washington."

"Go back to the house," Erin said, stepping to Gary's side. "Ye and the good Captain Tallmadge can protect the General. Leave us be."

Jenn dropped her guard, but held her ground. Horsey sounds from the courtyard drifted down from the hilltop. The guests were departing.

"Well?" Erin placing her hand gently on Gary's shoulder. "Are ye leaving?"

He nodded, handing his pistol to Erin. "I won't be needing this anymore," he said, leaning in for a farewell kiss.

Erin grasped the weapon, re-setting it to half-cocked for safety, but avoided the kiss. A bittersweet smile creased her lips. Gary knew it would haunt him forever. She reached into her skirt pocket and handed him a single folded page. "Take this. It's what ye wanted."

Gary unfolded the document and smiled. The Declaration of Independence.

"It was tacked to the wall of the commode," Erin said.

Gary was in another world now. He tapped the Watch face three times and recited, "TimeR2026."

"I won't watch ye go," Erin said, raising her chin before turning away. The moon slipped behind a cloud.

"What about me?" Jenn called out, hastening to Erin's side. "You'll come back for both of us, won't you?"

CHAPTER 68

Gary's left wrist spasmed. The ground tremored. Whitecaps rippled across the Hudson. He tensed, waiting to whisk away in a whirl of dust.

"Are ye gone?" Erin called from the river's edge, her arms crisscrossing her chest.

"No." The waters calmed. The embankment firmed. Gary dropped his arm to his side. "The Watch didn't work."

"Let me see," Jenn rushed forward, reaching for Gary's wrist. "Take it off."

"You are not leaving us, Mr. Johnson," a high-pitched hiss slithered from the trees.

Erin spun, slipped on the uneven ground, but regained her footing. She darted between Gary and the voice. "Who are ye?"

"No matter to you." Lai, swathed in black, advanced slowly from the shadows like a betrayed lover. He stepped past Erin without a glance. His piercing blue eyes targeted Jenn instead, undressing her from head to toe. "*You* were supposed to stop him."

"No," Jenn replied, gritting her teeth. She bounced on the

balls of her feet, her arms loose at her sides.

A cackle escaped Lai's spittle-soaked lips. "You are pathetic," he said, pointing a *nunchaku* first at Jenn then at Gary's Watch. "But, fortunately, quite predictable."

"You blocked..." Gary stammered.

"My country," Lai said, aiming his weapon at Jenn as he drew near, "... will not be denied its proper place in the world."

"Your country is..." Jenn started to reply. Lai slapped her face before she could finish. Jenn's head snapped back, her eyes flashing wide in surprise at the speed of his attack.

"Now, you both will have to die," Lai said, his foot lashing into Jenn's stomach, doubling her over.

"Not so fast, Chinaman," Erin called out from behind Lai. She planted her feet firmly in the dirt. The click of her pistol cock resounded in the still night air.

"And you are?" Lai's question went unanswered as Erin pulled the trigger. The muzzle flashed, its blast illuminating the riverbank. Lai's head exploded in a mess of blood and brains. His decapitated body spun once in a macabre dance before crashing to the ground at Gary's feet. Jenn vomited all over the carcass.

Erin shrugged. "He was more evil than Tarleton. We should throw what's left of him in the river before anyone comes."

"Not just yet," Jenn said. She slowly straightened and wiped her mouth on the sleeve of her dress. She patted down the body, powering through Lai's blood and her own mess.

"Did he promise a Watch for you?" Gary asked.

"If I stopped you." Jenn flipped the body over and searched it again, just as unsuccessfully.

"He lied to ye," Erin said. She pointed her pistol at the dead man's wrist. "What about that Watch?"

"Only Lai can time travel with it," Jenn replied, unfastening the band anyway.

"He won't miss it," Erin cackled as she reached for Lai's ankles.

The moon reappeared, providing just enough visibility for

Gary, Jenn and Erin to drag Lai's body to the water's edge. "One, two, three," they counted in unison as they swung it out into the current.

Erin searched the embankment, finally locating Lai's *nunchaku*. She tossed it far into the water, past the point where Lai's body had sunk from sight.

Gary doubted anyone in 1776 knew the Chinaman was here, so no one would miss him. He stared at his Watch.

"What are ye waiting for?" Erin called.

Jenn sat on a boulder, head in her hands. "It's all my fault."

"I can't leave you two here," Gary said.

"Ye feel an obligation to bring the Declaration of Independence home, don't ye?"

"I do."

"It's at risk, isn't it? In ye time," Erin asked, taking Gary's hand. "That's why ye came. Why ye were willing to risk ye life."

"Yes," he replied, looking back at the Mortier House. The candles in the Washington's bedroom were snuffed. "I won't let down our commander-in-chief."

"Ye must never give up the good fight. That's what Mamo taught me – what her Mamo taught her. That's what I'll teach my sons."

Gary had invented the Watch to seek fame and fortune but would leave 1776 with a much greater reward: a deep appreciation of the compromises the Founding Fathers reached to draft the Declaration of Independence and the risks they took to sign it. He prayed its lofty aspirations would unite Americans in 2026 as they did in 1776. "You're a brave woman, Erin."

"Godspeed," she replied, pushing him away. "Come back for us as soon as it's safe."

Gary started the launch sequence again. The embankment tremored, then shook violently, revealing a yawning crevasse. Erin and Jenn swirled away in a cloud of dust. Waves of energy radiated down his legs rattling the soles of his feet. He collapsed to his knees.

He awoke face down in the grass in what looked like a park.

The sun had just risen above the treetops.

A welt swelled on Gary's forehead. He forced himself up, first to all fours, then standing. His left knee wobbled as he tentatively stepped forward. Its familiar ache was back, too. He stripped off his jacket and unbuttoned his shirt. Sure enough, the scar from his rotator cuff surgery glistened with sweat. A trace of his appendectomy lingered on his abdomen as well. He smiled - no surprises so far.

A crimson Tesla zoomed silently by. The clamor of a descending airplane rocked the cloudless sky. Pickleballers shouted from the nearby courts.

A teenaged jogger in neon orange shorts stopped what she must have thought was a safe distance away, but wrinkled her nose as Gary's body odor assaulted her senses. "Are you all right?" she asked, lifting her sunglasses.

Gary nodded, still disoriented. He pulled the Declaration from his pocket, comforted by the grainy feel of the parchment. Instinctively, he set his tricorn on his head.

The girl turned away, tapping three digits on her phone. "There's an old guy wandering around the park. Hasn't showered in weeks. Dressed funny too."

EPILOGUE

"This guy stinks," Patrolman Frank Marciano called from the backseat of the police cruiser. Twenty-two, Italian Riviera handsome, he was only on his third week of street patrol. "The AC ain't helping much either."

"Whaddya expect? Rookies always get the shit jobs," broad-shouldered Rose Luzinski, his superior, answered without taking her eyes off the road. "I'll open the fucking window."

Frank gratefully sucked in a gust of fresh air. After his bacon, egg and cheese McMuffin settled in his stomach, he faced his handcuffed captive again. "When was the last time you took a shower?"

"Two hundred and fifty years ago," Gary replied, looking outside. "Where are we?"

"Wise guy, huh?" Frank said, raising his hand. "I should smack you upside the head, old man, but I don't want to ruin my manicure."

"Holy shit," Rose said, steering to the shoulder. "You're Gary Johnson? The Gary Johnson?"

"Gary who...?" Frank stopped mid-question, cranking his head to better view the sky. A news helicopter whirled in their direction.

"The time traveler?" Rose asked, reaching for her phone. "You went back to 1776."

"No shit?" Frank asked. "The President just posted about you: the brave American pioneer returning home in glory."

"Really?" Gary asked. "The President said that?"

"Called you a trailblazer, like Charles Lindbergh," Rose read out loud. "The embodiment of American exceptionalism."

"That jogger who found you posted a video," Frank added, tapping his own phone. "It's gone viral too."

"You've become the most Googled WHORM in America," Rose said.

"I thought I was a pioneer. Now I'm a worm?"

"W.H.O.R.M. White Heterosexual Old Rich Man," Rose replied. "There's a 'Revenge of the WHORM' T-shirt with your picture on it. A crypto-coin too."

"No more woke bullshit," Frank said, putting his arm over Gary's shoulder. "Real guys are in charge again. We take what we want."

"Huzzah!" Gary chirped, holding up his shackles. His right shoulder crackled like popcorn as he lifted his arms.

"Unlock him, Officer Cave Man," Rose ordered, snapping a selfie with Gary prominent in the background as soon as his hands were free. Both cops stared wide-eyed at the motorcade of network-logoed vans speeding towards them. "Before the whole fucking world sees us."

The vans encircled the police car. Photographers and reporters jumped out, whooping like Cheyenne warriors surrounding Custer at Little Big Horn. Within seconds, they aimed their microphones at Gary. Questions came fast and furious:

"Did you meet George Washington?"

"Benjamin Franklin?"

"Thomas Jefferson?"

"Did you bring back any proof?"

Gary stepped out and straightened his hat. "Yes. On all four counts."

He struggled to look past the jostling paparazzi for friendly faces. There they were – climbing from a Black Suburban. Lucie first. Then Molly. FBI agent Gibson led them through the throng.

"Welcome back, *mon brave vieux*," Lucie said, hugging him as cameras flashed. She wore dirt-stained overalls and a straw gardening hat. "We were worried about you."

"My Watch was stolen," Gary replied, squeezing his wife as if it was their first date.

"I can't wait to hear more."

"Let's get you out of here," Gibson said. "Air Force One is landing at Westchester County in an hour. Enough time to get you cleaned up."

Rob Mangano, silver-haired and dark-suited, waited by the Suburban. "Just wanted to make sure these guys treated you right," he said, nodding towards Gibson as he put an arm over Gary's shoulder.

"Thanks for looking after Lucie," Gary replied in hushed tone. "How'd you do it?"

"Just explained to the good agent here that the PR would be great whether you returned alive or...didn't."

Gary handed the Declaration of Independence to his lawyer. "I want every American to read it and form their own opinion."

"I wouldn't hold my breath waiting for that," Mangano chuckled as he tucked the neatly creased parchment into his jacket.

"Why don't you take the window seat," Lucie suggested as Gibson opened the rear door. Gary went in first and slid over. She took the middle, albeit a foot or two away from her husband. Molly seated herself at the far end. Mangano waved as the SUV pulled away.

"How does my famous husband feel?" Lucie asked, resting her hand on Gary's thigh.

"Like I'm seventy years old."

"C'est bien."

"If you say so."

"Did you come back alone?"

"Yes."

"And Erin Duffy? We read about your escape from jail with her in the Pennsylvania Gazette. Remy found it on-line."

"Where is Remy? And Maribel and the kids?" Gary stalled.

"Everyone's home waiting for you. I thought it best if they stayed away from the spotlight."

And this conversation, Gary thought. "The Committee of Safety in Philadelphia thought I might be a British spy. Without any high speed network, they had no way to verify my background so they locked me up, confiscated the Watch and sent it by horseman to the Continental Army headquarters in New York City. Ms. Duffy helped me recover it."

"And why would she do that?" Lucie asked, putting her hand back in her own lap.

"Erin was a waitress at the City Tavern where I stayed."

"Weren't you a little old for all that gallivanting?"

"Not really." Gary explained the rejuvenative effects of his time travel.

"Truly amazing," Lucie replied, fiddling with her wedding ring.

"I know you're skeptical, but it's true."

"He's right," Molly chipped in. "I ran the simulations myself. Thousands of times. Based on the power of the processors in the Watch, time travel should have taken between forty and fifty years off Gary's life."

"How did you know you were twenty-five, not say, thirty?" Lucie asked.

Gary's eyes sparkled. He could see the light at the end of the tunnel - and it might not be an oncoming train. "I had an appendectomy when I was twenty-five. Before I met you. When I landed in 1776, there was no scar."

"How old was Ms. Duffy?"

"I don't know for sure. Mid-twenties, I guess."

"An attractive woman?"

"For her times. Her teeth were black."

"*Pas de problème*, I'm sure. How did it feel to be so young again?"

"Wonderful," Gary said, rotating his arm above his head. "My shoulder didn't feel like a hot knife pierced it. My knee didn't ache all day. I could run and jump and ride horses."

"But you enjoyed your youth? Took full advantage of your physical prowess?"

"I guess so. It was exciting."

"I see."

"I will only ask you one more question." Lucie clasped his hand. Her eyes lasered on his. "Do you still have feelings for Ms. Duffy?"

"Not really. Not those kind of feelings at least," Gary sighed. "We helped each other. Saved each other's lives, actually. But, it was time for me to come home."

"So you don't plan to return to 1776?" Lucie released his hand.

"My time traveling days are over, my love."

"*Merci Dieu.*"

They drove for five minutes in silence. "There's one complication," Gary said. "Jennifer Tryon from TimeR. She's stuck in 1776 without a Watch."

"That bitch stole our code," Molly said. "Let her rot."

The Suburban braked to a stop in the Johnson driveway. "Twenty minutes for you to clean up," Agent Gibson said. "We can't keep the President waiting."

THE END

City of Philadelphia, 1776

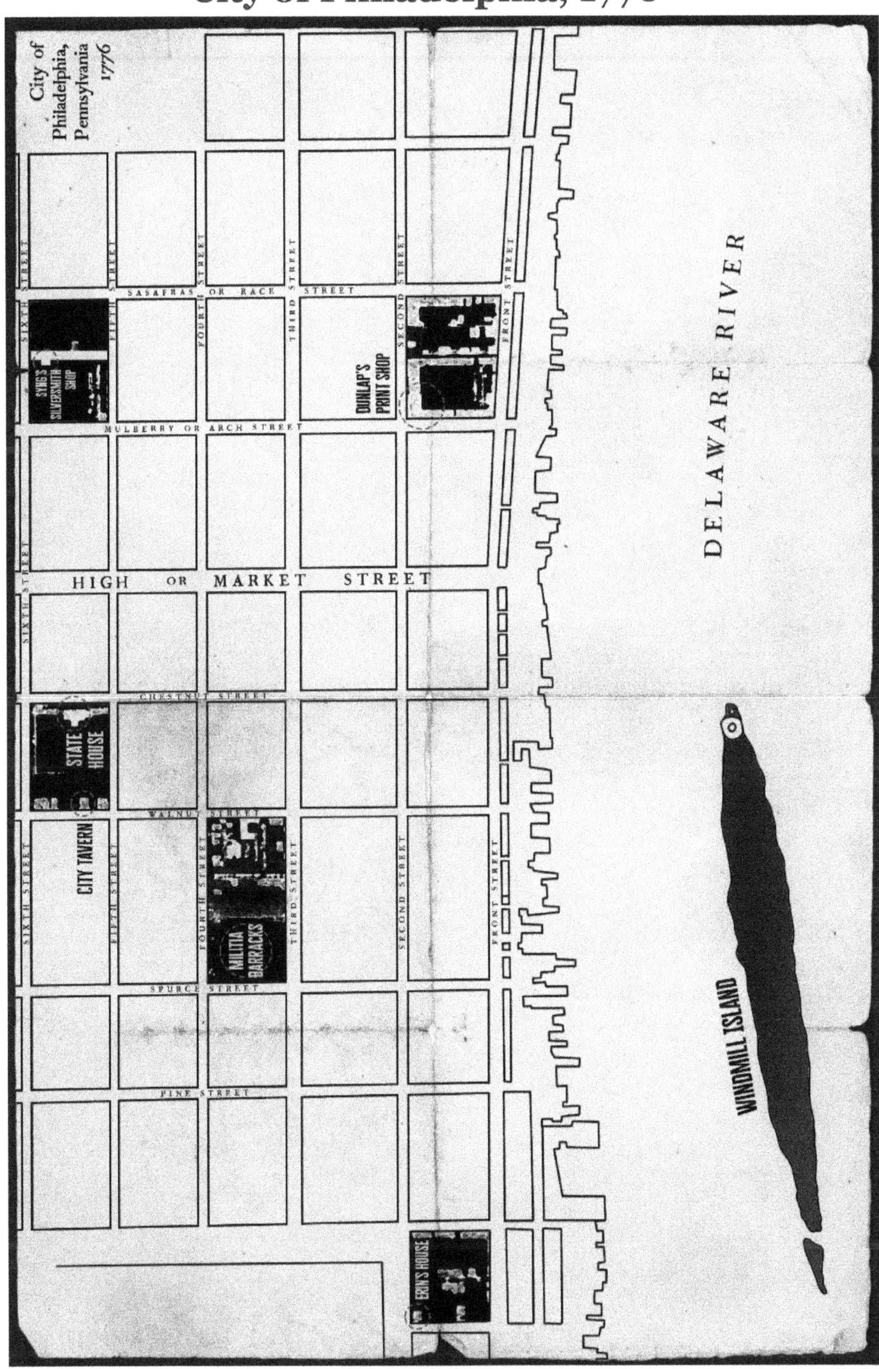

Historical Figures

Adams, Abigail	Loring, Betsy
Adams, John	McKean, Thomas
Chew, Benjamin	Milne, Edmund
Dickenson, John	Morris, Robert
Dunlap, John	Mulligan, Hercules
Franklin, Benjamin	Penn, William
Gates, Horatio	Robert Cary and Company
Graff, Jacob	Rodney, Caesar
Gwinnett, Button	Rogers, Robert
Hale, Nathaniel	Rutledge, Edward
Hamilton, Alexander	Sherman, Roger
Hancock, John	Syng, Philip
Hemings, Robert	Tallmadge, Benjamin
Hempstead, Steven	Tarleton, Banastre
Hickey, Thomas	Thomson, Charles
Humphreys, Richard	Trumbull, Jonathan
Jefferson, Thomas	Tryon, William
Kennedy, Archibald	Washington, George
Lee, Billy	Washington, Martha
Livingston, Robert	Wolcott, Oliver

Historical Events in Philadelphia in 1776

Friday, June 7 - Richard Henry Lee (VA) reads a resolution to the Continental Congress stating "these United Colonies are...free and independent states...absolved of all allegiance to the British Crown."

Monday, June 10 - Congress appoints a Committee of Five to draft a formal Declaration

Tuesday, June 11 - Congress votes 7-5 to postpone consideration of Lee's resolution (NY abstains)

Friday, June 28 - Committee of Five presents a "rough draft" of the Declaration to Congress

Monday, July 1 - Congress debates the draft for 9 hours; South Carolina and Pennsylvania vote against

Tuesday, July 2 – Lee's resolution of June 7 passes 12-0 (NY abstains)

Wednesday, July 3 - Congress revises the Declaration

Thursday, July 4 - Congress adopts the Declaration

Friday, July 5 - Congress inserts the Declaration into the record

Monday, July 8 - Declaration of Independence read in public for the first time

Tuesday, July 9 - NY approves the Declaration

Friday, July 19 - Congress orders the Declaration to be "engrossed" on parchment

Friday, Aug 2 - Congress signs the Declaration

Thursday, Dec 12 - Congress evacuates Philadelphia for Baltimore – Declaration travels along

The Declaration of Independence

In Congress, July 4, 1776
THE UNANIMOUS DECLARATION
of the
THIRTEEN UNITED STATES OF AMERICA

When, in the course of human events, it becomes necessary for one people to dissolve the political bands which have connected them with another, and to assume, among the powers of the earth, the separate and equal station to which the laws of nature and of nature's God entitle them, a decent respect to the opinions of mankind requires that they should declare the causes which impel them to the separation.

We hold these truths to be self-evident, that all men are created equal, that they are endowed, by their Creator, with certain unalienable rights, that among these are life, liberty, and the pursuit of happiness. That to secure these rights, governments are instituted among men, deriving their just powers from the consent of the governed, that whenever any form of government becomes destructive of these ends, it is the right of the people to alter or to abolish it, and to institute new government, laying its foundation on such principles, and organizing its powers in such form, as to them shall seem most likely to effect their safety and happiness. Prudence, indeed, will dictate, that governments long established, should not be changed for light and transient causes; and accordingly all experience hath shown, that mankind are more disposed to suffer, while evils are sufferable, than to right themselves by abolishing the forms to which they are accustomed. But when a long train of abuses and usurpations, pursuing invariably the same object, evinces a design to reduce them under absolute despotism, it is their right, it is their duty, to throw off such government, and to provide new guards for their future security. Such has been the patient sufferance of these Colonies; and such is now the necessity which constrains them to alter their former systems of government. The history of the present King of Great Britain is a history of repeated injuries and usurpations, all having in direct object the establishment of an absolute tyranny over these States. To prove this, let facts be submitted to a candid world.

He has refused his assent to laws, the most wholesome and necessary for the public good.

He has forbidden his governors to pass laws of immediate and pressing importance, unless suspended in their operations till his assent should be obtained; and when so suspended, he has utterly neglected to attend to them.

He has refused to pass other laws for the accommodation of large districts of people, unless those people would relinquish the right of representation in the legislature, a right inestimable to them, and formidable to tyrants only.

He has called together legislative bodies at places unusual, uncomfortable, and distant from the depository of their public records, for the sole purpose of fatiguing them into compliance with his measures.

He has dissolved representative houses repeatedly, for opposing with manly firmness his invasions on the rights of the people.

He has refused for a long time, after such dissolutions, to cause others to be elected; whereby the legislative powers, incapable of annihilation, have returned to the people at large for their exercise; the State remaining, in the meantime, exposed to all the dangers of invasion from without, and convulsions within.

He has endeavored to prevent the population of these States; for that purpose obstructing the laws for naturalization of foreigners; refusing to pass others to encourage their migrations hither, and raising the conditions of new appropriations of lands.

He has obstructed the administration of justice, by refusing his assent to laws for establishing judiciary powers.

He has made judges dependent on his will alone, for the tenure of their offices, and the amount and payment of their salaries.
He has erected a multitude of new offices, and sent hither swarms of officers to harass our people, and eat out their substance.

He has kept among us, in times of peace, standing armies, without the consent of our legislatures.

He has affected to render the military independent of and superior to the civil power.

He has combined with others to subject us to a jurisdiction foreign to our constitution, and unacknowledged by our laws; giving his assent to their acts of pretended legislation:

For quartering large bodies of armed troops among us:

For protecting them, by a mock trial, from punishment for any murders which they should commit on the inhabitants of these States:

For cutting off our trade with all parts of the world:

For imposing taxes on us without our consent:

For depriving us, in many cases, of the benefits of trial by jury:

For transporting us beyond seas to be tried for pretended offences:

For abolishing the free system of English laws in a neighboring province, establishing therein an arbitrary government, and enlarging its boundaries, so as to render it at once an example and fit instrument for introducing the same absolute rule into these Colonies:

For taking away our charters, abolishing our most valuable laws, and altering fundamentally the forms of our governments:

For suspending our own legislatures, and declaring themselves invested with power to legislate for us in all cases whatsoever.

He has abdicated government here, by declaring us out of his protection, and waging war against us.

He has plundered our seas, ravaged our coasts, burnt our towns, and destroyed the lives of our people.

He is, at this time, transporting large armies of foreign mercenaries to complete the works of death, desolation, and tyranny, already begun with circumstances of cruelty and perfidy, scarcely paralleled in the most barbarous ages, and totally unworthy the head of a civilized nation.

He has constrained our fellow-citizens, taken captive on the high seas, to bear arms against their country, to become the executioners of their friends and brethren, or to fall themselves by their hands.

He has excited domestic insurrections amongst us, and has endeavored to bring on the inhabitants of our frontiers, the merciless Indian savages, whose known rule of warfare is an undistinguished destruction of all ages, sexes, and conditions.

In every stage of these oppressions we have petitioned for redress in the most humble terms: our repeated petitions have been answered only by repeated injury. A prince, whose character is thus marked by every act which may define a tyrant, is unfit to be the ruler of a free people.

Nor have we been wanting in attentions to our British brethren. We have warned them, from time to time, of attempts by their legislature to extend an unwarrantable jurisdiction over us. We have reminded them of the circumstances of our emigration and settlement here. We have appealed to their native justice and magnanimity, and we have conjured them by the ties of our common kindred to disavow these usurpations, which would inevitably interrupt our connections and correspondence. They, too, have been deaf to the voice of justice and of consanguinity. We must, therefore, acquiesce in the necessity, which denounces our separation, and hold them, as we hold the rest of mankind, enemies in war, in peace friends.

We, therefore, the Representatives of the United States of America, in General Congress assembled, appealing to the Supreme Judge of the world for the rectitude of our intentions, do, in the name, and by the authority of the good people of these Colonies, solemnly publish and declare, that these United Colonies are, and of right ought to be, *free and independent States;* that they are absolved from all allegiance to the British crown, and that all political connection between them and the State of Great Britain is, and ought to be, totally dissolved; and that as *free and independent States,* they have full power to levy war, conclude peace, contract alliances, establish commerce, and to do all other acts and things which *independent States* may of right do. And for the support of this declaration, with a firm reliance on the protection of Divine Providence, we mutually pledge to each other our lives, our fortunes, and our sacred honour.

Revolutionary Works by Scott M. Smith

The Spy and the Seamstress

Contemporary Thrillers by Scott M. Smith
(Published under the name SM Smith)

Darkness is Coming
The Fourth Amendment

ABOUT THE AUTHOR

Scott M. Smith

After a thirty-year career on Wall Street, Scott retired in 2014 to pursue a lifelong passion to write. His cybersecurity novel, *Darkness is Coming*, won Distinguished Favorite in the Thriller category in the NYC Big Book Award competition. In 2017, he began researching the life and times of Nathan Hale, the official hero of his adopted home state of Connecticut. The effort resulted in *The Spy and the Seamstress,* as well as several in-depth articles published in the prestigious *Journal of the American Revolution.* Three of Scott's articles were selected for inclusion in the *Journal's* annual compendium of its best writings. Connect with Scott at www.scottmsmithbooks.com.